# Advance

"Two septugenarian si[...] [...]
addictive caper. . . . W[...]
The author's clever w[...]
will please Elmore Leo[...]
not to mention the C[...]
leads to a quick climax, making this a compulsive, enjoyable read."
— *Library Journal*, starred review

"Hilarious . . . A hypnotic and rollicking experience. Moore has got to be one of the funniest writers in or out of Glasgow."
— *ForeWord Reviews*

"I giggled my way through Donna Moore's *Old Dogs* . . . Filled with mayhem, torture, raw sexual banter, creepy chauffeurs, hired killers, and enough kilt-raising Scots profanity to shock a porn star . . . [A] ribald laugh-a-thon . . . I recommend *Old Dogs* highly to fans of Donald Westlake and Carl Hiaasen."
— Betty Webb, *Mystery Scene*

"Fast and furious with perfect timing and guaranteed to leave you smiling *Old Dogs* is one of my favorite books of 2010."
— Jon Jordan, *Crimespree Magazine*

"Liberally sprinkled with salty Glaswegian vernacular, the manically twisted tale reads like a contemporary but unusually bawdy Ealing comedy."
— Declan Burke, *The Irish Times*

"Like the perfect heist, Donna Moore's screwball caper is slick, audacious and hugely rewarding."
— Chris Ewan, author of *The Good Thief's Guide to Paris*

"[Donna Moore] has surpassed herself in her wit, insight and sheer turn of phrase in *Old Dogs*. Take Joan Rivers, add some less acerbic Susan Silverman and sprinkle with the sheer story-telling glee of early Carl Hiaasen and you'll have some idea of what to expect. Roll out the awards shelf, Donna is going to grab them all. Her wondrous artistry makes it seem so easy, and books this readable and compelling are anything but easy to achieve. This is true art. Beware, you may want to grab passers-by and insist they hear a passage read aloud, it's that good."
  —Ken Bruen, award-winning author of *London Boulevard*

"Very funny . . . Hilarious and exhausting; you can't help but love *Old Dogs*."
  —Valerie Ryan, Shelf Awareness

"Hilarious, irreverent and wryly observed. A classic screwball heist story ripped apart and reassembled from a uniquely female perspective, like Donald Westlake in high heels."
  —Christa Faust, author of *Money Shot* and *Choke Hold*

"*Old Dogs* is fresh and funny, a genuine load of laughs with a believably quirky, endearing, and hilarious cast of characters. It's the sort of a wild frolic you've come to expect from Donna Moore, and she hasn't let us down."
  —Tom Piccirilli, award-winning author of *Shadow Season*

"Oh, God . . . so funny! Donna is Scotland's answer to Donald Westlake with a Glaswegian accent and FABULOUS shoes! Wickedly funny."
  —Kat Richardson, best-selling author of *Labyrinth*

"Donna Moore proves that ...*Go to Helena Handbasket* was no fluke. *Old Dogs* is even better. You can't go wrong with two former hookers in their 70s, a great caper, and a cast of serious loonies. It's the funniest crime novel I've read in a long time, and if Judi Dench and Vanessa Redgrave don't star in the movie version, I'm going to be very disappointed."
  —Bill Crider, award-winning author of *Murder in the Air*

"*Old Dogs* is a dandy caper. Part *Hot Rock*, part *Absolutely Fabulous*. A thoroughly enjoyable read."

—Elliott Kastner, producer (*Harper, Angel Heart, The Big Sleep*)

**Praise for Donna Moore & her earlier book,**
**...*Go to Helena Handbasket*—winner of the 2007 Lefty Award for**
**most humorous crime novel.**

"It's like having Groucho Marx feeding you one-liners over your shoulder the entire trip. Author Donna Moore's debut is a laugh-riot of a read."

—Charlie Stella, author of *Johnny Porno*

"...*Go to Helena Handbasket* is a hilarious send up of the mystery genre. Donna Moore, with her trademark wit, has created a fast and funny read. I absolutely devoured it and anxiously await an encore."

—Barbara Seranella, author of the Munch Mancini crime novels

"Bridget Jones meets Raymond Chandler meets Jeffrey Dahmer in ...*Go to Helena Handbasket*, Donna Moore's brilliant absurd romp of a detective novel."

—Jason Starr, award-winning author of *Panic Attack*

"Donna Moore's debut rattles along at a manic pace. Sharp, snappy and very witty, the story starts at a sprint and never lets up its relentless pace. Moore is definitely one to keep an eye on."

—John Rickards, author of *The Touch of Ghosts*

"We all may very well be going to hell in a handbasket, but if we take Donna Moore's riotously funny ...*Go To Helena Handbasket* along for the ride, at least we'll go down laughing. Sam Spade in a skirt on acid."

—Reed Farrel Coleman, award-winning author of *Innocent Monster*

"Sharp, smart and flat-out funny. Donna Moore knows the genre, and she knows right where to stick the knife. The comedic debut of the year."

—Victor Gischler, best-selling author of *The Deputy*

# By Donna Moore

# OLD DOGS

## Donna Moore

Busted Flush Press
Houston 2010

*Old Dogs*
Copyright © Donna Moore, 2010

A Busted Flush Press paperback original.

Cover art © Julie Zarate
Cover design: Lisa Novak

ISBN: 978-1-935415-24-4
First Busted Flush Press paperback original printing, September 2010

**BUSTED FLUSH**
**PRESS**

P.O. Box 540594
Houston, TX 77254-0594
www.bustedflushpress.com

For my grandmothers—Floss and Betsy

# OLD DOGS

# Part One

BARRY SHEEHAN LOOKED at the diamonds sparkling around the wrinkled throat of the woman in front of him and surreptitiously adjusted his Y-fronts. Wealth gave him a hard-on and these two old bags were dripping with it. It wasn't so much the wealth itself, as the idea of separating it from its owners. In this case, La Contessa Letitzia di Ponzo and her sister Signora Teodora Grisiola, according to the gold-embossed card the Contessa had pressed into his hand. He held it between his thumb and index finger and transferred it easily from finger to finger and back again. It even felt luxurious and rich, passing through his fingers like silk.

Sheehan smiled at the two old dears in front of him and thought how easy this was going to be. His smile was the deal-clincher. He'd practiced it in front of the bathroom mirror and convinced himself he looked like Cary Grant—the sophisticated film star smile, the cheekily raised eyebrow, the twinkling eyes. How could they resist his charms?

"Well Mr Sheehan," the Countess stroked the diamond necklace with a liver-spotted hand, "Thank you for answering our advert. I think you will do very well as our chauffeur."

Her Italian accent was light and soft. It reminded Sheehan of some actress in an old black and white film he'd seen on video when he was last serving a stretch in the Bar L. "If you would like to come back tomorrow morning, we will have a uniform ready for you. As a . . . how would you say . . . trial run . . . we would like you to take us down to Ayr for the races."

"You ladies are interested in a little flutter on the horses?" Sheehan patted the crumpled *Racing Post* in his pocket. Things were looking better and better. The chance to drive a Daimler, a shot at stealing some rather fine diamonds *and* a day at the races.

"Gambling? No." The Contessa made a face like a bad tempered trout and her silent sister looked shocked at the thought, raising a jewelled hand to her throat as if to cross herself. "But we have an interest in fine thoroughbreds, yes. Now, Mr Sheehan. Many apologies for the lack of etiquette, but we have not yet hired a full staff. We have a full day's interviews planned for today. So in the absence of a butler I will see you out."

The Contessa picked an invisible speck of dust off her suit. Sheehan recognised the type, if not the actual designer—some flamboyant old queen who specialised in designing ill-fitting clothes

1

for frumpy old royals which made them look as though they had been upholstered rather than dressed. Sheehan stood up. He'd been dismissed. Fighting the dual temptations of bowing to them and nutting them, he allowed the Contessa to usher him to the door of the hotel suite she and her sister were currently calling *casa*.

THE CONTESSA CAME back into the living room and glided to the window. She looked down at the imposing gravel driveway of the very smart, very exclusive, country house hotel with its view of Loch Lomond. An unseasonably warm sunshine for late April made the water glitter as if it was covered in sequins. She watched as Sheehan appeared on the sweeping stone steps, paused to light a cigarette and climbed into a clapped out BMW, throwing his spent match carelessly onto the pile of pink and white blossoms which had fallen from the trees lining the steps. Her sister looked at her curiously. "Well, Letty, does he fit the bill?"

"He's a dodgy, rat-faced, little wanker who wouldn't know the word 'honesty' if it gave him a lap dance and bit him on the arse. He's pukka." Her accent was now more Isle of Dogs than Island of Venice. "Didn't he remind you of that punter you had in the late '60s, Dora? The politician who liked you to dress up as a milkmaid and squeeze his udders? Assistant to the Assistant of the Minister of Agriculture, Fisheries and Foods, weren't he?"

Dora giggled. "Old Marigold? Yes, Mr Sheehan *did* look rather like him. I do hope *he* doesn't want me to slap him on the buttocks and hit him with a fly switch. I'm getting too old for that sort of thing. Goodness, was that *really* forty years ago?"

Letty removed her necklace and threw it down on the antique Victorian coffee table. "That cheap tat is giving me a rash." She rubbed her neck. "Did you see Sheehan fixing his mince pies on it? And I thought he was going to crap himself whenever he smiled. That raised eyebrow and the facial contortions made him look like a constipated ferret. And did you see those nimble fingers with the business card—he's going to need watching, that one."

"Do you think he's a wrong 'un, Letty?"

"Wrong 'un? If he's not done time, I'll eat those hideous curtains."

"Then why did you give him the job, dear?"

"Let's put it this way, Dor'. I'd rather employ someone I *know* is dodgy but is as thick as two short planks, than have some clever bastard on the payroll and not be able to work out what he's going to do next." She pulled a packet of Rizlas and a pouch of tobacco out of her fake Chanel handbag from down the Leather Lane market, and rolled a cigarette one-handed, lighting it with a Zippo displaying a Hell's Angels emblem and the motto "Live Fast, Die Young." Reaching under the chintz cushion on the chair she pulled out a bottle of tequila. She opened the *Racing Post* which she had delicately picked out of Sheehan's pocket. Despite her advancing years, she still had the skills.

Letty put her feet up on the coffee table which groaned under the weight of her legs. "Me ankles are killing me. These shoes are a nightmare. I'll be glad when I can get back into the motorcycle boots again." She eased the navy blue court shoes off her swollen feet, flexing her toes with their silver nail varnish. "And this bleedin' corset is cutting off my circulation and making me fart. I had to keep it in with Sheehan here. And that's not healthy. If I'm gonna wear these clothes all the time we need to get a dog we can blame for the stink. Add that to the list, doll."

Dora pulled out a notebook and pencil, flicked through several pages, licked the tip of the pencil and took a note. "You remember we've got the property bloke coming shortly? And then we're interviewing for a chef and a butler this afternoon."

"It's all rock and roll, Dora." Letty plucked the pencil out of her sister's delicate fingers, circled a likely looking filly in the 5.30 at Catterick and handed the *Racing Post* and pencil to Dora. As Dora approved her choice of horse with a smile and a nod, Letty leaned over and picked up the property guides strewn on the table. "Are we agreed on this one?" She held up the brochure showing the tall, grey stone property with its tower and huge wooden door. "I've always wanted to live in a castle."

Dora glanced over, her porcelain forehead creasing into worry lines. "It's very expensive, dear. Don't you think we ought to rent something a little smaller and less . . . ostentatious?"

Letty looked at her sister. "Why in holy hell would we want to do that? The more ostentatious the better. You know what they say: 'if you've got it flaunt it'. And if you ain't got it you should flaunt it even more. The richer you pretend to be, the more people believe you, and the more they fall all over themselves to kiss your arse. Anyway, it's not as though we're going to be paying for it, is it?"

"I suppose not. But we *did* agree we should keep our heads low for a while. Especially after what happened in Australia . . ." Dora's cheeks paled beneath the thick layer of face powder she always caked on in the morning before facing the world.

"I keep *telling* you, Dor'. Stanislav has no idea *who* we are or *where* we are. He's thousands of miles away, doing all he can to try and recoup the fortune we diddled him out of. Bugger all chance of that, he'll be busy for a *long* time. Anyway, none of the other marks have ever worried you before. And they ain't caused us grief. Why are you so bothered about Stan?"

"He's dangerous. You remember what he said."

"Forget it, Dora, yeah? There's no chance of him finding us. These rich bastards don't want to admit they've been conned, and it ain't like he don't have plenty left. Don't worry about it. We're safe here."

Dora sighed. "If you say so. And that castle *does* look lovely."

"Good. Then that's settled then. We've come up in the world, Dor'. And we've got to play the game and look the part. We're not a pair of cheap tarts now you know. We're ladies." Letty reached over to the huge complimentary welcome basket filled with fruit and biscuits provided by the hotel management, and pulled out a packet of shortbread. "I'm so hungry I could eat a shite sandwich."

VICTOR STANISLAV PICKED his suitcase from the luggage carousel at Heathrow and made his way to the Customs Hall. He had no worries about getting searched. Even after a twenty-four hour flight he knew he looked as fresh and innocent as a daisy, thanks to Quantas' excellent Business Class facilities, some immaculate tailoring, his natural boyish charm, and the combined skill of Sydney's best plastic surgeons. He looked every part the successful executive on a business trip. Which, indeed, he was. The fact that his business was to find two elderly tarts, rip their heads off and take a dump in their neck cavities was neither here nor there.

The bored customs official glanced at him perfunctorily. "Anything to declare?"

"No." Stanislav had no need of anything but his suitcase full of fine tailoring and expensive cosmetic products, and a well-stocked bank account. He had left his arsenal safely locked up in his bank vault in Sydney and was planning to buy a suitable weapon in London. Call it his way of helping the British economy. Of course, no money from that little transaction would find its way into the Chancellor of the Exchequer's coffers, but that was irrelevant. Stanislav had always preferred the black economy anyway. Expedience, pragmatism and philanthropy—a serendipitous combination.

"London your final destination, sir?"

"Thought I might take a little trip up to Scotland while I'm here. See what the shooting's like."

"Grouse, sir?"

"Grouse, pheasant, woodcock . . . and hopefully a couple of old crows."

But the official was already looking over Stanislav's shoulder at the next passenger. Stanislav half-turned and glanced behind him. A scruffy young man was nervously fingering the zip on his backpack. The official stamped Stanislav's passport, "Enjoy your stay, sir, and I hope you bag your birds."

"Thank you, I'm sure I will." The official didn't reply. He'd already turned his attention to the young man with the guilty face.

"AND THIS, LADIES, is the Grand Ballroom." Gerard McIlroy, the sluglike representative of Franklin, Franklin, McIlroy and Franklin had saved the best until last. He threw open the doors to the ballroom of Cardieu Castle and ushered his 'rich clients' in, stepping back to let them get the full effect of the oak panelling, the magnificent chandeliers, the huge stone fireplaces, and the hideous paintings of chinless wonders wearing wigs and frocks and posing with meek looking women and dead animals—sometimes in the same picture.

Letty watched with a mixture of revulsion and awe as his nostrils flared and quivered. He waved a chubby little hand. "Just picture the romantic scenes from the past, dear ladies. The gorgeous *demoiselles* in rustling taffeta filling in their dance cards as the handsome *beaus* asked them to dance. Ah, the feasts and celebrations this historic place must have seen."

Letty heard Dora gasp behind her and turned to see her spinning on one petite foot, clasping her hands in wonder.

McIlroy half-bowed, giving Letty a close-up of his greasy comb-over. "Ah, how pleasant it is to be in the presence of two such discriminating ladies—a cut above the *petty bourgeois hoi polloi* it is normally my misfortune to deal with." His nostrils flared again, the long black hairs inside waving like the feelers of an insect sensing the presence of its Chanel-scented prey. McIlroy had been quivering with excitement and hovering over them like a fat spider since he had picked them up at the hotel. And Dora's reaction to Cardieu Castle had no doubt made him certain that the lucrative rental deal was signed, sealed and delivered.

"It is rather beautiful, is it not, ladies?"

"Oh, bugger me, *yes*." McIlroy shuddered and turned to Dora. Bless the soppy tart, her eyes were alight and Letty knew just what she was thinking. "I could roller skate in here to my heart's content."

Yep, as ever, Dora's inner child was out to play again. "Signora Grisiola, is, of course, having a little joke with you, Mr Franklin." Letty smiled at him reassuringly and then turned to fix her sister with a reproving glare. Dora grinned and mouthed a quick *"Sorry"* at her while McIlroy's attention was on Letty.

"McIlroy," said McIlroy. "I am the McIlroy of 'Franklin, Franklin, McIlroy and Franklin.' "

"Yes indeed, Mr Franklin." Letty knew full well what the slimy tosser's name was, but she also knew from dealing with slimy tossers just like him exactly how far she could push him. McIlroy opened his mouth to speak again. "We will take it, Mr Franklin."

"Certainly, dear ladies."

Letty had no doubt that she could call him Shithead now that they had agreed to rent this place. Quite frankly, it must have been a millstone around the firm's neck.

McIlroy coughed. "Now, whilst I appreciate that discussing financial terms is vulgar, there's just the little matter of . . ." he made a face and waved his hand regally, as though the Queen Mother had just farted in his face.

"Ah, of course, Mr Franklin. Now, I would give you a cheque right now but the Signora and I are in the process of getting our bank accounts transferred to the UK—with Coutts, you know. So I *do* hope that you will bear with us for a few days."

"Well, we do normally require a month's rental in advance . . ." McIlroy rubbed his eyebrow as he let the sentence drift. Why did the arseholes who regularly dealt with the upper classes so hate talking money?

"I do hope you will agree that that is *not* required in this instance, Mr Franklin. I believe you have the letters of introduction from Lady Kensington and the Duke of Worcester?"

Letty brought into play her haughtiest and most authoritarian voice, which she had practised after watching *The Godfather*. She was quite proud of it. Her fake Contessa accent lost its tones of honey and wine on a summer's evening in Tuscany, and took on the harsher tones of a back street bar in Sicily. The promise of sunshine and freshly cooked pasta was replaced by the idea of waking up to find a horse's head on the adjacent pillow.

"Certainly . . . certainly . . . oh, dear lady, I didn't mean to imply . . . it's just that the firm of Franklin, Franklin, McIlroy and Franklin insists on—"

Letty raised her hand. "I tell you what we will do, Mr Franklin. To show our appreciation for your firm's flexibility in this matter, we are more than happy to pay a premium over the rental. How does an additional ten percent a month sound?"

Bingo. McIlroy pressed an index finger to his lips to try to hide a huge smile. They had him—hook, line and sinker, like a big, fat pufferfish flapping ineffectually at the end of a line.

"Contessa, that sounds more than generous . . . *more* than generous." As McIlroy led them out of Cardieu Castle back to the office to sign the rental agreements, he completely overlooked the fact that he was now missing an even larger monthly payment in advance.

LETTY AND DORA were sitting in the upstairs parlour at Cardieu Castle. This was the room in which they could relax and be themselves. No visitors made it here, the staff knew that the parlour was off limits, and the Countess and the Signora were left to their own devices on the other side of the door. Letty stretched luxuriously on the red velvet chaise longue she had claimed as her own and took a long drag on the fat Cuban cigar she was smoking. A thick wedge of ash dropped onto the faded Ramones T-shirt. The names of Johnny, Joey, Dee Dee and Tommy were stretched to bursting point across her chest.

"Oh, bugger, I'm going to get ash all over this chaise longue."

Dora looked up from the Excel spreadsheet she was working on at the antique rolltop desk and jumped up to help her. As she leaned over Letty to scoop the cigar ash from the folds in her T-shirt, Letty admired with a mixture of pride and envy her sister's still taut and unwrinkled stomach in its tight black cut-off T-shirt.

"Dora, I've said it before and I'll say it again—you'd still be in demand if we were back on the game."

Dora giggled girlishly and patted her bottom in its tight black Capri pants. "I got mum's genes, love."

"Unlike me." Letty gestured at her own comfortable elastic-waisted jeans. "I got the jeans to fit Billy Smart's Circus."

"You know you were always the popular one Letty, dear. All the punters loved a bit of flesh. Your Rubenesque curves were always in demand. And look at you now. Not a wrinkle." Dora kissed her forehead, no doubt rubbing off the smudge of Chanel Pink Ballerina it had left behind as usual, and returned to her laptop.

Letty picked up the *Daily Record* from the side table. "That's cos they're all stretched out by my fat cheeks." She blew out her cheeks and made a face at Dora before settling back to open the paper.

The raunchy guitar sound of Black Rebel Motorcyclè Club belted out from the pair of enormous speakers that dominated the room, more than a little out of place amongst all the gilt and the representations of roses, lilies and orchids which fought like cat and dog on every piece of upholstery and wall coverings of the room. The lead singer exhorted Letty to "Spread Your Love," something which Letty and Dora had done with enthusiasm for thirty years from the late 1950s onwards, even though they were mostly lining someone else's pockets. Letty thought back with fondness to the day they had told their pimp, Big Al, that they were going into management for themselves. He had cried like a baby but they had persuaded him that, in their early 50s, they weren't going to be in demand for much longer. They'd given him a job as muscle in their new establishment—a little pied-a-terre in the Wimbledon suburbs and since then they'd spread their love only when *they* wanted to—for fun, rather than profit.

"What time you leaving for London on Monday, dear?" Dora's voice snapped Letty out of her reverie.

"I'm getting the ten-past-six flight down. Picking Gwen up at nine."

"She still determined to get the train back up?"

"Yep. She said in her last letter she wouldn't ever fly, that she wasn't ever going to be cooped up again. She's been inside that long, it's not surprising. Besides, all those people in a confined space—I don't think she'd do well. At least in the train we can get up and walk around. I've booked us into first class."

"I'll never forget what she did for me, Letty."

"For *us*, doll, for us. Now, enough of that maudlin stuff." Letty waved the newspaper at Dora. "Says here there's a big exhibition for the West End Park Museum in Glasgow, Dor'. Fancy going?"

Dora looked across. "Museum? Since when have you been interested in museums?"

"Since they started taking delivery of dogs."

"What sort of dogs?"

"Shih Tzu."

"Well, no need to be so bloody rude, Letty. I only asked."

"No, Shih Tzu dogs. Little yappy snappy things. Only these aren't real—they're the sort that are worth about fifteen million quid. Listen." Letty moved the newspaper closer to her eyes.

Dora tutted. "I wish you'd put your glasses on, dear."

"They make me look like Joe 90."

"It's only us here, Letty and I don't care what you look like."

"Well, I bloody do. Now, listen, there's some special exhibition at this West End Park Museum. Here's what it says.

" 'The Exhibition includes a gold necklace reportedly belonging to the Empress Livia, wife of the Roman Emperor Augustus, a vase from the Ming dynasty, and a collection of Inca treasures excavated from Machu Picchu. The most exciting and valuable items, however, are a pair of jewel encrusted gold Shih Tzu dogs, worth an estimated £15 million. The Shih Tzu is also known as the Tibetan Lion Dog and the breed originated in Tibet where it was kept in temples as a sacred dog.' Blah blah blah, some more stuff about them being owned by some Chinese Empress and guarded by eunuchs . . . I wonder why they needed to be eunuchs . . ." Letty contemplated that idea for a moment before continuing. "Anyway, they're apparently a great coup for the museum and there's some poncey twat rattling on about what an honour it is." Letty looked over at Dora. "What do you think?"

"Sounds lovely, Letty, but what exactly does all that have to do with us?"

Letty put the paper down next to her on the chaise longue. "It's bloody obvious, Dor'. We're going to nick them."

"CAMPBELL FINDLAY, CHIEF Curator of the Museum, said in a telephone interview today, 'This is a real coup for the West End Park Museum, and a real coup for Glasgow. We are honoured and delighted that museums from all over the world have donated such priceless and exciting treasures for our exhibition and we are looking forward to welcoming thousands of visitors through our doors during August.' "

Megan Priestly threw the *Daily Record* across her studio where it hit the cast for the pewter sculpture of a bird she was working on. The arrogant, slimy, back-stabbing, double-crossing, spineless bastard. "Campbell Findlay, Chief Arsehole of the Museum, Wanker and Dickhead Extraordinaire," more like.

It was no good, she could still see Campbell's smug face smiling at her from the pages of the newspaper, sandwiched between photographs of a pair of shiny jewel-encrusted gold dogs, and a rather elaborate but ugly looking vase. She could just imagine a similarly smug look, as he gave his interview to the *Daily Record*. Taking credit for all Megan's ideas, all her hard work. Well, she would see about that. Not to mention the more personal betrayal. She still had connections, still had clout, still had the means to make his life hell. She rubbed her stinging eyes.

Megan strolled over to the newspaper and picked it up. She couldn't abide mess for long. She was smoothing out the pages when the words 'Shih Tzu' jumped out at her. The dogs. Yes! Because, much *much* more important than the connections and the clout, she still had the keys to his flat. Oh, sweet Lord, yes. And she had one more thing—her hand cupped under Campbell Findlay's dangly bits, ready to grab hold, twist, and feed them to the stray cats roaming West End Park. For the first time in the last two months, since she'd lost both her job as Chief Curator of the West End Park Museum, and the love of her life in Campbell Findlay—both thanks to Campbell's sleazy deviousness—Megan felt herself smile. At last, after eight weeks of suffering, heartbreak and lack of sleep, she could finally get her own back on the slimy tosser. Megan felt the cloud of depression lifting—she had something to live for again.

SHEEHAN LEANED AGAINST the Daimler in the private enclosure at Ayr racecourse and watched Scotland's rich and famous swarm around his new employers like bluebottles around diamond-encrusted shite. Wankers. He had to admire the Italian pair though. Their scam was a good one. He'd been watching them for a while before it suddenly dawned on him what they were up to. From what he'd observed today they were selling certificates of part ownership in thoroughbred horses. Thirty thousand quid a share. The women had the right patter, references from top names in the horseracing world, the backing of Lord This and Duke That. Most of all they were talking the language of the greedy bastards drooling all over them. The language of cold, hard cash.

"A twenty-five- to thirty-percent return in three months," the Countess was saying in her clipped, lightly accented tones, airily waving a glass of champagne as Signora Grisiola tapped out strings of numbers on the slim laptop computer on the table in front of her. "Guaranteed. The stud fees on their own are worth a fortune in income. Why, the Duke of Chalfont was able to restore the family seat in a year from his returns. A hundred thousand, Mr Kavanagh? Certainly. Just give us your bank account details and we'll effect the transaction immediately."

To the uneducated eye it all seemed perfectly legit, but Sheehan's eye was anything but uneducated when it came to cons, grifts and scams. These rich tossers might not be able to recognize a whore with the clap when they saw one, but Sheehan certainly did.

He'd made a fair packet from this sort of scam himself until he'd gone to jail for it. His were on a smaller scale of course, but Sheehan recognized the signs. He'd sold dodgy TV advertising (he'd even got a film student friend to video a couple of fake adverts—and they'd made a porno while they were at it; Sheehan was rather proud of his starring role—OK, it was a short feckin' film and it was all wobbly cameras and badly dubbed sound, but they'd got the money shot and that was the main thing).

He'd guaranteed his investors a 30% return every 60 days. And, of course, he'd made sure to deliver to the first few investors. They spread the word and all the other suckers signed up. Needless to say, the other suckers never got their promised returns. Or their capital back, as it happened. It was risky, and you had to have balls to pull it off. For a while Sheehan had managed to juggle those balls as he robbed Peter to pay Paul, but eventually the whole thing had collapsed like a drunken sailor, and Sheehan hadn't managed to disappear before Strathclyde's finest came a-calling.

Sheehan lit up another cigarette and watched as his employers continued to play the crowd. These rich punters were falling all over themselves like champagne-swilling lemmings to sign up on the dotted line, each one trying to outdo the last in size of investment. The Signora was hard pressed to enter all the details fast enough after the Countess had reeled the marks in.

A red-faced Englishman with a braying voice staggered over, his arm around a huge mountain of a man. Sheehan pitied the hundreds of Cashmere goats now standing shivering on a bleak Mongolian plateau, bald as coots, their hair shorn to make the expensive suit worn by the newcomer. "Digby, old boy, I told these lovely ladies that you are as rich as Croesus and they made me promise to introduce them to you. I've just invested a hundred and fifty grand in their smashing little enterprise . . ."

If there was anything Sheehan hated more than an arrogant English shite it was a rich arrogant English shite. He ground out his cigarette under the heel of his boot. He was hot, uncomfortable and he'd nearly lamped the auld bitch one when she gave him the uniform. Green and gold—knife-edge creases in the trousers, gold buttons shining, black boots polished to within an inch of their life.

Green and gold? He was a Rangers man all the way. Green and feckin' gold? His mates in the main stand at Ibrox would rip the shit out of him if they knew. He hoped they never found out—his life wouldn't be worth living, and he'd never be able to play the flute on the Orange Walk again. He'd be thrown out of the Lodge and blackballed. His own balls tightened at the very thought.

If it hadn't been for that insult he might have stuck with his original plan of heisting the Contessa's diamonds and the Daimler. But he saw now that he should set his sights higher this time. No more of the penny-ante jobs followed by a stint in nick. No, he was going to make this job really worth his while. Sheehan had a grudging admiration for the old bitches. But it wasn't going to stop him relieving them of some of the cash they were collecting today. It would be like taking candy from a pair of wrinkled old babies.

LETTY HAD BEEN waiting outside for an hour when Gwen finally appeared, clutching a small bag to her chest, her knuckles tight.

Letty watched Gwen breathe in deeply as the heavy doors of Holloway Prison closed behind her. Letty felt as though her old friend had just reached into her chest and squeezed her flinty old heart. Well, Gwen *was* taking her first breath of free air in thirty odd years. They'd been horrified when the judge trying Gwen had turned out to be old "Hang 'Em and Flog 'Em" Fawcett-Smythe—but thirty years? The whole courtroom had gasped when he'd passed sentence. He'd said it was cold-blooded murder, that she'd planned it and used extreme violence. Planned it? Only if you could plan a murder in five seconds. And Fawcett-Smythe had referred to her past, said that she had a "history." Bugger me—you beat up one dodgy punter and they never let you forget it. Hardly a history. But the fact that she'd beaten up one man and killed another—no matter what the justification—hadn't been in her favour. Besides, it turned out the judge's wife had left him the day before. For a woman called Gwen.

Letty walked across the road, waving. Gwen's tired old face altered—her bright eyes and wide smile making Letty remember how she looked all those years ago. She held her arms open and Letty fell wordlessly into them. They stood there, hugging tightly.

Eventually Letty broke free, and held Gwen at arms length, looking her up and down. "Bugger me, it's good to see you Gwen, doll. You look much better than you did last time we came to see you."

Gwen nodded, reaching up to stroke Letty's face. "What are you doing here Letty? I told you they've got a hostel organised for me in Sydenham."

"Hostel? You think Dora and I would let you go to some crummy old hostel?"

Gwen shrugged. "It'll be better than I've been used to."

"You're coming with me. We've got a lovely room ready for you at home. It's nice and quiet, lovely countryside to walk round. And you won't need to worry about anything ever again."

"I've caused you and Dora enough bother—"

"Don't you ever bloody *dare* say that." Letty took Gwen by the shoulders and shook her gently. "We owe you *everything* Gwen. After what you did . . ."

"But I—"

"Just shut it." Letty took Gwen's left hand and kissed the dry palm. "Here, love, let me take your bag. This all you've got?" She felt her voice crack.

"It's all they let me bring out, Letty." Gwen opened the bag so Letty could see—the ancient cassette player, Bay City Rollers and T-Rex tapes, a dog-eared copy of *Anne of Green Gables*, a pair of purple velvet flares that she had been wearing when she entered and which would now no longer fit her. Why the hell did they bother giving her those back?

"We'll get you some new stuff, doll. Some lovely new stuff."

"I'm not bothered. But I wish they'd let me bring my letters. All those letters you and Dora sent me . . . and my family and friends too . . . before they forgot. But you and Dora never forgot. I loved those letters. Lived for them."

Letty swallowed. The lump in her throat felt as big as an apple. "You've got the real thing now. You won't need letters ever again." She took out a packet of cigarettes and offered one to Gwen.

"No thanks Letty. I gave up inside."

"Smart girl." Letty put the packet back in her pocket. "You're coming to live with me and Dora and we'll look after you right nice. And you wait until you hear about the little number we've got going on. Now let's get that train. Dora's wetting herself with excitement. She's dying to see you."

DUNCAN KIERNAN AND Raymond Bain were sitting on the immaculately kept lawn at the Western Crematorium having lunch and reading their newspapers in silence. Well, strictly speaking, only Duncan was reading. He looked over at Raymie, who'd been ogling the jugs on the Page 3 girl for twenty solid minutes, while stuffing his plooky face with six Greggs steak pies. Man, what a greedy bastard. Duncan took a bite out of his cheese salad sandwich and turned back to the paper.

The news was all bad. The Sons of William had been trounced by those Fenian bastards in the second Old Firm game so far this year, the drugs raid in Yoker that was reported on the front page of the *Daily Record* named Duncan's dealer as one of those who had been huckled, and new security cameras were being installed in parts of the West End. What happened to civil liberties, man? You couldn't carry out a harmless wee mugging these days without it being caught on seventeen cameras. Duncan turned the page to an article about an exhibition at the West End Park Museum.

He'd gone there a lot when he was a boy. It was a great place to dog school. Warm, quiet places to hide, huge-arse swords straight out of the fantasy computer games he loved, and the old biddy in the café was as blind and deaf as a baby rabbit so he'd had no problems nicking cakes from the counter. Come to think of it, she'd even had the whiskers of a baby rabbit too.

Duncan glanced over at Raymie who was now lying snoring, his skip cap covering his eyes, *The Sun* open at the fake boobs on page 3. He didn't know why Raymie bothered buying the paper every day. He never got past page 3. And he skipped pages 1 and 2 as well.

They had the Crem to themselves this morning. The big boss man Armitage was away on holiday today and Big Shuggie was picking up a body down in Dunoon. He would be gone for hours. Hence the reason Duncan and Raymond were taking it easy. While the cat was away the rats would play, and all that shite.

Duncan took off his shell suit top and draped it over the "Keep Off The Grass" sign. What was the point of grass if you couldn't sit on it? Besides, he had a problem with authority—he and Raymie both did. They weren't supposed to be on their lunch break. At least, not at this time of the morning they weren't. And they *definitely* weren't supposed to be drinking Buckfast and smoking draw on the job either but what the fuck, man . . .

Of course, Duncan wasn't actually drinking the Buckie, but Raymie wasn't to know that. Duncan had been teetotal since he'd caused the accident ten years ago. Vegetarian too, since he'd seen the mess the bodies were in. How was a thirteen-year-old boy supposed to cope with knowing he'd caused the deaths of two people? He hadn't been caught and he'd told no one. His big secret. He lifted the Buckie to his mouth and pretended to neck it before passing it to Raymie. Duncan looked at his watch—half ten in the morning and Raymie was steaming.

Still, it wasn't as though they were getting paid. That tight fisted bastard Armitage got most of his staff through the penal system, community service being such cheap labour. 'Course, you might not get any work out of the lazy junkie tossers you ended up with. Duncan classed himself in that category too. His lazy junkie tosser status was a source of pride.

He'd been arrested for breach of the peace and assaulting a police officer. Although he didn't see how peeing on the pig's shiny black shoes constituted assault. It served the bastard right for interrupting him mid-flow. No matter that Duncan was standing in the middle of St Vincent Street at the time and about to be mown down by a number 62 bus.

It wasn't his first offence, of course—he was never caught for the car crash, but he'd been nicked plenty of times since—and he'd been lucky to get off with community service. The judge had pointed out that at eighteen he was too old for Young Offenders and that he was reluctant to put him in the Bar-L where he might consort with . . . shock, horror . . . hardened criminals. The old dobber didn't have a clue, man. Most of the hardened criminals were on the streets these days. It was only the crap ones that got caught. Duncan had just been unlucky, of course. Raymie, however *was* one of the crap ones.

He and Raymie had hit it off when paired up to serve their community service at the Crem. Duncan had been a bit disappointed when he found out that they would only be cleaning, gardening and doing odd jobs, rather than actually burning bodies, but it was better than prison.

Raymie was a peach. Thick as mince and a clatty bastit, you couldn't trust him with the sugar in your tea—he'd have it out of the mug without his fingers getting wet. He was a right laugh, but. Raymie had been caught in the middle of a ram raid. Mind you, even a penguin with its head chopped off could have caught him. He'd expected to do a quick in and out on a jewellers in Clydebank but things had gone a bit tits up. The only vehicle he'd managed to break into was an ancient ice cream van with dodgy steering. And instead of ram-raiding the jewellers, his driving had been so shite that he'd ended up in the butcher's next door. According to Raymie, the polis had pished themselves laughing when they'd found him, concussed behind the wheel of the ice cream van, half a pound of liver in his lap and Greensleeves blaring out over the  sound system.They'd filmed it and showed it in Court. Duncan wished he'd been there to see that.

Duncan took a draw on his joint as he finished reading the article about the museum. "The Dowager Empress was one of the most formidable women in modern history. She started out as a concubine and ended up ruling China." Duncan rummaged around in his left nostril with his forefinger to help him think. Wasn't a concubine a bit like a hedgehog? How could a hedgehog rule China? He'd always thought the Chinese were a bit odd—the guy behind the counter at his local Chinese takeaway was definitely a weirdo, anyway.

He wiped his finger on the grass and carried on reading. "Tzu-Hsi squandered money on banquets, jewels, and other luxuries and on one occasion was served 150 different dishes at a single banquet. She invariably drank from a jade cup and ate with golden chopsticks." Golden chopsticks would beat those pishy wee wooden ones you got at the Shanghai Fortune, man. "At the end of her life, her personal jewellery vault held three thousand ebony boxes full of jewels. The most precious items in her collection were the two gold Shih Tzu dogs encrusted with emeralds, rubies, diamonds and sapphires." Three thousand boxes full of jewels. Fuck's sake, man. That was like . . . shitloads of boxes.

"Where the dogs originated from appears to be rather a mystery, but rumours suggest that they may have been stolen by a mysterious and shadowy cult in Tibet, following a savage massacre at a monastery high in the mountains in 1684. Over the next two centuries they changed hands on a regular basis, with several of their owners coming to violent ends, leading to theories that the dogs had been cursed." Pure brilliant stuff, man, just like in that old black-and-white film he'd seen last week with that Boris Karling guy all wrapped up in bandages. Duncan read the end of the article: "The Dowager Empress Tzu-Hsi, however, died at the ripe old age of 73 and was buried in splendour, covered in gems. She was reported to have wanted to be buried with the golden dogs and this was thought to have happened until the dogs turned up in the hands of an American collector in the late 1990s."

The cogs were turning in Duncan's mind. He swore to God he could feel the whirring in his head. What a fucking belter of an idea.

"Haw, fannybaws." He poked Raymie in the side.

"Fuck's sake, Dunk, I was sleeping. I was out on the randan last night and my head's loupin'. This had better be fuckin' good or I'll batter you."

"I'd like to see you try, ya mad rocket. You know that art gallery and museum place in the west end?"

"What? Art gallery? Do I look like that Picasso bawbag, ya mad nugget?"

Duncan looked at his friend. Raymie had an unfortunate coupon that *did* look like a Picasso painting. His nose had been broken so many times it was as lumpy as Duncan's maw's porridge. And he had a belter of a scar from where he'd been chibbed, which made him look as though he was permanently smiling on one side of his face. Yeah, Raymie looked as though his face had been set on fire and then put out with a frying pan. But Duncan wasn't about to say that, but. He didn't want to end up like the poor bastard who'd had "arsehol" carved into his arm with a Stanley knife. Even spelled right he didn't want to end up like that.

"Naw, man. They're gonnae have this exhibition thing there with shitloads of expensive stuff. Would be a skoosh to nick something."

Raymie raised himself on an elbow and looked at Duncan as though he had lost the plot.

"Nick something? What? Like a mummy? Or a soddin' great stuffed dinosaur?"

"Naw, ya tube, like these two wee gold dogs." Duncan passed over the newspaper, jabbing his index finger at the article.

Raymie read the piece, his lips and finger moving in tandem, very slowly. He frowned from time to time. English had never been his strong point at school. Raymie had said that he spent most of his time at school behind the science block where his strong points were smoking fags and sticking his hand up a wee slapper's blouse and copping a feel of her diddies.

"And what the fuck are we gonnae do with two wee gold shitty dogs that the whole world will be looking for? We can't exactly set up a stall down The Barras and put them on display now, can we?"

"Naw, man, of course not. But we can, like, melt them down, take out the jewels and sell the jewels and the gold separately."

Raymie shook his head. "Melt them down? You're no fuckin' real, you bawbag. How are we gonnae do that?"

Duncan gestured to the windowless white crematorium building behind him. "It's, like, two thousand degrees in them ovens. If that's not hot enough to melt gold, I'd like to know what is."

LETTY CROSSED HER arms, her ample breasts straining against the Kings of Leon T-shirt she was wearing. She peered out of the upstairs parlour window, watching Paul, the gardener, in the Japanese garden below. His muscles rippled against the tight white T-shirt as he plunged his spade into the soft damp ground. If only she were ten years younger. OK, maybe twenty years younger. She sighed and turned away from temptation. She was the Contessa di Ponzo, not Lady Chatterley.

"Gwen's still fast asleep. All that excitement."

"She looked shattered when she arrived. It was so good to see her."

Dora pressed a button on the laptop and sat back with a yawn, stretching like a well-groomed Siamese cat.

"So, Dor', what's the final total for Saturday's day at the races?"

"Best yet, Letty. Two hundred and forty grand directly into the account by telegraphic transfer, a further hundred and eighty grand in cheques which have been banked but are still to clear, and fifty grand in used fivers." Letty raised her pencilled-in eyebrows. Dora smiled. "The old geezer who looked like Harold Steptoe."

"The one ogling your tits?"

"He was admiring my brooch."

Letty snorted. "For an ex-tart, you're surprisingly innocent."

"Anyway, that was Lord MacDuff. He's got that manor house out by Stirling—part of the hunting, shooting and fishing brigade—grouse and salmon, you know. He also keeps pigs. Hundreds of them. I looked him up on the Internet. Apparently he's one of the richest blokes in Scotland but the rumour is that he doesn't trust banks and keeps a fair whack of his dosh on the premises. By the smell of these fivers, he keeps it in the pig sties." Dora picked up a crumpled five-pound note from the pile on the table next to her and delicately sniffed it, before replacing it on the pile and wiping her slim fingers on her pencil skirt.

"Good—that gives us a bit of working capital. Stick it all in the drawer." Letty looked at her watch. "Anyway, we'd better go downstairs. I asked Jeeves to gather all the staff in the kitchen so we could brief them on Gwen's arrival."

"I *do* wish you wouldn't call him Jeeves. That's *so* rude. His name is Mr Dixon. One day you're going to slip up and call him Jeeves to his face."

Letty snorted. "At least it's better than referring to the sodding butler as 'Mr Dixon.' Dora, you're supposed to be Italian aristocracy, not the housemaid."

"Well, he's a delightful man. He's been teaching me all about wine. Did you know we have the most amazing wine cellar in the basement? Mr Dixon and I have been down there every afternoon. I know the cellar intimately now."

"Well, doll, as long as you don't know Mr Dixon intimately, we'll be alright."

"And another thing—you know that chef doesn't like you in his kitchen."

"I know. That's why I asked them all to meet us there." Letty held the parlour door open for Dora who tapped briskly out in her stilettos. As they descended the wide, sweeping staircase of Cardieu Castle, overlooked by generations of Cardieu ancestors who Letty imagined were spinning in their graves like a troupe of bony whirling dervishes, she ran her hand lovingly down the highly polished banisters. This was the life.

VICTOR STANISLAV STEPPED off the train at Glasgow's Central Station. He looked around him, admiring the airiness, the glass, the marble, the spacious concourse. His knees buckled as he was bumped from behind.

" 'Sake, big man. Can ye no just stop dead like that, ya wanker." The man in the business suit stormed off, shaking his head.

That was the problem with people today. They had no thought for the comfort and safety of others. Victor *loathed* thoughtless and impolite people. Society was far too selfish, too self-centred, too intent on their own pleasures to be concerned about others. Philanthropy was dead. Even plain good manners had gone the way of the dodo. But best not to dwell on such matters. He was here for a reason and the sooner he completed his quest, the sooner he'd get back to his house in Sydney—back to his garden, his Vivaldi, his books, his well-appointed kitchen, made for a cordon bleu chef. And his collection of weaponry from around the world. The good things in life.

The train journey had been pleasant. The First Class carriage was practically empty and he'd spent the five and a half hours alternately reading a D. H. Lawrence book, one or two guide books on Glasgow, and some information on exhibitions and shows that he had printed off the Internet. A neat, leather-bound notepad now contained a list of places he wanted to visit once he had accomplished his primary mission. The Burrell Collection was, apparently, an experience not to be missed, the Cathedral was a fine example of Gothic architecture, and Victor was particularly interested in an exhibition opening at the West End Museum which sounded just up his avenue. There was a superb Ming vase, together with an intriguing-sounding pair of temple dogs which would fit beautifully into his collection of ancient Chinese art. The collection was locked away in a secure vault and Victor visited regularly to take them all out and look at them. He would sit in the cool vault with all those rich, fine things spread about him, the lighting system he had rigged up making everything sparkle and glow, drinking in their beauty and history. As the heat from the lights beat down Victor would gradually remove his clothing, placing it neatly on the back of a chair, until he sat there naked and sweating, surrounded by all that splendour. It was a shame his treasures could not be put on display, but many of them were too valuable to just leave lying around the house—no matter how good his security system. Not to mention that at least half of his collection was still being tracked down by various police and intelligence agencies throughout the world. Victor flexed his fingers as he waited in the taxi queue. Their skills hadn't been tested in far too long. He wondered what the security at the West End Museum was like.

His contact at the airline back in Australia had managed to track the two old tarts on a flight to Heathrow and then on to Glasgow. He had no idea where they were now, but Scotland was small and his skills were vast. He'd find them soon enough and then he'd make the old slags pay for stealing his money. He had plenty more, but it was the principle of the thing. Back in Sydney he felt that people had been laughing at him for getting taken in by the fake Countess and her sister. He couldn't have that. No one laughed at Victor Stanislav. *No one.* He stepped into a taxi. "Malmaison Hotel, driver, if you please." He would have a pleasant evening seeing what Glasgow had to offer, and then start his search in the morning after seven hours of deep and uninterrupted sleep in the best room the best hotel in Glasgow had to offer.

"Malmaison? Ah've been waiting in this queue for a fare for fuckin' ages, and you only want to go to Malmaison?"

As the taxi driver did a screeching U-turn, muttering under his breath, Victor came to the conclusion that Glaswegian people needed to be taught some manners.

LETTY SURVEYED HER staff in the regal manner she had cultivated expressly for the purpose. Dixon, the Butler, standing stiff and chinless in his dark uniform, next to his wife who acted as housekeeper and cleaner, Paul the hubba hubba gardener, Chef, glowering at this invasion of his precious "keetcheen," Sheehan, in his green and gold livery (Letty bit back a smile—she hadn't been able to resist when she had discovered he was a Rangers fan), and the Dixons' son, otherwise known as Odd-Job by Letty, since that was his role in the household. A motley crew, but they were coming along nicely and, more importantly, all of them seemed to be remarkably incurious about their new employers. Well, all of them with the possible, and slightly worrying, exception of Sheehan. Letty glanced at the subject of her concerns and found he was watching her with a slight smile on his face—or as much of a smile as his weaselly features could manage.

"So, Miss Ellis has arrived and she will be staying with us for the foreseeable future. I would request that you make sure that if you approach her you give her warning of that approach and that you don't make any sudden or frightening movements. Miss Ellis has a . . . delicate constitution and any surprises could have . . . unforeseen consequences. Treat her as you would the Signora and myself if you please. Now, as we have you all together, are there any questions?"

"Yeah . . ." Odd-Job got a poke in his skinny ribs from his mother for his impudence. "I mean . . . yes, ma'am . . . when are we gettin' paid? Ouch . . . fuck's sake, Mum. That wis sore." He rubbed his side with a thin hand, and turned his protruding eyes on his mother.

"You mean you haven't been paid yet?" Letty glanced at each of her staff in turn, seeing the heads shake. "Dora, please could you go and check with the bank and make sure the wages are paid into their accounts *immediatemente* . . . oh, and will you bring down that little bonus we discussed." She held up a finger to Dora. A thousand pounds each would go down a treat and keep them sweet. Letty beamed at the help. She felt like Robin Hood.

MEGAN WATCHED CAMPBELL Findlay double-lock the front door behind him and take the short flight of stairs down from his townhouse two at a time. She could feel her teeth grating as her jaw tightened. It was the first time she had seen him since they had split up. She was amazed to find that she really didn't fancy him anymore. In fact, his smug face made her wonder how she could *ever* have fancied him. He had been quite charming at the start—he was good at that when he wanted to be, and she'd always liked her men to have a bit of meat on their bones, but now she saw past the surface to the sleazy, backstabbing, job-stealing, two-timing egotistical turd he really was.

She placed a hand over her fluttering chest and took out the bottle of Kalms, twisting the lid open as she continued to watch Campbell. As he turned out of his path and walked along Hyndland Road towards his car, she saw his hairy belly peeping out over his trousers where his shirt was straining against the buttons. He'd definitely put on weight since they split up. All those expense-account lunches. He had constantly told Megan she was too pudgy and that she needed to diet. Pot, meet kettle.

Campbell swung his briefcase as if he didn't have a care in the world, and Megan could hear him tunelessly singing the words to Tom Jones' "Sex Bomb" as he made his way to his car. She had parked on the opposite side of the road to his red Porsche 928 or "The Fanny Magnet" as he had jokingly called it. Well, she had *assumed* it was in jest since he was supposed to be going out with Megan at the time but, given what she had found out about him since they had broken up, she thought that he may actually have been serious. Tosser.

Megan shook two of the tablets out of the bottle and swallowed them dry. She slid down in the seat of the ancient Volvo she had borrowed from a friend. It was unlikely that Campbell would spot her, he was too far up his own arse to take any notice of what was happening around him, but she didn't want to take risk it just in case. This would be her only chance to get inside the house. She had no doubts that he would get the locks changed after what she was about to do. Well, too late, she was about to hit him where it hurt.

Campbell threw his briefcase into the back of his car, got in and started the engine. As she expected, he drove off without even looking behind him, doing his favourite boy-racer start, and sped off down the road. She looked at her watch. Half nine. Bang on time. He was either off to his office at the museum or off for a meeting. She'd have a good few hours. She climbed out of the Volvo and went to the boot, looking around her before she took out the bucket of dog mess she had painstakingly collected from Kelvingrove Park the afternoon before, with the aid of a couple of Marks and Spencer bags and a pooper scooper. For the first time since Campbell had dumped her and she had lost her job Megan felt good about all the spare time she had. Collecting dog shit without drawing attention to herself had taken a remarkably long time. It would no doubt have been easier if she'd actually had a dog.

The street was quiet and it didn't appear that anyone was about to notice Megan and her eclectic collection—besides the bucket of dog shit, she had a restaurant-size bag of prawns, liquid laxative and a pair of scissors. She hurried up the steps and let herself into Campbell's house with the keys she still had from their two-year relationship. •

She closed the door behind her, humming happily as she pulled on a pair of rubber gloves. Now, she had a few important things to consider—such as where she should put the dog shit, how she was going to get the prawns into the curtain rails, and whether she should cut up *all* Campbell's suits or just his favourite ones. But first of all she would set the second part of her plan underway.

She picked up the phone, and dialled 141 before calling Campbell's mobile. "Oh, Campbell sweetie," she affected a low, breathy purr when he answered, "it's Hilary from the Burrell. Sorry about the voice—I have a bit of a sore throat. How do you fancy a nice early lunch today? I have a proposition for you. Lovely . . . My office in half an hour? Perfect, see you then." Smug-faced slimy bastard. He'd always fancied toad-faced Hilary, but she had invariably treated him with the contempt he deserved. Megan could almost sense the drool as Campbell accepted the lunch date.

She then rang Campbell's office phone, which was picked up after two rings by his secretary, Alison Anders. "Ms Anders? This is Nurse Ratched from Edinburgh Royal Infirmary. Nothing to worry about but your mother has had a wee fall and she'd like you to come through and collect her . . . She's fine, just a bit shaken . . . We'll make her a nice cup of tea, just come and collect her at Casualty. Cheerio, hen."

And then, continuing the medical theme, it was time to doctor Campbell's orange juice with a generous dose of laxative.


SHEEHAN LET HIMSELF into the upstairs parlour and quietly closed the door behind him. His employers had taken themselves off into the village with the new arrival, some weird old bag who seemed to wear nothing but purple velvet and who jumped at every bloody thing. The Countess and her sister treated the woman as if she was made out of some expensive china. The Signora in particular fluttered and fussed around her. But the Contessa was always there, watching her like an over-protective mother and quietly making sure she had everything she needed.

Sheehan wondered what the dowdy Londoner had that made his rich and regal Italian employers dote on her so much? He filed the question away for future consideration. Right now he needed to concentrate on the present.

He looked around the upstairs parlour. The sisters had been insistent that none of the staff set foot in their "*poco porto di tranquillity*," as The Contessa kept feckin' calling it until it was imprinted on his brain, and Sheehan had been champing at the bit to see what they'd got stashed in here. He idly thumbed through a selection of CDs—The Ramones, The Clash, Alien Sex Fiend, Rancid. He preferred a nice bit of Andy Stewart or Daniel O'Donnell himself.

The room was a tip. An empty tequila bottle and two heavy crystal glasses sat on a small antique table. An expensive-looking red dish that had some sort of Japanese design with dancing Geisha girls on it was overflowing with cigar ash and thick butts. He picked up the longest one and sniffed the end. It smelled fine. He tucked it into the breast pocket of his uniform jacket. Waste not, want not.

Shoes were strewn around the room. Delicate rainbow coloured mules with skinny little heels, sequin covered ballet slippers, a pair of Harley boots twice the size of the others. Sheehan couldn't imagine the Countess wearing the boots, but she had to be the one with the biggest feet, so the boots had to be hers. Interesting. There were newspapers everywhere. *News of the World* open to a page about a famous popstar bonking a politician's wife; a page ripped out of an old *Daily Record* about some museum exhibition; *Uncut Magazine*. Sheehan picked up a *Racing Post*. It was today's, a green highlighter pen singling out Two-Way Split in the 2.30 at Lingfield. And over the page, New Tricks in the 4.15 at Plumpton.

Sheehan tried to open the top drawer of a delicate-looking cabinet. Locked. He tried the other two drawers. The second one down was also locked. The third contained an empty gin bottle, a lipstick and a packet of corn plasters. He needed to get into those locked drawers. Now, where would they put the key?

Sheehan cast his eyes around the room. The mantelpiece—in one of those fancy looking vases no doubt. He moved swiftly over and picked up the nearest vase. Shook it. Nothing. Its twin at the other end sounded more promising. He tipped the vase upside down and a big white tablet fell out. He sniffed it cautiously. It smelled minty. Not drugs then—probably Steradent or something. A small box in the middle of the mantelpiece was also empty and the brass carriage clock revealed no hidden keys when he opened it.

Sheehan methodically paced the room picking things up, shaking them, feeling their nooks and crannies; pausing once as someone passed by outside the door. Feck. The old crones probably had the key with them. He'd have to force the drawers. But that would give the game away alright. He slapped the wall beside him, causing the tarnished frame of a painting of a huntsman in a red coat sitting on a horse and holding a dead pheasant to bounce against the wall.

Something slipped out from behind the frame and clattered to the floor.

Bing-fecking-o. Sheehan picked up the key and moved over to the locked drawers. The key turned smoothly in the top drawer and it slid out as Sheehan's clammy fingers clawed excitedly at it. A tube of Immac. A tube of fecking *Immac*? He'd wasted his afternoon only to discover that one of the old bags had a problem with unsightly facial hair? Disappointed, he turned the key in the middle drawer and pulled it open. A faintly unpleasant smell wafted out, but the sight that met his eyes was *extremely* pleasant. Hundreds and hundreds of used fivers. A sea of blue drink vouchers that made him quite light-headed.

He grabbed a handful from each drawer. It was careless leaving them there. The old bags obviously didn't have a scooby about the value of money. Rich bitches deserved to be parted from some of it. Fifty quid would do for now. He started to close the drawer and then hesitated. Well, maybe a ton. After all, he was going to have the whole lot at some point anyway. But for now a ton would be enough for a wee flutter while he made his plans to separate the two auld yins from the rest of their cash. Two-Way Split and New Tricks sounded like a nice each-way double.

LETTY CONSIDERED THE huge meringue filled with whipped cream and topped with a cherry. It was going to be tough to eat with any dignity. So why bother? She lowered her head to the plate, stuck out her tongue and licked the cream.

"Letty!" For gawds sake, you're supposed to be a sodding Countess." Dora was looking around the café, presumably to see if anyone had spotted Letty's lapse in manners. A family in the far corner was too busy dealing with a grumpy toddler, and a man in a business suit was tapping away at a laptop. Outside the café's large picture window the village street was deserted, apart from an outrageously dressed young girl with bright pink hair. She was wearing a fluorescent orange and black T-shirt that was several sizes too big for her, a pair of ripped black leggings covered in chains that Letty remembered from the punk days of the 1970s down the King's Road in London, and a pair of Doc Marten boots, painted turquoise. She was standing on the opposite side of the road, facing the window, holding copies of *The Big Issue*. Dora had taken pity on her on the way in and given her a twenty. She'd grinned and given Dora a thumbs-up before tucking the note into her jeans pocket.

Letty shrugged. "They'll just think I'm one of the eccentric upper classes, Dor'." She grinned at Gwen. "You alright, doll? Not too crowded in here for you, is it?"

"Nah, it's lovely, Letty. Just lovely." Gwen stirred her third cup of tea, steaming hot and syrupy with sugar. "I dunno what I would have done without you two. I was dreading coming out. I didn't have nowhere to go that was familiar to me, just some crummy hostel in Sydenham. I don't have no-one but you two. If you hadn't taken me in . . ."

Dora's lip quivered. "And why wouldn't we take you in Gwen? You're like family. I'll never forget . . . you know . . ." she trailed off and lifted her serviette to her eyes.

Letty cleared her throat. "Pair of soppy tarts. Dor', your mascara's running. You look like you're auditioning for a part in the Halloween version of *A Clockwork Orange*." Letty took a grey and crumpled handkerchief out of her pocket and licked the corner. She took Dora's chin gently in her hand and ran the handkerchief under Dora's eyes. "OK, let's get down to business. Gwen, doll, we've told you about the . . . ahem . . . little museum plan we have. Now, we'd really love you to give us a hand. While both Dor' and I can cope alright with basic locks and alarms, neither of us have your technical skills. But we completely understand if you'd rather not."

" 'Course I'm in, Letty. Just the three of us, is it?"

Letty looked at Dora, then slid out one of her cigarettes. Dora laid her hand on Letty's arm, her long, diamante studded fingernails glittering in the sunshine through the café's big window where they sat.

Letty sighed. "Bleedin' smoking ban." She took out a tin of snuff, twisted off the lid and took a huge pinch, sniffing it into each nostril. There was the usual anticipatory few seconds delay before she felt the burn of the tobacco and the almost icy rush of the menthol shooting up each nostril. The nicotine rush followed, making her heart beat faster, before it gave her the usual calming glow. "Well, see, Gwen, there we've got a little problem. We ain't as young as we used to be. We might think we're still twenty-five in our heads, but our bodies ain't able to keep up no more. We've got you for the technical stuff,

Dora with her organisational skills, and me for the planning. But what we're still missing is someone young and fit. Someone with a bit of cheek, more than a bit of charm and as cool as a cucumber to boot. And that's where we're struggling. We've got about two weeks to find someone, otherwise . . ."

They sat, contemplating the problem.

Letty looked up as the businessman's chair scraped back and she watched as he disappeared into the corridor leading to the toilets at the back of the café.

A minute later the café door opened and the girl who had been selling *The Big Issue* strolled in. Under the outrageous hair, her face was as delicate as an elf's and Letty watched her, intrigued. There was something light and insubstantial about her. Looking around, the girl walked confidently over to the businessman's table, closed the laptop he'd left there and tucked it under her arm. She took two steps back towards the door, then hesitated and turned back to the table again. Wiping the rim of the businessman's mug of coffee she lifted it to her lips and drank it down. Then she picked up the uneaten roll from his plate and lifted off the top to reveal a slice of ham and some salad. She picked out the cucumber and placed it carefully back on the plate, wiping her fingers on the napkin that lay on the table, put the top back on the roll and tucked it into her pocket. Ethereal—that was the word.

Letty noticed Dora and Gwen were watching the girl, too. Transfixed. It appeared that everyone else in the café, despite the girl's individual dress sense, had noticed nothing untoward. Cups were chinking, the muted hum of conversation and laughter carried on as normal.

The girl paused at their table. "Cucumber makes me heave." She picked up the Danish pastry that Dora had pushed to one side, strolled out of the café and off down the street. It wasn't just her clothes that were outrageous.

THE SUN STRIPED the steps through the narrow windows set high into the wall, cutting through the chill in this part of the museum, as Megan hurried up the spiral stone staircase to Campbell Findlay's office. His insistence on having an airy garret office, instead of one down in the bowels of the museum with all the other curators, worked in her favour. He'd said he was claustrophobic, and she'd felt awful for him at the time, making sure that if he needed anything from the windowless basement offices, she would go and get it. More fool her—she now realised he had just wanted to be—quite literally—above everyone else. But it had all worked out for the best. She knew that no-one else would be around. The hub of activity in the museum was down in the basement and nobody came up into the tower unless absolutely necessary.

Megan had half a bag of prawns and the remains of the liquid laxative in her carrier bag. Sadly, she had had to leave the bucket containing the rest of the dog mess in the boot of her car. While no-one would notice a woman with a carrier bag strolling into the museum, they *might* notice a woman carrying a bright yellow bucket of crap.

She poked her head around the door of the outer office at the top of the staircase. Alison's chair was empty and there was no noise coming from Campbell's office. Perfect. A few prawns tucked in the ventilation ducts, behind the ancient radiators and at the back of the drawers. And some laxative in Campbell's personal coffee machine. She would be in and out in a jiffy.

She closed the door behind her and let out a squeak as the phone rang. Her heart was pounding as though it was trying to jump out of her chest. Should she answer it? Although the office was away from the main part of the museum, the phone had a loud ring. A loud, accusatory, "there's an interloper in the office" sort of ring. Maybe someone would hear it and come up to answer it. Megan picked up the receiver and replaced it immediately. Silenced, but only for a few seconds as it started to ring again. She would have to answer it. "Campbell Findlay's office. How may I help you?"

"Oh, is Cammy around?"

Cammy? Megan almost gagged, whether from the twee nickname or from the sugary-sweet voice she wasn't sure. This sounded like one of Campbell's airhead bimbos. "I'm afraid that Mr Findlay is out for an appointment." Feeling reckless she added, "At the STD clinic."

"STD clinic?!" the voice sounded a little less sweet.

"Yes, I'm sure it's nothing to worry about. He has regular appointments."

"This is a regular thing?" Decidedly less sweet, more . . . vinegar.

"Oh, yes. He's on first-name terms with the staff. None of them will sleep with him, of course." There was silence on the other end of the phone. Shit. Megan wondered if she'd gone too far. Her brain was fogged from lack of sleep, but this was fun. And, after all, what did she have to lose? No-one had seen her come in, no-one would know she had been here. And if she could cause Campbell grief then . . . well . . . that had been her intention in coming here today, hadn't it?

"Well, here's another person that won't sleep with him." Megan put the receiver down as the woman hung up.

She opened all the drawers in Campbell's desk and threw some prawns at the back of each. The phone rang again.

She answered. A man's voice this time. "Mr Findlay is tied up at the moment," she said. Throwing caution to a force-ten gale, she added, "Quite literally, by this time, most probably. It's his Sex Fetishists Anonymous group meeting . . . Yes, I know, he really doesn't seem the type does he? Can I tell him you've . . . OK, bye bye, Bishop Cadwallader."

This *was* fun. Megan teased a small hole in the leather of Campbell's chair, opening up the seam in the seat back and, using his pencil, started poking in one prawn at a time. She'd managed five before the phone rang for a third time. An American voice drawled, "This is Alvin P Linklater the Third. I'm calling to let your Mr Findlay know that the Shih Tzu pair will be arriving in two weeks." Megan's good mood evaporated. This was the Treasures of the Globe Exhibition she had worked so hard on, that Campbell was now taking the credit for. "How can I help you, Mr Linklater? Can I give Mr Findlay a message on his return from the . . ."

"I know this is a lot earlier than we had planned but I have to head off on a business trip to Ouagadougou in about a week so I must bring the delivery forward. I need to make arrangements for someone from the museum to meet the security guy at the airport and collect the dogs from him."

"That's fine Mr Linklater, Mr Findlay is just . . ."

"I'm sure I have no need to stress to you, honey, how important it is that the little dogs are kept safe. I'm so goddamn thrilled to be able to loan them to a museum in the old homestead so to speak, but these puppies are my pride and joy. I would hate for anything to happen to them."

Megan was struck by an idea. An idea that would be *much* more destructive. She could do something to sabotage the exhibition and, with it, Campbell's chances of being taken seriously. What could she do? Steal the dogs? Hide them somewhere, maybe? Yes, that was a possibility. She would need to work on it but if she could do this right she could completely destroy Campbell's reputation and career, make him the laughing stock of the Scottish art scene, and maybe she could get her old job back. *If* she could do it right. It would be illegal, dangerous and a lot of hard work . . . but it would be worth it if she could pull it off.

"Certainly, Mr Linklater. Now, give me all the details of when the dogs are arriving and I will personally make sure they are taken very good care of."

She pulled a pen and paper from her handbag and wrote down the information given to her by the anxious Linklater. After hanging up she tipped the remaining laxative in the water cooler, emptied the last few prawns behind the tall filing cabinet in the corner and let herself out of the office.

She sneaked back down the stairs, pausing halfway down as an idea came to her. What if someone were to make replicas of the dogs and deliver them to the museum in place of the real ones? And maybe that person could leak information to the press that the dogs Campbell was gloating over were fakes. That would teach him. Megan hated being unemployed, but at least all this spare time gave her the freedom to do the things she needed to do today. Namely, dig newspaper out of the rubbish bin and start making a clay replica of a Shih Tzu using the photograph in the newspaper as a guide. After all, no-one knew what the dogs looked like in real life, did they? They'd been stuck in a collector's vault for years. Yes, she had plenty of things to keep her busy. Oh, and she would also need to find somewhere to dispose of half a bucket of dog shit.

DUNCAN PUNCHED RAYMIE in the arm. "Haw, Raymie, you gonnae stop eyeing up that bird and listen?"

"Look at her man, she's gaggin' for it. Play my cards right and I'm deffo gonnae get my Nat King Cole the night. She wants me, you can tell. She keeps lookin' over and giggling."

"That's cos you're a fugly bastard, not cos she's wanting your boaby." Raymie glared at him. As far as he was concerned he was God's gift. Duncan shook his head. Raymie looked as though he'd fallen out of the ugly tree and hit every branch twice on the way down. Plus, his face was full of angry red and white plooks and his teeth were rotten due to his heavy weed habit. Those munchies played havoc with your dentistry. To put it kindly, Raymie couldn't get his hole in a barrel of fannies. Maybe best not to dwell on that though, Raymie had a bastard of a temper. "Anyway, she's hackit, man," Duncan said. "A pure swamp donkey. She's got a face like a bulldog licking piss off a nettle and she's got to be about forty if she's a day."

Raymie shrugged. "A ride's a ride, man."

"Besides, her man's there. He's a big bear."

"Aye, he's blootered though, but. He's been on the bevy all night."

"He could still give you a good boot in the haw maws though, Raymie. Anyway, pay attention. We're here to discuss business, ya fud."

"So tell me again what we're gonnae do."

"I tell you Raymie, I've got a stoater of a plan. Can't fail, man. We're gonnae be rich. Those wee dogs is pure gold."

Duncan could almost see the cogs whirring as Raymie took a deep drag on his roll-up, narrowing his eyes as he sucked in the nicotine. He was the only person Duncan knew who could smoke a whole rollie in one drag. Raymie picked a piece of tobacco off his tongue and wiped it on his trousers, saying "So how do we steal them? We're not gonnae be able to just waltz into yon museum place and walk out with a pair of dogs worth millions. It's not as though we can put on a pair of sunglasses and carry a white stick and pretend they're dogs for the blind, Duncan man."

"It'll be a skoosh. We'll go in just afore closing time and check out where the wee dogs are, hide in the cludgies until it's dark, smash the glass case the dogs are in and then bolt."

Duncan thought his plan was a stoater but Raymie didn't look convinced. "You're pishin' out of your arse, you dobber. They're gonnae have guards and alarms and stuff. It's not like Tesco's. You can't just waltz in and stick things under your jacket, Dunk."

"I used to go to the Museum a lot when I was cutting school, man. They've got a couple of old geezers as guards. Big fat guys that can't do their jackets up for their bellies. They wouldn't be able to move faster than a slug if you stuck a rocket up their jacksies and put them on roller skates. They'll be sitting in their wee security guard place drinking tea and pulling their tadgers to the knicker pages in Kays Catalogue. They're no gonnae give us any hassle."

Raymie blushed to the roots of his spikey hair. "You fuckin' promised you weren't going to mention that again, you arse wipe."

"Most guys have a ham shank to *Playboy* or something. But not you, ya tube. Did your ma never wonder why the pages of her catalogue were all sticky?"

Raymie glared at him and gulped down the remainder of his fifth pint of the evening. "Anyway, maybe you're right about the guards, but what about the alarms? That place must be wired into the polis."

Duncan lifted his drink. It was really fucking expensive being a secret teetotaler. He had to get every round in so that Raymie wouldn't know that the vodka and Irn-Bru he was supposedly drinking was really just Irn-Bru. Raymie would have no respect for him if he knew Duncan didn't drink. Raymie lived for the bevy and measured everyone by how much drink they could hold, how many drugs they took, and how many people they'd chibbed. Anyone who didn't drink or take drugs or have a knife was a shitebag. Duncan took a gulp of the Irn-Bru.

"So what if there are alarms? There's *millions* of windows in that place. We just break one, jump out, and we're away across the park and out. By the time the polis arrive we'll be sitting on our arses with fifteen million quid of wee gold dog in our laps. Man, can you imagine? We'll be able to afford to get heavy bongoed in the pub every night." Raymie's eyes lit up under the solitary eyebrow. Duncan had obviously pushed the right button. "No, listen, man, we'll be able to buy our *own* pub. And we'll only let in the gorgeous lassies, no mingers. You'll not need to winch some wee hairy with a face like a smacked arse. With all that cash we'll be *hoaching* with fanny."

Raymie grinned. Dunk wondered if he should tell his pal it wasn't a good look. Raymie was addicted to deep-fried Mars bars, especially after he'd been on the weed. His teeth looked as though a psycho dentist had been at them with a blow torch. And his breath was boggin'. A mixture of sweet and sour, and day-old skittery shite.

"Well, I'm still not convinced, but it's worth a shot." Raymie's optimism had apparently got the better of him. Duncan knew he was deffo talking his language—birds and booze—what more could a red-blooded man want?

LOBSANG SAT HIS narrow single bed, meditating. He opened his eyes. The light from the candles cast flickering shadows through the darkened room, and the sound of chanting washed over him as he sat, cross legged, his hands resting on his knees, thumb and forefinger gently touching. He could feel the energy coursing through them. He glanced up and gazed at the image of the Goddess Nur-Lhamo, his heart feeling the usual warm and skippy way he always got when he gazed on her likeness.

He shook himself. Father Quang Tu always told him he had to concentrate when he was meditating, to stop thinking of earthly things and give himself up to the spiritual. He sighed. It was too late, his mind was altogether on the corporeal this evening. He picked up the newspaper clipping and read it once more. The holy temple dogs—resurfaced after all these years. His father, Quang Tu, would be blissfully happy if they were returned to their rightful home in the temple.

Since becoming High Priest of the Khang-pa Gser Khyi Tetsi Temple—The House of the Little Golden Dog—sixty years ago, Quang Tu had been driven by the thought of returning the sacred Temple Guardians back to their rightful place. Lobsang knew that he was the last hope of Quang Tu. He had to get those dogs back for the temple. He looked from the newspaper clipping to the small statue of the Goddess Nur-Lhamo on its plinth. He turned to the huge stone statue on the platform, draped in its yellow robes and freshly cut flowers, the mandalas on the walls framing her beauty.

"Nur-Lhamo—help me please." He hoped that the goddess knew that he took his sacred duty very seriously. The holy dogs had to be returned to the Temple where they belonged. Lobsang smoothed out the well-folded clipping from the *Daily Record* and placed it with the picture of the dogs by the statue's feet. "We'll get them back, I promise."

Quang Tu had written a carefully worded letter to the American collector who claimed that he "owned" the dogs. This had been answered with a curt response from the man's legal representative. That door was closed. Quang Tu had told Lobsang that he did not have the time for long drawn out legal battles. He wanted to see the dogs returned to their rightful place before he left these earthly realms. And, according to his doctors, that day was not many months hence.

Quang Tu had been Lobsang's inspiration and loved him like a true son. Returning the dogs to their spiritual home was Lobsang's destiny. He opened the thin paper containing the message from Quang Tu. "You will face many fears and tribulations on your journey my son. You must stay strong to your faith, but above all stay true to yourself and you will come through it a stronger man. You know that you were led to The House of the Little Golden Dog for a reason. I know that the Goddess Nur-Lhamo will protect you and keep you safe. We at the temple will pray for *ta-shi* for your journey. But you must be wary, young Lobsang."

Lobsang touched his lips to the paper. "I won't let you down, Father." He couldn't remember his real father and mother. He had pictures to remind him of how they looked, and he could remember laughter and happiness and games and trips and fun, but he couldn't remember their voices, or his mother's touch, or see his father's smile. No, Quang Tu was his only father now, and he didn't want to let him down.

"Kyle! Kyle, come and get your mince and tatties, son."

Kyle sighed. When was his gran going to remember to call him by his Buddhist name? Quang Tu had given him the name Lobsang, meaning "the kind-hearted one," but his gran insisted on calling him by his earthly name. Still, she did make brill mince and tatties. Kyle Naismith blew out the candles and opened the door of his bedroom. "Coming, gran."

"HOLD UP, DOLL." Letty was out of breath as she tried to catch up with the pink-haired girl carrying the plastic bag of *Big Issue* magazines in one hand, and the top-of-the-range laptop in the other. Letty's dogs were barking in the pointy-toed sequinned shoes Dora had persuaded her to wear for the trip to the tea shop in Luss.

Manolos were not meant for running down the street in. Especially when you were sixty-eight. Well, OK, seventy-eight.

The girl turned around suspiciously. "Just cos your pal gave me twenty quid lady, doesn't mean I owe you." She had a soft southern English accent that she was trying to make sound hard and don't-give-a-shit. It didn't really work.

"It's not like that, love. It's just that . . . well, my sister and I have . . . an interesting proposition for you. Come home with us, and we'll explain it to you."

"Oh, I *see*, like that is it? Well, sorry to disappoint you but I'm not interested in women. I prefer men." The girl turned away, surprisingly graceful in her Doc Marten boots.

Letty snorted. "Bugger me, doll, me an' all. Not saying I haven't done a little rug-munching when the situation called for it, or the client requested it, haven't we all, but give me a man any day." The girl turned back, her black-ringed eyes wide. She looked like a bush baby. Letty smiled at her and sighed. "It's been a bloody long time though . . ."

The girl let out a hearty laugh. "Well, you're a bit of a game old bird, ain't ya? So, you some sort of "tart with a heart"? An eccentric do-gooder, who's seen the light and now wants everyone else to mend their wicked ways then?"

Letty patted the girl on the cheek. "No, love, nuthin' like that." She tucked her liver-spotted hand under the girl's bony elbow and beamed up at the pale face with its delicate features. The dramatic make-up did nothing to disguise a bruised look that Letty recognised as stemming from pain, worry and lack of sleep. She *did* look like a bush baby—a vulnerable, heartbroken bush baby. Letty led the bemused girl off down the street to where Letty and Gwen were waiting. "Nothing like that at *all*. In fact, doll, it's exactly the opposite."

VICTOR STANISLAV SAT at his corner table in Glasgow's Rogano restaurant. The Rogano had been an excellent choice—Victor made sure that, wherever he went in the world, he dined out on the finest cuisine. He would have come here anyway, but it was serendipitous that his quarry had chosen to dine here this evening and when Victor discovered that, he'd immediately made a reservation. This restaurant had come highly recommended, and with good reason. His monkfish-and-leek parcels with the delicate mousseline of scallops had been a melt-in-the mouth delight, and the dessert of frangipane tart with griotines was wonderfully complemented by the sharpness of the accompanying cherry sorbet.

He closed his well-read copy of Descartes' *Discours Sur La Methode*, finished the last drop of the excellent *Chateau d'Yquem* dessert wine with its heady overtones of honeyed tropical fruits, and signalled for his bill. Descartes' *Discours* was the bible by which Victor lived. He applied its concepts in every circumstance, including the situation in which he currently found himself. Descartes' first precept was to accept only that of which you are sure.

Victor was definitely sure that the so-called Contessa Letitzia di Ponzo and Signora Teodora Grisiola were a pair of deceitful elderly harridans. He was equally sure that they would pay for their transgressions, and that he, Victor Ignatius Raskolnikov Stanislav, was the ideal man to make them pay. According to Descartes, precepts two and three were to divide the difficulties into small parts, and to solve the simplest problems first. Well, Victor was well on the way to achieving those aims—he had taken the initial step of making sure that he was inhabiting roughly the same geographical space as his prey. Descartes' fourth precept was to make as complete a list as possible of what needed to be done to ensure that nothing was omitted. Victor's list was dazzling in its simplicity. It was, in fact a very short list. Item one was "Find the bitches," item two was "Kill the bitches." Of course, item two was further subdivided into sub-section a ("disembowel aforementioned bitches with a sharp knife"), sub-section b ("force-feed them their still warm livers") and sub-section c ("tear their wrinkly heads off"). Victor was nothing if not thorough in his planning.

While enjoying his dinner and his book, Victor had paid attention to the muted hum in the restaurant around him—the clink of cutlery on fine china, the chink of glasses, the laugher and conversation of Glasgow's glitterati. As he waited for his bill, the world encroached again. His ear was, by now, finely attuned to the annoying voice at the next table, which belonged to the object of his attentions. A red-faced and chinless English man was holding court over his two well-dressed and rather bored-looking companions.

". . . made an absolute *killing* at the Races. Old Jonty was on top form and I had three winners in the first four races. It was champers all round I can tell you!"

One of the other men at the table said something that was too quiet for Victor to catch.

"Oh, it was top hole, old chap. Had myself a little investment while I was there. Hundred and fifty grand in a *super* little investment opportunity. Thirty-percent return not to be sneezed at, what?"

Victor closed his eyes as if in pain as the obnoxious loudmouth snorted and guffawed. Somebody should have done something about the dreadful inbreeding in the English aristocracy before it had got to this stage. However, this seemed to be the proof he needed that he was on the right track. Victor had spent the days since his arrival in Glasgow trying to track down the Countess and her sister. He had been busy researching Glasgow society. It wasn't too much of an effort. He had visited some excellent restaurants, one or two gentlemen's clubs, chatted with doormen and waiters and trawled the Internet. It appeared that this . . . blowhard . . . at the next table knew everything and everyone in west of Scotland society and if anyone would know where his prey was located, this man would.

"Oh, of *course* I can introduce you, Alastair, old chap. The Countess and her sister are two of my *dearest* friends. I'm taking the Laird of Stradavullin there for dinner next week. Lovely little pile they have. Wouldn't mind a bit of that myself in this part of the world. So near Glasgow and yet super for grouse . . ."

Well, well, well. Victor was a great believer in serendipity. And here was a perfect example. With a little bit more luck he could cross item one off his list.

"Your bill, sir." Victor smiled at the waiter and took his wallet from the jacket of his bespoke Saville Row suit. He slid out a credit card halfway, hesitated, pushed the card back and took out a thick wedge of cash instead. His credit card was in a false name but he would rather there was no record of even one of his pseudonyms being in the restaurant that evening. Just in case. Victor placed the notes in the folder provided, including a large, but not overly large, tip, and left the restaurant.

Victor moved towards the arch leading to Royal Exchange Square and stood in the shadows, enjoying the pleasant evening breeze. From his breast pocket he took a limited edition Cohiba Double Corona, unwrapped it and ran the cigar under his nose. Beautiful. It smelled of rich undersoil and spices. He lit it and took a long soft draw. A herbaceous, piquant taste, with an intriguing undernote of florals and young leather. He hoped the Englishman was in no hurry to leave the restaurant.

SHEEHAN PACED IN front of the door of the upstairs parlour pausing to listen fruitlessly at the door from time to time. The old crones had brought home some scruffy wee jakey and now the Countess, her sister, the weird silent one and the teenager had been closeted in there for hours. Sheehan feckin' *hated* not knowing what was going on. What did they want the junkie girl for anyway? She was probably a thievin' little bitch and would fleece the daft auld bags if they weren't careful. And if there was any fleecing to be done then *he* was the one to do it. No little junkie punk tart bitch was going to elbow her way into *his* cushy little number. Not a feckin' chance.

And he wished they'd get to feck out of his personal bank vault. He wanted to relieve the drawers of another wad of fifties. He'd put a wee punt on the horses that had been circled in the sisters' *Racing Post*. Two-Way Split had romped home at 15-1 and New Tricks had beaten his nearest rival by a short head, coming in at 3-1. Sheehan had been minted, for all of half an hour until the donkey he backed in the next race fell at the first fence. It had broken its leg and Sheehan hoped the bastard had been melted down to make glue. He'd lost every penny. And more besides.

So he needed some more stake money for tomorrow, and his bookie was refusing to let him have tick, the miserable feck. He put his ear to the door. Frustratingly, he could hear the soft buzz of voices, and the occasional laugh, but he couldn't make out anything that was being said. Feck it, he would go out and take the Daimler for a spin into Helensburgh, see if he could find some wee bird on her way home from the dancing, in her shag me shoes, and give her a bit of the old Sheehan Sausage. By the time he came back the old biddies would have gone to bed and he could nip in and get some cash from the drawers. Might even fire up that laptop that the Signora was always tapping away on, see what all the fuss was about.

\*     \*     \*

THE OBNOXIOUS ENGLISHMAN and his companions rolled out of the front door of the Rogano.

"So, chaps, anyone fancy that lap-dancing place in Mitchell Street? Some top totty there and the girls all love me. I have to fight them off."

One of the men laughed. "No thanks, Charlie. It's alright for you single men, but some of us have wives to go home to."

"Well, you know what they say Alastair—what happens in The Pink Pussycat Club stays in The Pink Pussycat Club. I'm one of their best customers. The owners know me—I can get us the best seats in the house doncha know."

"You just go on, Charlie. We'll see you at rugger tomorrow." Victor drew back further into the shadows as the Englishman's two dinner companions passed by. "For God's sake, Alastair," he heard one of them say, "that bloke's a wanker of the first order. Where did you pick him up?"

Victor pulled on a pair of fine tan leather gloves, gloves that had been tailored especially for him and which had been moulded to fit his hands like . . . well, like the finest glove . . . and he watched as Charlie set off in the determined but staggering gait of a drunk, humming tunelessly to himself. He crossed the pedestrian safety of Buchanan Street, and into Gordon Street.

Victor followed him at a distance. There were very few people around and, as Charlie turned left into Mitchell Street, Victor increased his speed. Mitchell Street was narrow, dark and quiet at this time of night. Which were the exact attributes Victor was looking for. As Charlie passed a multi-storey car park, Victor started running, slammed into Charlie and hustled him inside the entrance and up some stairs, his hand over Charlie's mouth. The place was closed for the evening and deserted but Victor wasn't taking any chances. He slammed Charlie's head into the door of the lift.

He stood behind Charlie and put his mouth close to the man's left ear. "I'm going to take my hand away from your slobbering mouth. If you so much as breathe loudly I will snap your neck. You will speak only when I tell you to and you will do it quietly. Is that clear?"

Charlie made an unintelligible noise and nodded. Victor slowly took his hand away from Charlie's mouth and wiped it on the jacket of Charlie's pin-striped suit. Charlie remained with his head pressed against the lift door.

"Turn round."

Charlie reluctantly did so. "I say, old chap . . ."

Victor held up his hand to stop the bleating. "Did I *tell* you to speak?"

Charlie shook his head.

"What is your name?"

"Charles Hamilton-Kirkspriggs. I'm a—"

". . . Wanker who's about to have his neck snapped if he doesn't shut the fuck up when I tell him to. Yes, I know. Now, I overheard you mentioning that you may know two . . . ladies, although I use the term in its loosest sense—the Contessa di Ponzo and the Signora Grisiola. Is that correct?"

Charlie nodded.

"They are good friends of yours?"

"Well . . . not really . . . I mean, I hardly know them. I only met them—"

Victor stopped him with a blow to the stomach that made Charlie bend double and retch. Victor neatly sidestepped the stream of vomit. "So you were lying to your friends? Trying to make yourself out to be better connected than you are?"

Charlie nodded, wiping a strand of drool from his mouth.

"Tut tut, Charles. Lying is a *very* bad habit. I shall add that to the list of things that annoy me about you." Charlie opened his mouth to speak. "And, I must say Charles, that list is getting rather long." Charlie shut his mouth again with a sob.

"Now then, Charles. Do you know where the old bitches live?"

Charlie's head bobbed up and down like the annoying nodding dogs Victor hated so much when he saw them in the backs of cars. What *made* people purchase such crap?

"Charles, you may speak. But only to tell me where they live."

"C-C-Cardieu Castle. Along the A82 towards Loch Lomond. It's on the—"

"Thank you. I will find it. Now, that wasn't difficult was it?"

Charlie's shoulders relaxed slightly.

"Oh, by the way, I'd like your wallet please, Charles."

"Oh, I *say*, old chap, I've given you—"

Charlie's braying protestations ceased abruptly as the bones in his neck snapped. Victor lowered him to the ground, removed the wallet from Charlie's inside pocket using a crisp linen handkerchief and exited the empty car park. The handkerchief was just a precaution—the same plastic surgeon who had fixed Victor's face had also replaced his fingerprints with skin from his feet—a painful procedure but well worth the effort. Victor had taken the opportunity of the enforced bed rest to have extensive dental surgery. Again, no records existed. He had made sure of that. As a result he was anonymous and untraceable. He could do what he liked, with impunity. And he did.

Victor strolled back up Mitchell Street and turned onto Gordon Street. It was a pleasant night, still, so he decided to walk back to his hotel a few streets away in Blythswood Square. As he passed the front of Central Station he noticed a skinny youth in a baseball cap and one of those horrendous nylon outfits that Glasgow's drug addict population seemed to favour, according to an article he'd read in the *Glasgow Herald* that morning. That the scumbag's left trouser leg was tucked into his white athletic sock outraged him all the more. The youth appeared to be watching him, sizing him up. Victor put a slight stagger into his walk, took the dead Englishman's wallet out, again using his handkerchief, and dropped it, as if by accident, behind him. When he reached the corner he turned back. The face of Glasgow drug chic was holding the wallet in his hands. Good. He would hopefully try and use the credit cards, or pass them on to someone else. That would confuse the police a little. And with any luck the drug addict would be arrested for the murder.

Victor strolled towards his hotel, pleased with his evening's work. A good dinner, a nice cigar, the world was one blowhard lighter, and a thieving drug addict would be removed from the streets if the police did their job properly. And, above all, he now knew where his prey lived. Almost time for item two on his list.

"SO, DOLLFACE, TELL us some more about you." Letty offered the pink-haired girl a cigarette. The girl, it turned out, was called Katrina and Letty was pleased to see that she had taken being picked up by three elderly ladies, brought back to a castle and fed on Chinese takeaway, completely in her stride.

They were now in the billiard room on the lower ground floor of Cardieu Castle—the green baize-covered snooker table dominating the room with its oppressive dark-red walls covered in photographs of Cardieu ancestors through the ages with their hands full of dead animals. Heads of the same animals dotted the walls and looked down on the four women as they each took their turn at the snooker table.

Letty and Dora had sounded Katrina out while Gwen, as ever silent in the company of strangers, had looked on, occasionally wafting away the cigarette smoke, but otherwise totally still, only her eyes darting from face to face as she took everything in.

Letty took pride in being a good judge of character and it was seldom that her snap decisions about people were proved wrong. They hadn't yet told Katrina their plans but Letty was convinced that, even if she didn't want any part of them, she wouldn't grass them up to the rozzers. She hadn't yet asked *them* any questions, but Letty had noticed that her eyes were darting about all the time and she didn't seem to miss anything that was going on around her. Those eyes were stunning but looked far older than the nineteen she had admitted to and Letty recognised some of the experiences she could see in them.

Katrina waved away the offer of the cigarette. "No thanks, Letty, but I'll have another of those margaritas. They're smashing." She held out her glass for Letty to give her a refill from the pitcher next to her. Snooker balls clicked as Dora and Gwen played a well-matched game. "Not much to tell, really. After my dad buggered off and left us we were living in Folkestone. My mum met this guy from Edinburgh on the Internet and we moved up here to live with him and his son when I was thirteen." She paused, then shrugged. "I didn't like his son, so I ran away shortly after. Spent a couple of years on the streets in Glasgow, then moved out here—I prefer the countryside. Got a bedsit, sell *The Big Issue* to tourists. Do this and that, you know. Whatever I have to."

"Like nickin' laptops?"

Katrina grinned. "Yeah, well, if you're stupid enough to leave two grands-worth of equipment on the table in full view, what can you expect?

"Too right, dollface." Letty held up her glass. "Here's to crime!"

"Talking of which, I'm assuming I'm not here for totally legitimate reasons. So what's the score?"

Letty looked at Dora and raised her eyebrows.

"I think she can be trusted, Letty, love. Black ball, corner pocket."

As Dora walked around the table to take her shot, Gwen muttered, "Were playing snooker. You don't need to say which pocket. You only do that in pool."

"Oh, sorry, Gwen, dear. I always get that wrong, don't I?" Dora smiled at Gwen and patted her on the leg as she passed her.

Letty refilled Katrina's margarita. "Well, treacle, if these two old tarts have quite finished debating the finer points of the game, let me just put it this way. How much would you risk for a couple of million quid?"

"Letty, some days I'd cover myself in chicken liver paté and jump into a pond full of piranhas that hadn't eaten for a week if there was a five-pound note at the bottom."

"Well, dollface, if all goes to plan, you can buy all the paté you want, and the Arsenal football team to smear it on if that's what tickles yer fancy." Katrina raised her glass as though she was toasting eleven paté smeared hunks and Letty clinked her own glass against it. "Dor', you'd best let that slimy git Sheehan know that we'll need him in the morning for a run into Glasgow. Us girls are going to get us some culture. But first, we need to get Katrina here kitted out with some new togs. And, I think, a trip to The Rainbow Room for a new hairdo." She gingerly patted the top of Katrina's brightly coloured head. "Doesn't this get you more notice than you want?"

"Actually, it has the opposite effect." Katrina ran a hand through the spikes. "People tend to notice the hair and the clothes but never the person in them. It sort of makes me invisible, in an in-your-face sort of way . . ." She shrugged.

"Well, doll, for *our* purposes, I think we want to tone you down a bit. Summat a little less spiky and not quite so . . . pink."

MEGAN DRAINED THE last of her glass of wine and twirled the stem of the glass in her fingers. "Certainly, Mr Linklater, I will be at the airport to pick the dogs up personally. You have absolutely no need to worry. I can assure you that an insurance policy is in place and the museum is picking up the tab for the premium . . ."

"Little lady, the insurance is not my primary concern. These little dogs are my pride and joy. I need to be sure that your security is second to none. Otherwise I will send my own men over."

"That is very kind of you, but really not necessary, Mr Linklater. Our security staff are top notch. We have hired extra staff for the period of the exhibition and I will ensure that the dogs are given special treatment. Please don't worry, we—"

Dear God, was the man *ever* going to shut up about his precious sodding dogs? Megan placed the receiver gently on the coffee table and went into the kitchen to refill her glass from the cheap but tasty bottle of Tesco's Rioja. She'd been on the phone making final arrangements for the last half an hour, trying to reassure the American that the precious pooches would be treated with kid gloves. Her phone bill was going to be massive. Still, it would be worth it, to get her own back on that slimeball ex of hers, Campbell Findlay.

Back in the living room, she put the phone to her ear. The American was still droning on about his "babies." She could probably have left the phone while she cooked herself a three-course meal and he would still be rabbiting on when she came back.

Megan took a huge gulp of wine, almost choking as she swallowed it in a hurry when Linklater ran out of steam. "Rest assured that I will be at the airport tomorrow to collect the dogs from your security man . . . No, no. Absolutely no need for him to stay. I will have our own men with me and the dogs will be perfectly safe . . . Oh, I'm terribly sorry, Mr Linklater. That's the Czar of Russia on the other line about the Fabergé egg the Imperial Russian family are loaning us for the Exhibition, I'm going to have to go."

Whoops. The wine and lack of sleep must be getting to her. Even Linklater must be aware that the last Czar of Russia died almost a hundred years ago. But no, it was OK, he hadn't noticed. Just a final exhortation to ensure that the dogs were displayed on the Chinese silk cushions he was sending over with them. After a breezy "Give my regards to His Czarship," Linklater ended the call.

Megan put the phone down with relief and rubbed her ear. She looked at the concrete and iron dogs on the table in front of her. The casts had turned out . . . well, they had turned out. That was about all she could say. Megan was, even if she said so herself, an excellent artist and very much in demand. Since her abrupt departure from the museum she had been keeping herself busy and financially afloat with various commissions, mostly via word of mouth. The dogs, however, had meant that her paid work had been put on hold for the last couple of days. Megan was a perfectionist but she hadn't had time to create a masterpiece which was up to her usual standards and, whilst the dogs closely resembled the originals in all important aspects, one of them had a squint and the other a wonky nose. They looked ugly and a little bit grumpy. However, they would pass and tomorrow she would paint the fake dogs with gold paint and stick on the array of cheap stones she had bought from the art supply shop—rubies, emeralds, sapphires, diamonds. They wouldn't be exact copies, and they wouldn't fool an expert in Eastern art. But then, Campbell Findlay was no expert. This would expose him for the useless tosspot he was and hopefully he'd get the sack. And if she wasn't arrested for theft, forgery and God only knew what else, she might get her job back, and maybe get a sleep for the first time since the whole sorry mess happened. Yes, well, she should look on the bright side. She picked up one of the dogs. Dear merciful heavens but it was hellish ugly.

IN THE UPSTAIRS parlour of Cardieu Castle Letty was tucking into a full Scottish breakfast—bacon, sausage, fried eggs, fried tomatoes, white pudding, tatty scone, toast—a heart attack on a plate but it suited her constitution. She'd started her day with a fry up for at least sixty of her seventy-eight years and it hadn't done her any harm. And sausages always reminded her fondly of the good old days. She took the last piece of fat, pink sausage and used it to wipe up the bright yellow egg yolk. She popped it into her mouth and chewed, sitting back in the floral easy chair with a sigh.

Letty picked up the *Racing Post* and lit a cigarette, resting her feet on the tiny Edwardian coffee table in front of her. Ah, life was good.

Dora gasped, almost spilling her tea on the *Glasgow Herald* she was reading. "Letty . . . you know that Charles Hamilton-Kirkspriggs bloke who's supposed to be coming to dinner with the Laird of Stradavullin on Saturday?"

"Bleedin' hell, Dor'. I can't stand that big-mouthed twat. But he knows most of the rich gits up here. I dunno if I can stand yet another evening in his company. I wish we didn't have to have him over. But he's too valuable a contact to just drop, more's the pity."

"Well, Letty dear. It looks as though the wish fairy has smiled on you. He's been murdered."

Letty sucked on her cigarette. "Murdered?"

"Yes. Listen to this. 'The body of Charles Hamilton-Kirkspriggs—well known bon vivant and nightclub entrepreneur—has been found dead in a city centre multi-storey car park. Police believe it was a murder motivated by robbery.  A youth is helping police with their enquiries.' "

"I dunno, Dor'. It's shocking how young people behave these days. In our day there weren't—"

"Oh, shit." Dora raised a trembling hand to her mouth. "Oh, my God, Letty, listen to this. 'Hamilton-Kirkspriggs parted from his dining companions outside the Rogano Restaurant in Glasgow's City Centre and was found dead shortly after. Police are trying to trace a man who was eating on his own in the same restaurant and who was seen by the dead man's friends as they left. Police believe he may have valuable information in connection with Hamilton-Kirkspriggs' death.' " Dora held the paper up and stabbed a pink fingernail at the page. "This bit . . ." She pushed her glasses further up her nose. " 'He is described as being very smartly dressed, approximately six-feet tall and athletic-looking with wavy black hair. Restaurant staff noted his accent as being distinctive—either Russian or Eastern European, mixed with Australian.' " Dora looked at Letty, a look of horror on her face.

"You think it's *Stan*? Don't be daft, Dora. There's no way he could have found us. It's probably some Aussie tourist. You know they get everywhere. In some parts of London you're tit deep in them."

Dora ran a hand over her forehead and back over her neat French pleat. "I just think it's a bit of a coincidence. You know how angry he was."

"I think it *is* a coincidence. Don't worry. We'll keep an eye out, if that will make you feel better, girl. And once we get the dogs we'll disappear. We'll have so much bleedin' dosh we'll be able to have plastic surgery that'll turn us into Halle Berry and Angelina Jolie. Bugger me, maybe we'll even treat Sheehan to a facelift too. Turn him into Johnny Depp and buy him a lorryload of Viagra."

Dora gave a weak laugh. "Well, Letty, if you don't stop eating all those fry-ups, you're going to end up looking like Margaret Rutherford rather than Angelina Jolie."

Letty ignored her and turned back to the *Racing Post*. She wasn't going to discuss this nonsense about Stan anymore. Dora was overreacting and Stan was back in Australia where they'd left him. She was sure about that. She folded over the page. Absolutely certain. Just as certain as she was that Saturday's Child was going to win the 2.10 at Folkestone.

THE ISLAND OF Creagsaigh had been Kyle's home for the last ten years and now he was getting ready to leave. He'd hardly set a foot off the island since he was seven. Kyle hadn't told his gran why he was going, just that he had to go to the mainland for a few days. She hadn't been happy. In fact, she had cried, which had made Kyle feel sad. But she was his gran and she was here to see him off. In fact, the whole island was here, waiting with him for the boat to arrive to take him over to Lewis. He would then get on the plane from Stornoway to Glasgow. His stomach flip flopped at the thought—it would be his first plane trip.

It would be nice to see more than six people in one place at any one time—and people his own age too. On Creagsaigh he was the youngest islander. By about forty years. His gran had taken him there after the death of his parents. It was the island she had been born on and she had taken Kyle back there after the accident. She had said that Kyle would be safe there. She wasn't going to let *him* be mown down by a drunk driver. Kyle had submitted to her cosseting willingly. He'd been in the car when his mum and dad were killed and he missed them very much. On the island he knew he was safe and loved. The nightmares had only stopped about two years ago. And now he was getting ready to leave. His stomach felt fluttery and his hand tightened over his gran's. He was going to miss her.

She had home-schooled him—every couple of months a big box of lessons and supplies had arrived from the mainland. Kyle had an aptitude for maths and science but his real love was English. He loved books—particularly books about adventure and excitement, and especially those with proper heroes. He'd got that from his gran, who also loved to read. She wouldn't let him have anything too modern though. She vetted all the books that arrived, reading them first and tut-tutting over some as she sat in her hard wooden chair by the fire. So he'd grown up with John Buchan and Leslie Charteris and

Raymond Chandler. He had roamed the small island imagining he was Biggles, or The Saint. Saving the world and falling in love.

He could feel himself blushing, and put a hand on his cheek, feeling it hot under his fingers. The boat was nearing the shore, bobbing up and down gently on the grey water. He knew that some bits of his education were sadly lacking. His gran had locked up one of the biology books in the dining room cupboard. Kyle had received an education in life by the other islanders—old Fraser the Fish, naturally enough, had taught him to fish; Morag had taught him to weave. He could birth a lamb, and repair a boat, and cook a hearty stew. But he still didn't know whether the funny feelings he had got in his groin since hair started to grow there were natural. He'd seen the bull mount the cow of course, but then, the bull had a purpose. Kyle didn't think that touching himself there was something he should be doing. And he couldn't ask his gran. And when he asked Fraser the Fish, Fraser just cleared his throat, gazed out to sea and muttered something about sin.

Kyle checked his luggage for the fiftieth time. He'd been to Lewis before but even that was exciting. He'd gone over to do an exam last year. His gran had come with him for a wee operation as a day patient. She had told Kyle to wait for her in the library where his exam was being held. He had been tempted to go to the pub but the sour smell outside had put him off, so he had done as she had asked and gone back to the library where he had people watched for a while. That was good. There were girls there. They made him feel funny. Nice funny though. But he had to hold his coat over his groin when he got up to leave. The librarian had also showed him how to use a computer and he had surfed the Internet. The computer's previous user had been looking up Buddhism and Kyle had been interested to read up about it. That's how he'd found his father and the temple. He'd written down the address and sent a letter. His friendship with Quang Tu had started from that moment.

Kyle was startled out of his reverie by his gran squeezing his hand hard. She was looking up at him, a wee tear running down her weatherbeaten face. Kyle suddenly wondered if he was doing the right thing. Glasgow wasn't for him. Maybe he should just stay here. He put his suitcase down. Aye, he would stay. Look after his gran. Tend the sheep. Sit out on the cliffs and watch the birds.

"Well, son, this is it." His gran reached a cool hand up and stroked his cheek. "I've put *The Thirty-Nine Steps* and *Mr Standfast* in your suitcase. You can read them at night, because you'll not be sitting in the pub, son, will ye?"

"Gran, but I—"

"I'm proud of you, son." His gran looked at the silent islanders, who surrounded Kyle in a circle. "We all are. And we know you'll come back a bigger man than you went. It's only right that you go away from us, Kyle—then you will know that you belong here."

Kyle looked at her shining eyes and then looked away—unable to bear the pain he saw there. His gran didn't want him to go, but if she could be strong about it then so could he.

"I love you, Gran."

"I love you too, son. Stay safe, Kyle. Ring me every evening when you're safely back in your hotel. At 7 p.m., mind."

"Aye, Gran." Kyle raised his eyebrows at Fraser.

"Don't you be going into any pubs, now."

"No, Gran."

"And no talking to any girls."

"Aw, Gran, course not." Kyle felt his face burning.

"And mind and go to church on Sunday. I've told the minister at the Church on St Vincent Street to expect you. And he'll come by your hotel and see you too."

"Thanks, Gran." Kyle awkwardly hugged his gran, suitcase in one hand. She was getting awfy frail.

She stood on tiptoe and gave him a kiss on the cheek. "Doesn't seem long since you were just a wee totty boy" She ruffled his hair. "Here's the boat, son. I'll let you say goodbye to everyone else." With a final hug, she stepped back as Kyle received pats and hugs and kisses from the rest of the islanders. Fraser helped him into the boat and then handed him his ancient suitcase. As the boat pushed off from the shore Fraser whispered, "The Snaffle Bit in Sauchiehall Street. Nice wee boozer. Tell them I sent you and they'll look after you there, laddie."

As the boat pulled away from the small dock, Kyle felt lonely and miserable. The lump in his throat was huge. He wondered if it would choke him. He waved to the dwindling specks on the jetty and turned away towards the Isle of Lewis.

"Off for an adventure, young Kyle?"

Kyle nodded at the boat's skipper and then smiled, "Aye, Skip, I am that." And he was. And he realized he was looking forward to it.

"LADIES AND GENTLEMEN, welcome to Glasgow. You may now disembark the aircraft using the forward door. Please ensure that you have all your belongings with you."

Kyle was excited. And he was also desperate to go to the loo. He hadn't dared get up during the journey and had sat with his seatbelt on the whole time. Luckily, it was a short flight from Stornaway. He clapped his hands in glee and then turned apologetically to his seat companion. "Sorry, madam, this is my first time on a plane and my first time in Glasgow. I can't wait to see all the buildings and the shops. And everyone says the people are so friendly."

The elderly lady in seat 56A smiled at him sweetly and put her cross stitch into the bag at her feet. "Fuck me, son, but you're in for an awfy shock."

Kyle handed her down her capacious carpet bag from the overhead locker and she pushed her way into the aisle, shaking her head. Kyle beamed at his fellow passengers as he let them past and then made his way to the front of the plane.

Two of the pretty air-hostesses were at the front saying goodbye to people as they left the plane.

"Goodbye, sir, enjoy your stay."

"Have a nice visit, madam."

"Goodbye, sir, thank you for flying with us."

As Kyle got to the front of the plane he dropped his rucksack and shook each of the girls' hands in turn, as his gran had taught him, although perhaps a little too enthusiastically and definitely for too long, but he couldn't help it.

"Goodbye, sir, enjoy your stay in Glasgow."

As Kyle left the plane he wished he had had the courage to ask one of the stewardesses out for a meal. He followed the crowds along the corridor and down a moving staircase to the baggage carousel. He ran back up the stairs a few times, just so he could come down the moving staircase again, before finally reluctantly moving to the baggage carousel. It was brill too. By now, Kyle's was the only case left on and he ran after it and picked it off the conveyor before it disappeared behind the plastic curtain. He headed for the door marked "Exit," wondering where to find the bus into Glasgow. He stopped to look at the myriad of signs and someone thumped into him from behind, causing them both to yelp.

"Hey, man, you should watch where you're going." He turned towards the owner of the deep voice behind him and found himself staring into the stomach of an immense man. Kyle, the tallest on the island at five feet eleven inches, had to tilt his head backwards to look up into a pair of muddy green eyes under a blonde buzz cut. Kyle was intrigued. The man had a square silver-coloured case chained to his wrist. The case was fairly small but the man was carrying it as though it contained something heavy. Kyle had never seen such a thing. Was the man really forgetful or something, that he had to chain his belongings to his body?

"Sorry, sir." Kyle smiled at the man and held his hands up in apology. But the stony-faced giant just pushed past him towards the exit. Kyle hoped everyone he met in Glasgow wasn't going to be that rude.

MEGAN PRIESTLY SCANNED the faces of the incoming passengers as they exited the baggage reclaim area. She was having difficulties seeing, what with the oversized sunglasses, and the overly large hat, but she had thought it wise to disguise herself, since she was just about to commit a crime. She wasn't sure what jail term impersonating a museum official and stealing priceless antiquities carried, but it was bound to be substantial. Probably slightly less than murder or rape, but still not to be sniffed at. She didn't think she was cut out for a life slopping out and sewing mailbags. She'd watched *Prisoner Cell Block H* and it wasn't pretty. Unfortunately, she hadn't thought about a disguise until she was leaving the house, so all that she had was the outfit she had worn to a recent fancy dress party. The Dolly Parton wig and pink sequined cowboy hat were calling rather more attention to her than she would have liked. At least she had thought twice and left the 38DD plastic chest at home.

She took the sunglasses off and looked around. Ah, this might be her man. A tall broad-shouldered and muscular bloke with a military bearing was striding through the doors. He kept turning round to glare at a fresh-faced young lad who was looking around him with a mixture of confusion and excitement.

She put the sunglasses back on and walked towards the big man. "Mr Linklater's security man?" He nodded. "Good afternoon. I'm from the museum. Campbell Findlay has asked me to collect the exhibit."

She motioned the man towards the coffee shop just outside baggage reclaim. The young lad the security guy had been glaring at smiled politely at her as he walked past, carrying a battered suitcase and a crisp new rucksack. Megan turned and watched him curiously as he bounded off, looking like an overenthusiastic puppy.

DUNCAN STOPPED DIGGING long enough to take a drag on his cigarette. Next to him, Raymie leaned on his spade. "I've been thinkin', Dunk."

"Oh, aye, man. I thought your coupon looked as though you were constipated." Dunk plunged his fork into the rose bed. The grounds of the Crematorium were perfectly kept, thanks to a series of community service "volunteers."

"Shut it, you dobber. I've been thinkin' about those wee dogs. You sure we can melt the gold down in the ovens?"

Duncan turned his attention from the flower bed and to his cigarette. " 'Course we can, man. They stick the bodies in there and they're all burned to a crisp in no time."

"Aye, man, but my maw can do the same with a joint of beef on a Sunday. That's not to say she could melt all her sovereign rings at the same time."

"Ya balloon. She's not cooking, like, a whole cow though, is she? She's just cooking a wee bit of a cow. I tell you man, these ovens are pure dead fierce. Look, there's the boss man, let's ask him . . . Haw, Mr Armitage, me and Raymie have got a question for you."

Armitage, red-faced and sweating in his tight black suit, waddled over. "What are you two lads doing smoking? You know I've told you not to smoke in the public areas. And it's not your tea break is it?"

"Aw, sorry, big man. We was just wondering how hot them ovens in there get?"

"Up to two thousand degrees Fahrenheit, laddie."

Raymie nodded thoughtfully. "Is that hotter than my maw's oven at home?"

Armitage laughed. "Aye, son, about ten times as hot."

Duncan flicked his friend playfully on the ear. "I tell't you, ya wee nyaff. See you, you don't know heehaw about heehaw. Thick as two short planks, so you are."

Raymie ignored his friend and fixed his gaze on Armitage. "Could you melt gold in it?"

Armitage looked puzzled. "Why do you want to know that?"

Duncan glared at his friend. "Well . . . he just wanted to know what would happen if the body had, like . . . gold teeth or summat."

Armitage's face turned slowly white and then purple, putting Duncan in mind of that wee fat Violet from the Willy Wonka film he'd been to see six times. "What the hell are you trying to say? Are you accusing me of something underhand?"

"Naw, man . . . Mr Armitage . . . we was just curious is all." Duncan could kill Raymie. "Just taking an interest in our job an' that."

Armitage moved closer. His breath was honking. Duncan could feel it almost searing his eyebrows off. "Well, don't. Remember, if it's *my* business, then it's definitely none of *yours*. Now, you two get back to work and stop poking your shitey noses in where they don't belong. Or I'm gonnae stick my hand down your throats and swing you about by the ershole hair, you monkey sacks. And put those cigarettes out." Armitage moved off, rolling from side to side like a weeble.

Duncan punched Raymie in the arm. "Haw, chin head. How did you not just come right out and tell him what we were up to? Ya mad rocket."

Raymie shrugged. "Aw, shut it, fannybaws. An' look what I half-inched out of his pocket while he was talkin'." Raymie opened his hand, revealing a ring with two keys on it. "Keys to the crem. *Now* who's the mad rocket, ya fud?"

CAMPBELL FINDLAY PUSHED back his expensive black leather chair and slid open the top drawer of his desk. That horrible smell was getting worse, he could swear it. None of his colleagues wanted to visit his office and his secretary had stopped flirting with him. It was just as bad at home. He'd taken to sleeping with all the windows open, but it wasn't helping. And the woman he'd brought home from Clatty Patty's nightclub the previous evening had asked him if he was a fishmonger. He sighed. The evening had been a washout. He'd opened a bottle of champagne and used some fresh orange juice to make a jug of Bucks Fizz which they'd downed before going to bed. Well, Campbell had downed it. She'd wanted voddy and Irn-Bru. Unfortunately he'd got a severe and very noisy dose of the runs and when he came out of the bathroom the woman had gone.

Campbell pulled out the cuttings from the *Glasgow Herald*, the *Daily Record* and the *Evening Times*. They would look marvelous, framed and hung on the walls of his office. He looked very debonair in the photos, even if he did say so himself. And the articles themselves were excellent. He had been heavily quoted and he sounded very important. He had been hoping for some national coverage, from the broadsheets down south. This *was* an important exhibition after all. But they didn't seem interested. Too interested in war and politics. The arts and culture just weren't hot enough topics these days.

He would need to get his secretary to call STV, arrange an interview with *Scotland Today*. The exhibits had started arriving, and his staff was busy setting them up in the Exhibition Hall on the ground floor. He would go down soon and ensure that they were being installed to his exacting requirements. He liked to show his face at least once a day. Keep them on their toes. The special exhibit cases had arrived, additional security had been hired, and the guides were all swotting up on the new exhibits.

If he was honest, Campbell didn't have a clue about any of the exhibits. He didn't have to; he had minions for all that. As Chief Curator he was ostensibly supposed to know about all the exhibits within the museum, just like Megan used to. But, well, he had better things to do, quite frankly. He was the handsome public face of the museum. He enjoyed the schmoozing, the jollies, the freebies, the women throwing themselves at him.

He wasn't that interested in art, when it came down to it. He'd been employed for his marketing skills. He didn't need the work, the menial stuff, the tedious cataloguing. And he *definitely* didn't need to know all the crap about paintings and exhibits. Why keep a dog and bark yourself? But he knew he talked a good game—after all, it's how he had got to where he was today. By unashamedly clambering over other, weaker people in his quest to get to the top of the greasy pole, and now he was there he was going to superglue himself to the top.

As far as Campbell was concerned, planting his shiny, black, size 10, Kenneth Cole-shod foot on the back of some poor history geek's hunched back was just a case of survival of the fittest. Campbell studied himself in the full length mirror he had had installed in his corner office. Yep, there was no doubt about it—he was, most assuredly, the fittest.

The phone on his desk rang. His secretary, to let him know that the gold dogs had arrived from the States. Campbell had to rack his brains for a few moments before he recalled the exhibit in question. He hadn't heard from Linklater for a week or so. Strange, because the boring fart had been pestering him mercilessly for the last couple of months, wanting reassurance after reassurance that his precious pooches would be well looked after. "Bring them in would you, Alison."

The door opened and his cool blonde secretary walked in. The silver case in her hand was small but obviously heavy as she struggled across the room with it. Campbell made no move to help her, just tapped the empty desk in front of him. Alison grunted with the effort of lifting the case onto the desk.

"Who delivered them?"

"Dunno—apparently some woman who looked like Dolly Parton, only without the chest."

Campbell's eyes flicked down to Alison's chest. He could see the outline of her lacy bra underneath the sheer cream blouse. She saw him looking and arched her back a little.

"When are we going out again, Campbell? I'd love to try that new Persian restaurant in the Merchant City."

She would need to go. She was becoming too demanding. Shame, she was rather a good secretary too. "Bit busy at the moment with this exhibition, Alison. Soon though." He undid the clasps on the case and opened the lid. Inside, two rather garish gold statues, studded with jewels, stared up at him. Jesus. Amazing what passed as art these days. They didn't even *look* that much like dogs. More like hairy rats. They looked like some cheap rubbish you could buy at the Pound Shop. If he was Linklater he would be quite glad to see the back of them. They certainly didn't look like fifteen million quids worth.

Alison peered into the case and her top lip curled. "Quite," said Campbell, closing the lid. "Ugly little buggers, aren't they?"

\*     \*     \*

SHEEHAN WAS SERIOUSLY pissed off. He'd nicked some more of the fivers from what he now considered his personal stash in the parlour and put a ton on Saturday's Child in the 2.10 at Folkestone, after he'd seen the name circled in the *Racing Post* that the Countess had left lying about. The donkey had been beaten by five lengths by The Big O. And now his access to the cash was seriously curtailed. The old dears, plus their young visitor, had been almost permanently closeted in the upstairs parlour.

And now the Signora one had told him that they wanted to go into Glasgow just after lunch, and that they were to be taken to the museum. Sheehan wondered if they were going to offer themselves as exhibits. But they were more like the cheap old tat you could find in any stall in the Barras, rather than fine antiques. They were *definitely* up to something, Sheehan was convinced of it.

His employers had emerged in all their finery. The Contessa was dolled up in flowered taffeta. She looked just like a sofa his parents had had back in the 1970s. The signora was wearing black Capri pants, a tight black top, and a pair of pink and black polkadot shoes with four inch silver heels. Sheehan had to admit that she was a fine looking woman despite her age.

The weird Gwen one was, as usual, wearing purple velvet—this time a long skirt and flowing coat and scarf. Sheehan had to hold back a whistle when he saw the young punk girl. The girl's pink hair had been transformed into a demure blonde bob. The black eye makeup had been replaced by something pale and shimmery, and the nose, lip and eyebrow rings had been removed. She was wearing a close-fitting navy blue suit with white trim, and a pair of navy high-heeled shoes with ankle straps. As she came out to the car she was pulling the hem of the short skirt down, as though she was not used to showing her legs. And a fine pair of legs they were too. She was a fecking stunner.

The Contessa tapped him on the shoulder. "Sheehan, you had better take care. Your tongue will be getting dirty from the gravel on the drive. You might wish to put it back in."

Sarky cow. Sheehan held the doors of the Daimler open for his employers, shut the doors behind them and got into the driver's seat.

In the back, he heard Katrina say "So, Letty, tell me . . ." The Contessa put her pudgy finger to her lips.

Sheehan was sure he heard her say "Little piggies have big ears," before the privacy screen between him and the spacious back of the car shut her voice out.

"DID YOU SEE the weasel checking out your arse as you climbed in, Dor'?"

Dora giggled. "Oh, I don't think it was *me* he was checking out, Letty. I think it was young Katrina here." She patted Katrina's stocking-clad knee. "You *do* look rather lovely, my dear. You really are a beauty, you know, and so . . . fragile."

"I feel weird. Not like myself at all. I haven't worn a skirt since I was at school. I'm really not sure I can pull this off, you know."

"You'll be *fine*, doll. You're a natural. Just remember to keep crossing and uncrossing your legs so that the dog can see the rabbit. Findlay won't even be listening to what you're saying. You got the notebook and pen?"

Katrina rummaged in her new Versace handbag. "Yep. All present and correct."

"Good. Just ask the questions we discussed, stun him with your beauty, and go as far as you need to go short of letting him give you one over the desk." Letty opened the drinks cabinet, took out four lead crystal champagne flutes and a bottle of Veuve Clicquot. "Now, let's go and get ourselves some culture, ladies."

STANISLAV SAT IN his hired BMW outside the gates of Cardieu Castle. He had been waiting outside all morning, just assessing the lie of the land and biding his time for the perfect opportunity. His fingers were itching to rip the old bitches' wrinkly heads off, but he also wanted to make the most of this opportunity. He didn't want to kill them too quickly. He wanted to make them realize *why* they were dying. They wouldn't try and con *him* again. Not in the short-but-painful period before death, which would be their only opportunity.

Stanislav had noted the comings and goings at the castle. A young gardener had been weeding the gravel driveway all morning. A sandy-haired man with a face like a dingo had washed the Daimler on the long gravel drive, and a Sainsbury's lorry had made a grocery delivery. Through the binoculars, it looked as though at least half of the delivery had come in bottles.

The dingo-faced man had gone inside the castle and re-appeared some time later, having changed his green overalls for a smart green and gold suit. He was followed shortly thereafter by four women. Stanislav's heart raised a beat. Two of the women were the Countess and her sister. The third was a big woman dressed in purple, and with hair that looked as though she had stuck her finger in an electrical socket. And finally, a young, smartly dressed girl who looked a little like Grace Kelly. Stanislav had never seen the latter two before. The sisters must have picked them up over here.

As the Daimler pulled out of the driveway, purring smoothly, Stanislav slid down in his seat. He had two choices—to sneak into the castle and wait for the sisters to return, or follow them and see what they were up to. And, knowing them as he did, they were definitely up to *something*. Stanislav turned the key in the ignition and pulled out a few car lengths behind the Daimler. There was more than one way of skinning a pair of wrinkly old cats.

"CAMPBELL, THERE'S A journalist here from *The Independent* to interview you. Shall I tell her you're not available?"

Campbell didn't like being disturbed after lunch, as his secretary knew very well. He'd been out to lunch at the Ubiquitous Chip with a catering representative. Campbell always made sure that he arranged his meetings for late morning, and then inveigled his companion into taking him out for lunch. The roasted quail had been delicious. Back in his office though, Campbell was feeling decidedly queasy. His dining companion had chosen the sea bass. Campbell's stomach had churned. He was beginning to really hate the smell of fish. He could still smell the damn slimy things.

The three glasses of red wine that had accompanied lunch were having their usual effect and he was feeling the urge to have a wee nap to sleep it off.

However, his secretary had just uttered two words which made him salivate—"journalist" and "interview." And the fact that she was from one of the nationals made his groin tighten. "No, Alison, please send her in. I think I can spare her five minutes." He checked out his profile in the mirror and wondered if she had brought a photographer with her.

STANISLAV WATCHED THE long legs of the girl as she disappeared up the second flight of stairs, through a barrier marked "Private." The women apparently had some business to transact here. Knowing the fake Countess, the only business they could possibly be transacting in a museum was funny business. He decided that he would try and find out exactly what that funny business was. It might serve him better than just killing the women straight off. Besides, this visit to the museum was also serendipitous—he'd read up on it—this was going to be where the exhibition with the Chinese vase and precious dogs were. This would be a chance to have a look around. He walked back the way he had come in, down the stairs to the car park at the rear of the museum. As he passed the display of leaflets and brochures his attention was attracted by a poster advertising the Treasures of the Globe exhibition. The poster showed the Chinese Ming vase that he had read about, an Egyptian statue that looked to be one of the Pharoahs, the pair of gold dogs that had so intrigued him, an Aubusson rug, a thick Roman necklace made of gold, and a beautifully decorated Lombardy bureau. The marquetry was ivory, satinwood and palisander, Stanislav thought. Early 18th century. It would look wonderful in his hallway back in Sydney. He loved fine things. The exhibition would certainly be something special for the museum, full of valuable treasures. Stanislav stopped dead in his tracks . . . valuable treasures. *Now* he knew why the Countess and her sister were so interested in the museum.

CAMPBELL FINDLAY WAS in love. The young journalist in front of him was gorgeous. A top piece of totty. Blonde hair, stunning eyes, slim, legs up to her armpits. Legs that were currently crossing and uncrossing in front of him every few minutes. She had asked the usual questions about what exhibits they had received, when the exhibition was, etc.—questions that he was able to answer off pat from his previously prepared list while he enjoyed the view in front of him. He turned to the left, to make sure she got a good look at his profile.

"So, Mr Findlay, I assume you have hired additional staff to assist during the exhibition?"

"Please, my dear, call me Campbell. Yes, we have hired five new guides to tell people the history behind each of our donated exhibits."

"And security . . . Campbell?" The girl's long eyelashes fluttered like a butterfly landing lightly on Campbell's groin.

"We've hired an extra couple of guards . . . I say, how would you like to have dinner with me tonight?"

"That sounds delightful, Campbell. And the exhibit cases . . . are they alarmed?"

"Oh, yes, we have motion sensors around some of the displays, plus plinth alarms with sensors . . . wireless transmitters to the security guards' pagers and to Anderston Police Station. I know this lovely little restaurant you would love. Very intimate."

"Sounds perfect, Campbell. So, how does this wireless system work?"

"Oh, you don't want to know about all this, Miss Lane. Let's talk about dinner."

The journalist leaned forward so that her breasts rested on Findlay's desk like two soft pillows. Campbell wished he could rest his face between them. "Oh, but Campbell, I find it fascinating. I love to hear a man talk about . . . his equipment. And our readers will be fascinated by the inside workings of a museum." Her voice was breathy. "And please, call me . . . Louise."

"Well . . . Louise . . . beautiful name by the way . . . Louise Lane . . . it sounds somewhat familiar, perhaps I've read your columns before? Now, what were we talking about?"

"We were discussing how fascinated our readers would be when they heard all about the little inside tidbits you can share with them. Hmmmmm, maybe I should speak to my editor about a regular feature . . . so, tell me more about the security system."

"Well, obviously, I can't go into too much detail, but essentially the museum has about three hundred sensors. If an object is moved off its plinth, then the sensor detects that there is no weight on it and a signal is sent to a receiver high up on the wall. That then triggers the alarm system, telling the guards which sector of the museum they should go to. Plus, the CCTV system homes in on that sector, and on the exit doors. It's all very high end."

He trailed off as she played with the top button of her blouse. "And, say a person wanted to circumvent the system . . . how would they do that?"

"Oh, it would be impossible." He cleared his throat, running a finger under the tight collar of his shirt. My, but it was hot in here. "The system is password controlled. Plus, there are defences against cable cutting, and signal jamming. All the wireless devices transmit a 'check-in' signal which registers in the security room every ten minutes and the central computer monitors that." The journalist's wet lips parted and made the most delightful pouty shape. "But enough of that, my dear. Suffice to say that if anything untoward were to happen, all hell would break loose. The system is unbeatable. I checked into it all myself in great detail and took bids from several companies before we settled on this one." Campbell preened—neglecting to mention that the security company who developed and installed the system was the winning bidder not because they were necessarily the best. In fact, he had a sneaking suspicion that, in cowboy terms, they probably wouldn't have been out of place in a Spaghetti Western, but they were the only bidder to have offered him the chance of a three day cruise to Spain if they won the bid. Besides, who would want to go to all the bother of stealing antiquities from a museum when there were so many easier targets? And all the security systems in the world hadn't helped at the Kelvingrove Art Gallery when someone slashed the Dali, had it?

"And is the system ever turned off?" The journalist licked the tip of her pencil.

Campbell's penis started to stiffen. He hoped he wouldn't have to stand up any time soon. "I'm sorry . . . ?"

"I asked if the system is ever turned off, Campbell."

"It's on stand-down when the cleaners are in, or when the staff are working on the exhibits, but at those times we have a heavy guard presence in that area. So . . . Louise, are you staying in one of the hotels up here?"

"I am indeed, Campbell. I have to go back down to London the day after tomorrow."

"Well, that's very nice. Maybe after dinner we could go back to your hotel for a drink . . . ?"

"That sounds delightful, Campbell. I shall look forward to it very much. Now, I just have one or two more questions and then I can get out of your hair. But first . . . do you keep fish?"

KYLE WALKED THROUGH the park, happy to see trees and greenery and space again. He was loving Glasgow but it was so crowded and busy. The buildings seemed to bear down on him and made him feel a bit claustrophobic. His senses had been overloaded with the sights, sounds, tastes and noises of the city. His ears were still buzzing from a morning spent in Virgin Megastore. He hadn't known what to expect when he went in, he'd thought the shop was selling something completely different, given its name, but it had turned out to be a music shop. His gran had an old record deck back on the island and some records by Perry Como, Andy Williams, Sidney Devine, Bill Haley and the Comets. Kyle had particularly loved Bill Haley and had worn out *Rock Around the Clock*. They had an old radio too, set to the World Service. But the music shop had been something else.

A cacophony of sound had greeted him when he went in and he just hadn't known where to start. The staff had been very nice, giving him suggestions and playing samples of music he might like. When he told them he was a Buddhist they recommended some exciting bands —The Shamen, Lemon Jelly, Hot Chip, Devendra Banhart, and had shown him how to listen to them through the earphones. It was all very clever, very exciting and he had learned a new word . . . trippy, which he liked very much.

In fact, he had learned several new words, and many new things. After leaving Virgin he had walked along Sauchiehall Street, going into shops where the names or window displays appealed to him—a shoe shop called Schuh, where he had bought some totally trippy trainers, a clothes shop where he had spent ages choosing a big baggy pair of jeans that already had creases in them—his gran would spend ages trying to iron the creases out—a place called Starbucks where he had drunk something called a Caramel Macchiato. In fact, it was so nice he had drunk three. His head was spinning. He'd bought his gran something in a very nice shop called Ann Summers. The girl serving him had been very giggly and had shown him a buzzing massage machine called a Rampant Rabbit. It was blue, his gran's favourite colour, and it would be really good for the arthiritis in her neck. The girl had giggled even more when he told her he wanted one for his gran, and asked him what his gran wanted with a dildo. That was the second new word Kyle had learned today—dildo. It rolled off the tongue and sounded musical. Trippy dildo.

After all the coffee he'd felt hungry so he had stopped off and had a pizza. It was trippy and delicious. He had asked in the restaurant for directions to the West End Museum and they had told him just to keep walking along Sauchiehall Street and catch a bus at Charing Cross.

He got off the bus and walked through West End Park, past a lake with ducks and swans and little paddle boats, before going into the museum. He could see the top of the museum from his vantage point in the park. It was a beautiful building—breathtaking and imposing— pale sandstone, statues of long maned lions guarding the huge doorway, four little turrets, and lots of windows sparkling in the sun.

He hadn't really thought about what he was going to say to try and persuade the museum people to let him have the Shih Tzu, so that he could take them back to their spiritual home. He was hoping that the people in charge would realize the importance of the dogs to the Temple and just . . . give them back. He sat in the park next to a big stone fountain. Some young people were laughing and talking loudly as they cooked some wonderful smelling food on a barbecue. Kyle watched them. He both enjoyed and envied their camaraderie and easy closeness. He loved his gran and the other islanders, but seeing the young people made him wish he knew people of his own age. Looking at the young people he realized both how much and how little he knew. His heart felt funny. He closed his eyes and meditated.

LETTY OPENED THE car door and ushered them all in. Katrina shook her head as she climbed in after the others and squeezed her dainty form between Dora and Gwen.

"It's no good ladies. The whole caper looks to be a no go." Katrina sighed and looked glum. She sat back in the rear seat of the Daimler as Sheehan pulled it smoothly away from the kerb.

"Why, dollface?" Letty had closed the privacy screen so that Sheehan couldn't earwig. She, Dora and Gwen had been eagerly awaiting Katrina's report, having spent the time waiting for her to return in the museum's café, drinking tea and eating the museum's famed Danish pastries. They had waited until they got into the car before discussing what she had discovered.

"The security system is state of the art. I've got the details of it, so that we can look it up on the Internet, but . . . well, it just looks as though they have all bases covered." Katrina took out her notebook, and relayed to the three elderly ladies everything she had gleaned from her conversation with Campbell Findlay—including his lecherousness, the fact that she had agreed to meet him for dinner later, and the nasty smell of stale fish about his person and his office.

"Oh, dear." Dora's shoulders slumped. "And I was so sure this was a perfect opportunity to make some big money."

Letty eased off her court shoes. "Bloody hell. I dunno why, but I thought it was going to be a lot easier than this. Maybe we're getting too old for this lark—we're just not used to all this technology—things were a lot easier in the old days. That safety-deposit box robbery we did back in the 'seventies was so much simpler. Maybe we should just stick to the thoroughbred con, and not go for anything more ambitious. Shame. This would have set us up nicely in our retirement. But . . . if we can't, we can't."

" 'S'alright." Letty, Dora and Katrina turned to the usually silent Gwen, who blushed at the attention she was getting.

"What do you mean, Gwen, love?"

"Detection transmitters have a flexible software scheduler with a remote key switch. Manual interruption is a feasible option."

Letty leaned forward, scratching under her left armpit. "Blimey, dollface, what the bleedin' hell does that mean?"

"Simple." Gwen beamed an infrequent smile at her friends. "All we need to do is turn the bugger off."

DUNCAN WATCHED AS Raymie breathed on the display cabinet and gently polished the glass with the sleeve of his shell suit. "C'mon, Raymie, I want to see the spears and daggers and swords and that."

Raymie had his face close to the case, his breath continuing to steam up the glass. "Aye, but look at these, man. They're amazin'. All those colours. I didnae know there were so many different types. They're pure dead brilliant Dunk."

Duncan shook his head. "You turnin' into a poofter? I'm wanting to go and look at weapons and stuff and you're interested in fuckin' butterflies, ya fud."

"It's nature, Dunk. It's a fascinating thing nature. All those different animals living with each other and eating each other. That evolution stuff. Survival of the fattest an' that. Stuff growing." Raymie tailed off, unable to put his thoughts into words.

Duncan snorted. "Aye, bawjaws—the only growing thing *you're* interested in is weed."

"Naw, man. You never watch any of those nature programmes, the ones with that David Attenborough?"

" 'Course, man. I wouldn't miss all them animals eating and shagging each other. Man, you seen some of them giving it laldy? It's like . . . animal porn. Pure radge, so it is."

Raymie dragged himself reluctantly away from the case of brightly coloured butterflies and moths. "Anyway, bawbag, we gonnae go and look at this room where the wee dogs are gonnae be kept?"

Duncan bounced on the balls of his feet. This place was amazing. He hadn't felt so excited in ages. "Aye, and then we'll go and look at the mummies, Raymie. They've got real dead bodies in them sarco . . . saro . . . sarphogacuses you know. Hundreds of years old so they are, and all wrapped in these bandage things just like you get from Boots. Pure dead mental."

CAMPBELL FINDLAY STARED in puzzlement at the young man opposite him. His secretary had told him that a Buddhist monk was here to see him on a matter of international importance, and Campbell had been intrigued, but this guy had the soft lilt of the Scottish Highlands and Islands.

The supposed monk was gazing around the office with interest.

"So . . . errr . . . Karl . . . what exactly can we do for you?"

"This is a lovely building, Mr Findlay. My gran would love to see all this." The young lad screwed up his face as if he was concentrating. "Smells trippy though. Where do you keep the fish?"

Campbell was getting distinctly fed up of the fish thing. "So, you've had a chance to look around the museum?"

"Yes. I've had a good look round. I haven't seen the dogs though. Where are you keeping the Shih Tzu?"

"Ah! You've come to see our Treasures of the Globe exhibit? The gold Shih Tzu dogs?" By the beaming smile that spread across the young man's face, Campbell guessed that he had hit the nail on the head. "Well, the exhibition hasn't started yet, so they aren't on display." The beam subsided. "Can I ask what your interest in them is? My secretary said that you had a matter of the utmost importance to discuss with me. I am rather busy at the moment so . . ." The beam had now completely disappeared.

"Oh, I'm sorry, Mr Findlay. I have a letter of introduction from the temple in Tibet. The one that the dogs originally came from." The lad handed over a thin airmail envelope.

Campbell Findlay gave the letter a cursory glance, noting the Tibetan stamps. Maybe there was some publicity potential in this. "I can give you a sneak preview of the dogs if you like?" The beam was back, full force.

Campbell rang for one of the security guards to accompany them and then ushered his visitor out of the office and up a narrow flight of stairs that led to a short corridor. "While the exhibition is being set up we are keeping the pieces in here." He unlocked the two heavy metal doors that led to the secure storage room and knelt on the floor in front of the silver case that had been delivered that morning. The security guard watched the proceedings carefully, breathing noisily as he did so. Campbell opened the case and displayed the contents to the young man who stared at the golden dogs for several minutes in silence. Campbell assumed he was praying, or whatever Buddhists did when they came face to face with sacred relics that had been lost to them for hundreds of years. Finally, the lad looked up at him and shook his head.

"They're not very pretty, are they?"

LETTY TAPPED THE ash off her cigarette into the palm of her hand and looked around the room for somewhere suitable to deposit it.

"I've told Sheehan we're going out this evening but that we won't need him and he can have the night off. He didn't look best chuffed about it until I told him we weren't taking the Daimler. I think he takes it into Luss or Helensburgh and acts like a boy racer to try and impress the birds. I believe he considers it his own personal knocking shop."

Dora looked up from painting her toenails. "What a horrible thought, dear. And don't put your ash in that vase again. What car *are* we taking, anyway?"

"The gardener's old Escort. Something nondescript that won't draw attention to ourselves." Letty gave up looking for a suitable ashtray and tipped the ash into her open handbag. "Katrina, I've booked you into the Hilton under the name Louise Lane. If you can, after dinner, get Findlay up to your room."

Katrina snorted. "I honestly don't think that will be a problem, Letty. He was looking at my legs as though he'd never seen a pair before. I think it's probably more likely that I won't even *get* dinner."

"You be bleedin' careful. I've booked Dora and me into the next room. Just in case he tries any funny business."

"You've not used your own credit card have you, Letty?" Katrina bit her lip."

Letty patted Katrina's translucent cheek. As the girl relaxed with them she was losing the hard edge that Letty had known was just a front, and becoming more and more solicitous of them. She almost treated them as though they were a trio of fragile grandmothers. "Katrina, love, I've not used my own credit card since 1979. It's amazing what you can do if you know the right people." She held out a small box. "When you get him up to the room, slip one of these into his drink. Shouldn't take him long to conk out. He'll be out like a light for a good twelve hours. When he falls asleep, have a rummage through his trousers. Keys, cards . . . anything to do with the Museum, bring 'em next door. Dora and I will do the necessary and get them copied."

Katrina nodded. "OK. Just one question, I don't have to stay there with him all night, do I?"

"Blimey, no, dollface. We'll be back with the stuff while he's still snoring away like a good un. You can leave him a note saying you had to get back down to London sharpish. The room'll be paid for. We can have it away on our toes and he won't be any the wiser. Bit of a sore head when he wakes up, but that's all." Letty tossed the box into the air. Katrina caught it smoothly and tucked it into her pocket with a flourish.

\*    \*    \*

VICTOR STANISLAV HADN'T had this much fun since his days as a mercenary in Angola. He'd almost forgotten what it was like to be lying hidden under a camouflage net watching his targets through a pair of binoculars. He was camped out in undergrowth at the side of the loch, with a good view of the main front entrance of Cardieu Castle. He was prepared for the long haul. After the Daimler had disappeared in the direction of Loch Lomond he had gone back into the city centre. He'd kitted himself out in a shop on Buchanan Street which sold climbing and hiking gear, and they'd told him of an army surplus store along Argyle Street where he picked up some camos and a water container.

It had been a long time since he'd done this and he might be out of practice but—to paraphrase the old adage—once a French Foreign Legionnaire, always a French Foreign Legionnaire. He was proud of his Képi blanc and it had been a wrench for him when he left. But the Legion didn't look too kindly on one of their number murdering a fellow Legionnaire. Murdering anyone else . . . not a problem—in fact, it was mostly how one got promoted—but not one of your own. So he'd taken an early discharge and the not so subtle hint to get as far away as possible. That was how he'd ended up in Australia. He'd taken it easy since then. Maybe *too* easy.

He'd become soft and let his guard down. Back in Australia when he'd met the two old ladies, he'd taken them at face value and considered them to be eccentric but harmless, and had allowed himself to be relieved of a small fortune. However, it wasn't the money that bothered him—he had plenty of that. It was the fact that he was now a laughing stock amongst people he considered to be his inferiors—Sydney's nouveau riche.

Stanislav shook himself. That sort of thinking wouldn't get the job done. He dug his fingers into the dirt and rubbed them over his face. It was time to get back to what he knew best.

He trained his binoculars on the drive. He could see the door and the Daimler. Any movement and he would be able to reach his car before the Daimler could disappear. An ancient blue Escort which he knew belonged to one of the Castle's staff appeared from the side of the Castle and sped off down the drive. Stanislav checked the copious notes he had made. The Escort belonged to the gardener, no doubt off home for the evening.

Stanislav hunkered down in his ditch and opened a silver foil pouch containing beef casserole. He didn't think it would be wise to heat it up, and it wasn't his usual filet mignon with foie gras but it set the blood coursing through his veins, as it took him back to the old days in the blazing sunshine of the desert, being shot at as he curled up in a foxhole, adrenaline pumping and testosterone raging like a bull elephant as he ate his meager rations.

LETTY OPENED THE hotel room door to a grinning Katrina.

"Well, he's sleeping like a baby. The world's ugliest, slimiest, most obnoxious baby—one that any sensible mother would have drowned at birth—but he's sleeping." Katrina threw herself down onto the easy chair in Room 806.

"I hope it was worth it treacle—I wouldn't like you to have gone through all that for nothing." Letty opened the mini bar. "I haven't got a bleedin' clue why they put the alcohol in such small bottles." She removed three mini bottles of vodka from the fridge and poured them into a glass.

Katrina grinned. "Oh, it was most certainly worth it." She opened her handbag. "Here, I've come to drop these off before I go back and listen to him snoring again. I have a load of keys, a keycard and . . . pièce de résistance . . . a notebook containing what, amongst other things, could be usernames, passwords and PIN numbers. Of course, they might not be for the museum, but with any luck we'll have got the whole lot and hopefully they'll come in useful. He's not very security conscious, is he?"

"Brilliant, my dear." Dora took the haul from her. "I'll go and get these copied. I'm not sure what I can do about the keycard. We might just have to keep that, and hope he thinks he's mislaid it." She patted Katrina on the cheek. "Was it really awful?"

Katrina raised her eyebrows and shuddered theatrically. "I feel as though I have been coated in that slimy stuff slugs leave behind and lightly sautéed in three inches of lard. If you can believe it, when he came to pick me up he kissed my hand and said 'Well baby, I'm here. What were your other two wishes?' "

Letty made gagging noises and Dora giggled. "Not an auspicious start. Did the evening get any better, my dear?"

"Hardly. We went to this restaurant where they seated us next to each other rather than opposite. It was like going out to dinner with a limpet. He kept touching my knee and he insisted on ordering for me. Oysters." She crossed her eyes and stuck her tongue out in a face of disgust. "I bloody *loathe* oysters. It was like eating a plateful of snot—I thought I was going to heave. Especially when we arrived back here. I asked him if he wanted to come up for a nightcap and he leaned over and whispered in my ear 'I'm going to be your Fred Flintstone, baby—I'll make your Bed Rock.' " Dora whimpered and put her face in her hands, her shoulders shaking.

Letty gave Katrina a quick hug. "Bleedin' hell. I think we ought to go and stick a pillow over his face. That would be an act of human kindness to women everywhere."

"I'm going before I have to hear anymore." Dora stood up and walked to the door. "If he wakes up before I get back, just make an excuse and get in here, Katrina. Don't stay in there with him."

Katrina waved her off as Dora left the room. "Will do, Dora. I don't think he'll wake up though. He's had practically a full bottle of champagne and one of those magic pills Letty gave me to knock him out. What were they anyway, Letty?"

"Horse tranquilisers. But I bet he don't wake up feeling like a stallion."

THE PHONE ON Kyle's bedside cabinet rang. He was just about to take a huge bite out of his room service sandwich. He put it down reluctantly, his stomach rumbling, and picked up the remote control to mute "Pimp My Ride" on Channel 5. He loved television. Only one of the islanders had TV. When there was anything exciting happening—mostly Scotland playing football—they would all head round to old Mac's house with sandwiches and fruit and homemade soup and watch the event on Mac's 52" state-of-the-art flat screen TV. Kyle lifted the telephone receiver—it was probably his gran, ringing to check that he wasn't in the pub, or out with a girl or something. Not that Kyle would know what to do with a girl.

"Hello, Kyle's room, Kyle speaking."

"Kyle, my son, how lovely to hear your voice. I am down in the library in the village and they let me use the phone. The whole temple is agog to hear how you are getting on. How are you enjoying Glasgow?"

"Quang Tu! How lovely to speak to you."

"And you too, my son. Now, Kyle. Do you have any news of the dogs?"

Kyle's face fell. "It's bad news, Father. The man who runs the museum told me that the American millionaire who owns them would never let them out of his possession. And the temple could never afford to buy them. Mr Findlay told me that they are worth, like, millions of pounds. "

On the other end of the phone Quang Tu sighed long and hard.

Kyle desperately wanted to make him feel better. "I've seen them though."

"You have? That must have been a wonderful experience for you, Kyle. How did you feel when you laid eyes on their sacred golden beauty?"

Kyle grimaced. He didn't want to tell Quang Tu that the dogs would be humanely put down if they were real, and that he had never seen such horrible things in his life. "They're very . . . uh . . . shiny," he said, summoning up as much enthusiasm as he could. Then, not wanting to lie to Quang Tu he added, "They don't look totally like they do in the pictures and paintings you have of them though."

"No, my son. I am sure that the spiritual significance strikes you and they are so much more splendid."

Kyle was thinking more of the squint and the off-centre nose, but he held his tongue.

"I am very sad, Kyle, my son. Very sad indeed. I was hoping that we would be able to get the dogs returned to their spiritual home during my lifetime. They belong here with us. Kyle could hear the pain in Quang Tu's voice. The old monk continued. "Will you speak to the gentleman at the museum again? Ask him to contact the collector and try and appeal to his finer feelings. The dogs may have a monetary value which we cannot, of course, afford, but to us, they are priceless."

"I'll try my best, Father." Kyle said his goodbyes and put the phone down. He had grown to love Quang Tu through their correspondence, and he felt as though the other monks were his friends. He felt a spiritual bond to them and really wanted to get the dogs back for them, and for the temple.

Kyle decided that he would have to give the problem his consideration and see if he could come up with a plan. He turned the sound on the television back up and settled back on his bed to watch the film which had just started. *The Italian Job* it was called. The newspaper reviewer gave it four stars and described it as a film about a criminal mastermind who stages a gold bullion robbery. Kyle put his half-eaten sandwich on the plate and scooted forward on the bed to get closer to the screen.

CAMPBELL FINDLAY WOKE up with a groan. He felt as though an orchestra of woodpeckers was using his skull to play a particularly manic rendition of "The Flight of the Bumble Bee" and his tongue felt as if someone had fed a family of hamsters a Chicken Vindaloo, waited for all hell to break loose and then tipped the cage contents into his mouth—exercise wheel and all. That was it—he was never going to drink again.

He swung his legs off the bed and dashed into the bathroom, hitting several walls on the way. Where the hell was he? Oh, yes. Louise Lane's bedroom at Glasgow's Hilton Hotel. He hoped she hadn't heard him vomiting. It was hardly romantic. He poured water into one of the glasses on the sink and rinsed his mouth before going back into the bedroom. Maybe he could give her a little bit more of the Campbell magic.

No Louise. But on the pristine pillow next to his sweat stained one was a note written on Hilton notepaper. '*Campbell baby, you were amazing. I hope the earth moved for you as much as it did for me. Sorry to dash but I got a call in the early hours about a big story breaking down south and had to head back down to cover it. The room is paid for. Enjoy breakfast. Check out is 2 p.m. I hope we can do that again some time. Mwah, Louise.*'

Campbell smiled a self-satisfied smile. Of course he had been amazing, he always was. It sounded as though he had outdone himself last night though. It was a shame he couldn't actually remember it. And why had he dressed again afterwards? He looked down at his wrinkled suit. He was still wearing his tie and shoes as well. Maybe they had played some kinky sex game of boss and secretary. Yes, that must be it. He looked at his watch. It was just after 6 p.m. How on earth had he managed to sleep all that time? He'd missed not only breakfast but a full day at the museum. He took his mobile phone from his jacket pocket and saw that he had also missed several calls from his secretary. Worst of all, it was past checking-out time and he was now going to have to pay for an extra night.

CLINT EASTWOOD WAS on the trail of vigilante cops in *Magnum Force* on Megan's plasma TV screen. However, his audience was distracted. Megan was beginning to worry. She had come up with the plan to substitute the golden Shih Tzus in a combination of anger and lack of sleep. Now, she was beginning to think that she had made a huge mistake, and that she should have just stuck with her original plan of putting prawns in Campbell's curtain rails and cutting up his suits. Instead what had she done? She had stolen fifteen million pounds worth of precious artifacts. It wasn't just the monetary value, it was the fact that the dogs were items of great historical, cultural and religious significance. And where were they now? They were sitting on her coffee table next to a glass of red wine and a half-eaten plate of sweet and sour chicken with fried rice. And every time she looked at them she felt ill.

Megan was thoroughly stressed about the whole thing. Sleep still eluded her and she was becoming more and more fatigued. When she closed her eyes all she saw were the dogs; when she opened them, there they were too. Her mind was racing but not in a logical way. That was unlike her. She couldn't concentrate on anything. The reason she was watching a film was that she'd seen every film Clint Eastwood ever made so many times that she knew what was coming next.

She'd never had trouble sleeping before. It was only since she had lost her job and Campbell had dumped her that she'd started to suffer. And becoming a criminal had *really* set it off.

What would she do if the police banged on her door right now? She would go to jail for theft is what would happen, where she would no doubt become some butch lesbian's bitch—she'd seen *Prisoner Cell Block H* and *Bad Girls*, she knew the score. And her mother wouldn't be able to hold her head up down the bingo ever again. Megan broke into a sweat as an even more horrendous thought popped into her head. What would she do if she got burgled?

She jumped up from the sofa. She had to hide the dogs. They were too big for under her mattress and her wardrobe was too obvious. She needed somewhere that a burglar would never think of looking. Suddenly she had a flash of inspiration—under the kitchen sink with the cleaning products. Most house-breakings were committed by men. That cupboard would be the last place a man would look. Megan took the dogs off the coffee table one by one and carefully carried them into the kitchen where she tucked them into the cupboard under the sink—one on each side of the waste-pipe—draping a pair of yellow rubber gloves over one dog and a chamois leather window cloth over the other. She arranged a couple of bottles of Mr Muscle and a can of toilet-cleaning mousse in front of the dogs and stood back. A perfect temporary home.

As for resolving the problem permanently . . . well, she had to do something. There was no way she could keep the dogs—she would never ever be able to sleep again. She couldn't dump them—it was tempting, but it would be so, so wrong for the dogs to just disappear. They belonged to the public and had to be on display. And she couldn't just walk into the museum and return them . . . could she? Megan played that scene in her head. No, that wouldn't work. Maybe she could return them to the American collector. She shuddered as she thought of them getting lost in transit. The only plan she could come up with which would make everything right again was one which could get her into a lot of trouble if things went wrong. But it had to be done. She was going to have to break into the museum and replace the fake dogs with the real ones.

CAMPBELL FINDLAY LOOKED at his watch. It was just before closing time on the first day of the Treasures of the Globe exhibition. The day had gone very well with a steady stream of visitors in and out all day. The café had made a mint, and the shop had been a hive of activity from the time it opened. It had been an inspired idea of his to have a range of keyrings with miniatures of all the treasures on them. Well, strictly speaking, it had been Megan's idea, but he had claimed it as his own. No sentiment in business after all.

Campbell walked through the main foyer of the museum. He stopped in front of one of the temporary signs which had been placed there and swore under his breath. The sign read "MUSEUM CLOSED

SUNDAY MORNING DUE TO STAFF TRAINING." Someone, probably one of the ubiquitous school children, had changed the T of "TRAINING" to a D with a black felt-tipped pen. Campbell made a mental note to have the sign replaced and continued into the exhibition hall. He surveyed the last of the visitors. A motley crew if ever there was one. A class of small and exceedingly annoying children had their grubby little fingers all over the glass cases. He would need to make sure that the cleaning staff was told to pay special attention in here. He hated school parties. They treated the museum as a place to play hide-and-seek—running around all over the place screaming, spilling drinks everywhere, getting lost. One of the little brats had once had to be rescued from inside the sarcophagus in the Egyptian room. Campbell had no idea how he and his little pals had managed to slide the heavy stone lid aside far enough for him to climb in, but they had. Then the little horrors had run off and left their companion stuck inside to fend for himself.

Campbell moved his shiny Ferragamo-clad foot aside as two small boys sped past him, and considered the other visitors in the room.

The most popular attraction appeared to be the rather ugly Shih Tzu dogs. One of the visitors had been there all day, firmly planted in one spot, just looking at the dogs, the waist of his oversized jeans practically around his knees. It was the young lad who had visited him with a plea from some monastery in Tibet. Campbell had rather liked him and almost felt sorry for him. He felt a twinge in the area of his heart which was unlike anything he had felt before. He put it down to indigestion from his slap-up lunch courtesy of the *Glasgow Evening Times*. The newspaper was going to do a big spread on the opening day—a behind the scenes look at the most important exhibition in Glasgow since the opening of the Burrell Collection.

Apart from the lad . . . Kevin . . . Colin . . . Campbell couldn't quite recall his name . . . there were some other rather odd characters hanging around the Shih Tzus. A pair of young men in shell suits and baseball caps—Campbell believed that in common parlance they were known as neds—were eyeing the dogs and the innocent country boy and nudging each other. Campbell thought he might warn the naïve lad to watch out that he didn't get his pocket picked.

Three elderly ladies were also hovering around the glass case containing the dogs. One looked a little like Margaret Rutherford; the slimmest one was mutton dressed as lamb—she must have been nearing eighty, but she was wearing a rose-coloured pencil skirt and matching jacket, with a pair of high-heeled navy shoes with a bow on the front. The third, who seemed more interested in something high up on the walls, was covered in purple velvet like an overstuffed chaise longue.

A very smartly dressed man who looked to be in his early forties was standing to one side, partially hidden by a pillar. Campbell thought he was staring rather more intently at the elderly ladies rather than perusing the exhibits. He was obviously a student of human nature rather than history.

As Campbell watched the museum visitors milling around the room he suddenly had the uncanny feeling that someone was watching *him*. He turned round. The only person there was a woman who looked a little like Dolly Parton. Blonde hair and oversized sunglasses which were a little out of place in the shady museum. Perhaps the woman had an eye infection. Campbell couldn't see her face, but there was something about the curvaceous figure that reminded him of someone. One of the previous notches on his bedpost perhaps.

The tannoy system sputtered to life. "Ladies and gentlemen, the museum is about to close. Please make your way to the exits."

The remaining children scurried away to find their teacher and the rest of the visitors dragged themselves away from the exhibits. Campbell caught odd snippets of conversation as they passed him.

"Aw, I was hoping we would have time to go back and see them wee butterflies."

"Fuck's sake, Raymie, get a grip, you knobdobber . . ."

"Blimey, Dor', those dogs are bleedin' ugly little sods . . ."

The young man ran a hand gently over the glass case and turned away reluctantly. He smiled sadly and nodded slightly as he passed Campbell. "They're not very pretty, but they really should go back to where they belong, Mr Findlay." He walked off, turning occasionally to glance back at the exhibit.

The well-dressed man and the Dolly Parton lookalike seemed to have melted away too. Campbell was left on his own in the roomful of exhibits from all over the world. The visitors' footsteps faded away. He walked slowly around the room—the gold Roman necklace, the

Fabergé egg said to have belonged to the last Czar of Russia, the Aztec treasures, the ancient Egyptian cat, the Ming vase—items of great beauty and historical significance. Campbell had to admit that Megan had done an amazing job putting this exhibition together. Not that he felt one single pang of guilt for taking the credit. When you were climbing the stairway to success, the aim was to remove the rungs as you went so that those following couldn't overtake you. Megan had been one of those rungs. He had stepped on her with one of his highly polished shoes and then . . . removed her. All's fair in love and business.

Campbell stopped in front of the central case, housing the jewel in the collection—the golden Shih Tzu dogs. He shook his head. The old woman was right. They *were* bleeding ugly little sods.

LETTY STOOD WITH Dora and Gwen outside the museum's back door. Sheehan, waiting in the Daimler, gunned the engine.

"What's his bleedin' problem? Wanker. He can wait a few. I think he's going to be trouble, you know—I've caught him looking at us funny a few times, and I think he's cottoned on to something. Anyway, we'll cross that bridge when we come to it—let's get back to the task at hand. Well, Gwen? What do you think?"

Gwen shrugged. "Not a problem once we're inside. We got the keys and pass card to the security room and system. I know exactly what I'm doing once I get in there. Getting inside is going to be a bugger though. That's where the security system seems to be tightest. We don't have the keys or codes to the doors, the windows are alarmed up the wazoo, and there's an external security perimeter which I can't fathom out without getting into the security system. Rock and a hard place. The internals are a piece of piss once we actually get in. That's the big problem."

"It's not just big, Gwen, doll. It's a bleedin' enormous problem. Like an elephant in a hamster cage."

Letty looked up at the imposing blonde sandstone building, pondering the problem of breaking in. Her attention was caught by a pale green van drawing up beside them. Six women and two men piled out of the back, chattering. They rang the bell set into the wall and were buzzed in. Dora and Letty turned as the van pulled away. Big blue letters on the side of the van read: "Scrubbers of Glasgow—for all your cleaning needs."

"Well, Letty, dear, I think your elephant has just shrunk down to the size of a fieldmouse. All we need to do is for one of us to get hired by the Scrubbers."

"Don't look at *me*, Dor'. I haven't used any elbow grease since I stopped giving hand shandies to all those tight bastards who didn't want to pay for a full shag."

Dora hoisted herself onto a low wall and crossed her enviously slim ankles. "Oh, well, I've always been a dab hand with the rubber gloves dear. Looks like it will be me then. Once a scrubber always a scrubber."

"Don't worry, you won't have to hold down a proper job for long, Dor'." Letty put her hands around Dora's waist and plucked her off the wall as if she were a budgie on a perch. "I was thinking we could do it Saturday night. It'll be busy with visitors during the day, so lots to clean up in the loos and café. The cleaning squad will be engrossed. Plus, the museum's closed on Sunday morning, so it will be that much longer before the theft is discovered." Linking an arm with both Dora and Gwen, she led them slowly away from the museum. "You can say you don't feel well and need to leave and then let the rest of us in while the alarms are off and there's plenty of activity and we'll hide out somewhere until the van's taken the rest of the cleaning staff away."

Dora tucked a stray curl behind her ear. "Well, I'm going a bit stir crazy anyway. This castle lark is lovely and all that, but it makes me feel a bit awkward having people drive me everywhere, cook for me, and clean out the bath after me, so a bit of honest hard work will be a nice change."

"*Dishonest* hard work, Dora, doll. Right, let's go before Sheehan has apoplexy. Look at that ferrety little face. The more I look at him, the more he creeps me out. I think he's gotta go."

DUNCAN AND RAYMIE sat on the steps of the museum and watched as the Daimler pulled away.

Raymie, the clatty bastard, spat after the car. "Rich old bags."

"Nice motor though, Raymie."

Raymie lit a roll-up. "I'm dying for a fag, Dunk. I hope we don't have to sit in the cludgie for hours on Saturday without a smoke." Raymie gestured to the times posted on the door of the museum. "Place closes at half five. What time do you think we'll be able to nick the dogs?"

"Not until it gets dark. But just think Raymie, man, after Saturday night we'll be able to smoke all the smokes we want. And no more rollies. It'll be Superkings all the way, man. We'll be up to our oxters in pure nicotine."

"Aye, Dunk. We can get our own ciggies made. Half hash, half tobacco. And marooned in Tennants Special Brew. Minted, man."

"Marooned? What's marooned, bawbag?"

"You know, soaked in it until it sucks up all the flavour. Like that Jamie Oliver tosspot does with meat."

"Fuck's sake, you mad rocket, it's not marooned, it's marinated."

Raymie shrugged and ground out the remains of his cigarette on the museum step. "Whatever, fannybaws, and watch who you're calling a mad rocket or I'll batter your melt in."

Duncan watched Raymie's face as it screwed up like a bulldog's arse, apparently in thought. He was obviously contemplating the possibilities of cigarettes marinated in lager. He held out his cigarette towards Duncan. "Maybe we could get some made that taste of kebabs, Dunk."

Kebabs. That would give you the boak. Minging things that you only ate when you were drunk. Duncan was glad he was a vegetarian. "Aye, Raymie, whatever you like, pal."

"I cannae wait. How can we not do it before Saturday night, Dunk?"

"Cos the Crem's shut on Sunday. There'll be nobody around and we'll have the whole day to melt down them wee ugly dogs."

KYLE SAT CROSSLEGGED on the grass at the back of the museum. He had spent the last 24 hours watching some mega heist movies— *Ocean's 11*, *The Taking of Pelham 123*, *The Asphalt Jungle*, *How to Steal a Million*, *The Italian Job*, *The Great Muppet Caper*.

He was nervous, excited and his head was buzzing with ideas. The only things he knew for sure were that, in order to steal the dogs from the museum, he had to wear a suit, tie and hat, not sneeze, somehow manage to engineer a city wide blackout, find a subway train to escape on and blame a talking pig for the theft. It was confusing and trippy. He had to get the dogs for his father, Quang Tu. Leaving Glasgow empty-handed wasn't an option.

Kyle looked up at the building in front of him. He had spent some time inside the museum trying to work out how he was going to get in and he knew that the roof of the big hall at the middle of the museum was made of glass. That was good. One of the movies had dealt with that . . . he couldn't quite remember which one—by about the tenth movie all the storylines had started to merge into one . . . but all he would need was a glasscutter, some rubber suction pads and a climbing rope. This wasn't going to be a problem. Unlike his home on the island, in Glasgow you could get *anything*. Some young man wearing a rustling white shell suit, trainers and a baseball cap had, only five minutes before, come up and asked him if he wanted some weeds. Kyle wasn't quite sure why he would need them, so he had said no, but the young man seemed to be having success elsewhere as Kyle watched him move off. The weeds appeared to come in very small bags. It just went to prove that in Glasgow you could sell weeds to people sitting in a park surrounded by beautiful flowers. If you could do that, you could buy and sell anything. Glasgow was brill. No, Kyle didn't think he would have any problems getting what he needed to rescue the dogs. Sweet.

Kyle hadn't quite thought beyond getting into the museum. He knew that if he could get in everything else would follow on from there. The Goddess would provide. She always did. And she'd been good to him so far—he'd seen a sign about the museum being closed on Sunday morning, so he would have longer to get in and out.

MEGAN SCRATCHED HER head which was sweating like mad under the Dolly Parton wig. And her insides were churning. She'd almost thrown up on Campbell Findlay's shiny shoes as she'd walked past, the smug-faced git. Seeing him again, close up like that, reminded her of what she used to feel about him before her eyes were opened to what a complete twat he was. He'd given her a passing glance. Well, he'd given her tits a passing glance and she thought she had seen a flicker of recognition in his eyes. She would need to be more careful when she came back.

Megan had walked around the museum to keep herself awake and every one of her ideas for the Treasures of the Globe exhibition was being used—the exhibits, the posters, the layout, even the bloody keyrings for sale in the museum shop, for God's sake. She had almost cried standing in the shop and seeing those keyrings. She had grabbed a miniature Ming vase and a miniature gold and turquoise Roman necklet and stuffed them into her pocket, her hand tight around them. The thought flitted through her mind that she was getting altogether too good at this criminal lark.

She had no doubts that Campbell was passing all her ideas off as his own. Come to think of it, she wished she *had* thrown up all over him. Would have served the bastard right. But that would have been drawing more attention to herself than she needed. She'd almost gone to pieces when she'd seen Campbell and that just really wouldn't do. Focus, she needed to focus. It wouldn't be too hard. She would come back on Saturday night—she still had the keys that would let her into the museum and unless Campbell had changed his code word for the door entry keypad she wouldn't have a problem. She didn't think he would have—since she had known him he had always used MrCool. He was a creature of habit, as were the guards. She knew their routines, as well as all the little cubby holes they sat in for a chat or a wee nap to avoid the onerous task of wandering round the museum. The guards were always most tired after a busy day shift and their hours were long. Saturday night would be best. She could be in and out in ten minutes, it would be simplicity itself. Remove the fake dogs, replace them with the real dogs, dump the fake dogs into the Clyde, and nobody would be any the wiser, mission accomplished. If anyone noticed the change . . . well . . . it wouldn't really matter, would it? After all, nothing would have been stolen. Quite the opposite, in fact.

With the dawning realization that this wasn't going to be as much of a problem as she thought, Megan's stomach started to settle. She could be back home in her wee flat in half an hour chilling out with a glass of wine. Maybe, just maybe, she would then be able to get some sleep.

STANISLAV LEANED AGAINST the wall of the museum and watched the Daimler with its four mismatched passengers pull out of the car park. He placed his left hand on his right wrist and checked his pulse—his little finger with its jade and gold pinky ring delicately outstretched—his heart rate was just above normal, despite the fact that he could feel every fibre in his body vibrating like a tuning fork. He was aching to shred the old women into pieces. Every time he saw them the urge got stronger and stronger—once he got his hands on them he was going to make sure they suffered. Theirs would not be the usual swift, passionless, efficient, businesslike death that he prided himself on and was paid handsomely for. No. He was going to take his time and enjoy this immensely.

He looked down at his well-cared-for hands with their buffed nails—it had been a long time since he'd got his hands dirty. And this would be a real hands-on job. The pretty young girl and the purple woman he remembered seeing at the train station were minor irritants to his plan. Call them collateral damage.

Stanislav pushed himself away from the wall and brushed off the sleeve of his cream linen jacket. He could feel his lip curling as he walked past two spotty and badly dressed youths standing on the front step of the museum. One of them pressed a finger to the side of his nose and cleared out the other nostril. A glistening, green blob of phlegm just missed Stanislav's highly polished shoe by a matter of inches. Disgusting. They deserved to be taught a lesson in manners. And if he didn't have something more pressing to do, he would be just the man to teach them. He continued to walk past, catching a snippet of conversation in a whiny nasal voice ". . . marooned in Tennants Special Brew. Minted, man."

SHEEHAN ADJUSTED HIS rear view mirror. He could feel his blood pressure rising. The auld bitches had climbed into the car and the Countess had snapped "Home, James" before pressing the button that closed the security screen so that he couldn't hear what they were saying. No please or thank you, just "home fecking James." Who the feck was James anyway? Not content with the indignity of the green and gold uniform, was he now going to get stuck with some poncy name to boot? Not if he could fecking help it he wasn't. Time these posh bints were taught a lesson. Sitting in the back there swilling down champagne and eating the horses' doofers that the chef had put in the limo's fridge for them earlier that day.

No. Sheehan had had enough. He was going to tell them he was onto their little scams and that they were going to have to cut him in for a slice of the pie. And he wasn't talking a dainty little slice either—he wanted a big piece, crust, filling and cream on top to boot.

As Sheehan turned into the quiet country road leading to Cardieu Castle he reached his hand into his pocket and stroked the reassuring cold metal of the gun he'd taken out that morning from its hiding place in his room. He turned round and tapped on the window separating him from his employers.

The window slid down and the Countess leaned forward, her horse face showing puzzlement at their unscheduled stop. Sheehan raised the gun and pointed it at her wide nostrils. This was going to be good—the auld bags were going to wet themselves. He had practised several one-liners and thought he had come up with one worthy of Michael Caine in *Get Carter*. He put on his best Michael Caine voice. "Now, ladies, not a lot of people know this, but I'm onto your little scams and I think it's time you and me had a little chat."

The three elderly ladies looked at him silently for a few seconds. Yep, they were obviously frozen with fear at the menace in his voice. They would be pissing their drawers. Well, they were old, they probably did that anyway. Then the Signora spoke. "It's 'you and *I*' you uneducated, ferret-faced little shit."

# Part Two

"FUCK'S SAKE, DUNCAN, get your arse out of my face, man. It's bad enough being crammed into this cludgie without your shitty arsehole pointed at me."

"Shut it, ya bawbag—do you want to bring the guards in here?"

"Can't we at least spread out a bit. Surely we'd be OK sittin' in the main bit rather than cramped in this wee cubicle."

"An' what if the guards come in to check, ya tosser? Naw, we're best off in here. This cubicle is out of the way. If they check the cludgies they're only going to give them a wee swatch, not look in every cubicle. Now shut it, I'm trying to read. Did you bring a book like I told you to?" Duncan took a well thumbed copy of *Big Jugs* out of his pocket and opened it at his favourite page.

"Aye, I nicked one from Borders earlier today." Raymie pulled out a small white book. Duncan glanced at the title and shook his head. *Butterflies and Moths of the British Isles.* Fuck's sake. Big Raymie was turning into a right poof.

LETTY WAS SEETHING inside. She, Katrina, Gwen and Sheehan sat in stony silence in the white van Sheehan had stolen earlier that day. He had swapped the number plates with ones he had stolen off a smashed Renault Megane in a scrap yard along South Street. They were parked up on the tree-lined road around the back of the museum. It was near enough to the service door that they would be able to see Dora when she came out, but not so near that it would be obvious. The houses lining the road were set apart from each other and back from the road.

Dora, ever the optimist, had looked on the bright side of having their new partner on board. They still had a driver, they now had unobtrusive transport that couldn't be traced back to them (whoever noticed a ubiquitous white van?) and they had someone to do the dirty work. On the minus side, Sheehan was a complete arsehole. Letty sighed. He'd threatened to go to the police and tell them about their nice little horseracing con if they didn't let him in on the deal. And, having sussed out their weak spot—Gwen—he'd threatened her with the gun until they told him what they were up to at the museum. Dora, soft tart, had blabbed the whole caper.

So now they had a new partner. A very demanding partner. And his first demand had been a new uniform to replace the green and gold one. He wanted blue, with red trim. Dickhead.

The back door of the museum opened and Dora appeared, fanning herself, accompanied by a huge mountain of a security guard. The armpits of his cheap white nylon shirt were stained yellow with sweat and with his bald head, neck rolls and big belly straining against the buttons of his shirt he looked like an out of shape Buddha. He was patting Dora on the shoulder ineffectually as she leaned against the wall, wafting her hands in front of her face in a feminine way. Letty grinned. She could almost see Dora's eyelashes fluttering. As she wound down the window of the van, Dora's tinkling voice reached her through the still summer air. ". . . you very much, you dear *dear* man. I'll be fine in a couple of minutes, I just need a little fresh air and a sit down." Dora sank gracefully to the ground, half in and half out of the door. Clever old tart. She'd made sure that the guard couldn't shut the door, leaving it open for them to make their way in when the coast was clear. The only problem was, he was hovering around Dora like a bluebottle around shite.

Dora raised her head to her knight in sweaty armour. "Would you mind awfully being a darling and getting me a glass of water? I'm *sure* that will get me back on my feet again."

The security guard by this time looked so smitten that he would have slit his own throat if Dora had asked for a sip of his blood. He patted Dora's arm once more and stood up, looming over her awkwardly. His voice rumbled like a heavy goods train. "You just wait there, hen. I'll be back in a few minutes."

"Oh, and if you could find me a wee block of ice to put in it, that would be lovely." Letty looked on as Dora craned her neck back to watch the security guard as he disappeared back into the dimly lit museum and then jumped up, belying her seventy-something years.

"That's us," said Letty, opening the van door. "Sheehan, you stay here, we'll get the dogs. Not sure how long we'll be—we'll need to wait until the cleaning staff leave."

"Not fecking likely. I'm not your skivvy now, lady. I'm an equal partner in this little escapade and I'm not going to let you crafty auld bitches out of my sight until those dogs are sold and I have my share."

"Oh, just shut the—"

"Katrina, doll, it's OK. Do whatever you like, Sheehan. We haven't got time to argue, that guard could be back any time. Just keep quiet once we're inside."

As they moved towards the door of the museum, Dora beckoned them in "What bloody kept you? I thought my heart was going to burst out of my chest waiting for you all to take your time and wander over as though you were going on a picnic. And what's *he* doing here?" She glared at Sheehan as though he was something nasty that had stuck itself to the bottom of one of her Manolos.

Letty put a hand on her sister's shoulder. "Never mind that now, doll; where do you want us?"

Dora motioned them into the cool darkness. "Up the staircase on the left hand side and into the room with the model of the big dinosaur in it—we've already cleaned in there. I'll just get rid of the guard when he brings my water and then join you. I sowed the seeds so that the rest of the cleaning crew will think I've gone home."

"DUNK?"

"What?"

"Is it no time yet? We've been here fuckin' hours, man."

"We've been here exactly half an hour, ya knob."

Raymie sighed and turned the page of his wee book. Man, that Silver-studded Blue butterfly was pretty.

STANISLAV REACHED OUT and stopped the door closing as the Signora and the sweaty security guard disappeared up the corridor. The others were already inside, he had watched as the Signora had ushered them in after her little Oscar-winning performance for the guard. Stanislav lay on the grass, one finger in the gap between door and frame. The door was steel, and the mechanism wanted to close, making the heavy door press painfully into his finger, squeezing it mercilessly. But Stanislav didn't move a muscle. He lay motionless until he could no longer hear footsteps or voices and then slowly pushed the door of the museum open and slid in, closing the heavy door soundlessly behind him.

"DUNK?"

"What now?"

"I'm dying for a ciggie. I've not had one for *hours*."

"We've only been here just over an hour and you had one just before we came in. See that wee metal thing in the ceiling? That's a smoke detector. You light up and there's going to be alarms going off and water all over the place. Just get back to your butterflies and gies peace, you mad rocket."

KYLE STRUGGLED UP the hill to the front of the museum. All this stuff was really weighing him down. He had rope—lots of rope—glasscutters, a crowbar, and these really brill little suction hooks that the man in the store had told him would let him walk up walls like Spiderman. The man had been a big movie buff and they'd got to talking about heist movies. He'd fixed up Kyle with some mega stuff and he was good to go. It had cost him a whole load of money though. He didn't have much left from the neat pile his gran had given him before he left. It had seemed like a fortune but, wow, Glasgow was an expensive place—what with the hotel and pizza and souvenirs and stuff you needed to break into a museum. He'd never allowed for that when planning the trip. And he felt bad enough about his gran giving him some of her savings. He would pay her back.

At the top of the slope Kyle collapsed gratefully to the ground between the wall of the museum and a thick bush. He knew what he had to do. Climb up the wall, over the roof, cut a hole in the glass ceiling of the exhibition room and lower himself down to the floor. It all sounded so simple when he was watching Audrey Hepburn in *How to Steal a Million*, but now he was here, he wasn't quite so confident.

Kyle lowered his head as a small door almost hidden in the wall nearby creaked open. A lady with a mop and bucket came out, propped the door open with the bucket and moved over to a bench at the edge of the grass, lighting a cigarette. Maybe he wouldn't need the lycra Spiderman outfit he'd hired after all.

"DUNK?"

"*What?*"

"I need a piss."

"Fuck's sake, Raymie, you cannae go out there. The guards could come in mid slash."

"What about in here?"

"Jeez . . . ok, change places. Slide past me and use the pan. An' don't flush it."

"Dunk?"

"Jesus H . . . what is it *now*?"

"Can you hum or something? I can't take a pish while you're listening."

LETTY, DORA AND Katrina were were playing poker, in one of the museum's alcoves, using a pterodactyl wing as a table. They knew that this position was one of the museum's blind spots, thanks to Gwen. Gwen herself had been studying the plans she had drawn up after their previous visits to the museum, showing the placement of cameras and alarms throughout the public areas of the building and was now hiding in the ventilator shaft near the security room, checking on the movements of the guards. Sheehan paced nervously round and round the huge brontosaurus that dominated the alcove. Dora looked up at him and nodded, before saying quietly, "What are we going to do about him?"

Letty grimaced. "Don't worry. We'll think of something. Right now, we'll just go with the flow. And you never know, he might come in useful if we need some muscle."

Katrina snorted quietly. "Muscle? I've seen more muscle on a dead sheep."

"DUNK?"

"Aye. What is it *now*?"

"This place gives me the creeps. Do you think it's haunted?"

"It'll be haunted by *you* if you don't shut the fuck up, ya fanny."

VICTOR STANISLAV HAD located most of the Contessa's party in the Prehistory room—very fitting for a pair of wrinkled dinosaurs who would soon be extinct—and was now taking the opportunity to visit the Symbolist room—best enjoyed in the peace and quiet of the after hours museum. Carefully avoiding the fixed cameras he was surveying the artwork. He was very impressed with the grouping of Symbolist art and literature in one exhibit—the original manuscript of Mallarme's poem "Les Fenêtres," the drawing of Arthur Rimbaud by Paul Verlaine, paintings by Henri Fantin-Latour, Gustav Klimt and Edvard

Munch, a pictorial display of scenes from Maurice Maeterlinck's play *The Blue Bird.* Yes indeed. Most impressive. He would write to the curator and express his gratitude for such an excellent exhibit once all this was over. Stanislav returned to the display case containing *Nuit de l'Enfer,* his favourite work by Rimbaud. "*C'est le feu qui se relève avec son damné.*" So beautiful. Now, a quick trip to the Egyptian exhibit and then he would check up on his prey. He wondered where the woman in purple had disappeared to.

"DUNK?"

"Aw, man, we've only got to stay in here another hour or so and then we can get going and nick they wee dogs. You can't have a ciggie, you've had a pish, I know it's creepy, I've not got any more food—you've drank all the Irn-Bru and eaten all six Mars Bars."

"It's no' any of that, big man."

"Then what is it?"

"I need a Barry White."

"No fucking *way*, Raymie. You'll need to hold it in."

"I cannae, Dunk. I'm touching cloth."

IT WAS THE first time Kyle had ever prayed inside a dark, musty coat cupboard but then this trip to Glasgow was full of firsts. He pressed the little button on the new watch he'd bought. He'd only ever had an old one with Mickey Mouse on the face. Pressing the button made the watch glow all green. It was brill. He did it again.

"FUCK'S SAKE, RAYMIE, your arse is boufin', ya manky bastit. That's no' a shite, that's a weapon of mass destruction."

"Shall I flush it?"

"Flush it? That keech isn't going to go down the stank. They're going to find it floating here tomorrow and put it in the museum as an exhibit. Man, that's pure rank. Have you been to the doctor about that stomach of yours? That can't be healthy. And no, you can't flush it, more's the pity. That'll bring the guards in. Mind you, they're going to be here soon enough wondering what that hoachin' smell is."

LETTY'S EYES FLICKED from one crew member to another as an animated Gwen stabbed a stubby finger at the plans on the floor in front of her and spoke decisively—much different from her usual silent demeanour. "Three guards. Two of them do a tour of the museum every hour and or so. It takes twenty-five minutes and they start on the first floor, go down to the ground floor and then to the offices, shops and café in the basement and then come back up the rear staircase. The other guard—the one that fancies Dora—is now in the security room. He's not come out at all, he's presumably watching the screens. Danger points for cameras are here, here, here and here. Next security visit to the Treasures exhibition room is due at 22.10. The guards will leave the security room at twenty-two hundred hours which means we need to be in position at 21.50."

"Thanks, Gwen, doll. OK, are we all clear on our roles?" Letty looked at each of them in turn before turning to her unwanted crew member. "Sheehan, you're going to go up with Katrina and Gwen and subdue the guard in the security room."

"Don't hurt him." They all turned to Dora, who blushed under her face powder. "We have a date on Wednesday night. He's taking me greyhound racing."

"Tie him, gag him and blindfold him and put him in one of the rooms at the top of the tower. Gwen, love, you can then do your magic on the alarms and cameras. Turn them off as the guards leave each exhibit on their tour. I'm going to need the alarms switched off in the Treasures room by quarter past ten, just after the guards have done that room. Dora and I will then take the dogs from the case. You three need to be out of the security room by twenty past ten at the latest. We'll then have about five minutes before the guards go into the security room. Say another five minutes before they realise that the other guard hasn't just gone to the loo. Ten minutes to get out of the museum while the alarms and cameras are off. It's going to be tight. Any questions?"

"Well, that all sounds very nice, but . . ."

Letty was getting distinctly sick and fed up of the sound of Sheehan's voice. She turned to face him and raised an eyebrow. Yes, *Mister* Sheehan?"

"Well, if you don't mind, I'd rather be there when you two take the dogs from out of the case. It's not that I don't trust you or anything, but . . . well . . . ok, that's exactly what it is. I wouldn't trust the pair of you as far as I could throw you." Sheehan grinned his weasel-like grin at Letty. "And, quite frankly, that wouldn't be very far now would it . . . *Countess?* So, we're going to do things slightly differently if you don't mind. Listen up, ladies . . ."

"I'M GONNAE HEAVE. I can't stand that stink anymore. Jeez . . . another half hour stuck in here. I'm never going to get the smell off me. That's not right, Raymie. There's some alien inside of you waiting to burst out or something. You need to see a doctor. Or an exorcist, you minger."

STANISLAV MELTED AWAY into the shadows behind a pillar. So, the old harridans appeared to be well prepared. He found himself reluctantly impressed by their panache and flair. They seemed to have covered all bases. Well, he would just have to take advantage of that. They also seemed to have some dissension in the ranks. He would see if he could take advantage of that, too. As the great Chinese mercenary General Sun Tzu once said, as circumstances are favourable, once should modify one's plans accordingly. Stanislav was expert in the art of taking advantage of favourable circumstances. And this particular situation excited him greatly.

"DUNK?"
    "Aye?"
    "You OK, big man?"
    "Aye."
    "You look a bit peely wally."
    "Aye."
    "Can we go soon?"
    "Aye."

MEGAN SAT ON the number 62 bus, the rucksack containing the two gold dogs, keys to the museum and the pair of bright pink rubber gloves clasped between her knees. Bloody car. What a time to break down. She hoped she didn't faint, get mugged or get stopped and searched by the police for looking suspicious. The dogs were heavier than they looked. She would be glad when this was over and done with. Megan ran over her plan again in her head. Unlock the door, swap the real dogs for the fakes in the case, get out as fast as possible, get rid of the fake dogs, go home, open a bottle of wine. That sounded too simple. There must be something she was forgetting. Right—she needed to stop off at Oddbins and get some more wine. No, something else was niggling her.

Unlock museum door—no problem. She had the keys, she knew the password. Swap the real dogs for the fake dogs in the case. Again, not a problem. Get out . . . wait. The case. Oh, shit, the case. It would be alarmed and impossible to open—her brain was turning to mush through lack of sleep. She now had a constant buzzing in her head which was driving out all logical thought. She knew that returning the dogs was a stupid idea, but taking them in the first place had been even more ridiculous. And now she had to suffer the consequences. But her mind just wasn't functioning properly. She hadn't even been able to count out her £1.15 bus fare. The bus driver had asked her what was up with her and the other passengers had started to tut. And now she'd overlooked something like that. How the hell was she going to get the fake dogs out of the case and the real dogs in? She couldn't exactly leave the real dogs on top now, could she? That would sort of give things away. And she would have to leave the fake dogs there. There would definitely be some sort of investigation if that happened. Two sets of dogs would raise suspicion. If she could just get the fake dogs out of the case and the real dogs in, she could see Findlay just keeping the whole thing quiet. Out of embarrassment for not spotting the fakes, if nothing else. What was she *doing*? Maybe she should just go and hand herself in to the police now.

Megan let out a long, loud, slow moan.

The old wino sitting next to her quietly crooning "My Way" stopped in mid-verse and turned to the rest of the bus, "Ah never even *touched* the lassie, so ah didnae."

"IT'S JUST NOT right, Gwen." Dora's lower lip quivered uncontrollably. "That horrible man is taking over. And I just *know* he's going to be trouble down the line. I can see everything that we've worked so hard for just disappearing. The dogs, the castle, the scams . . . we're just trying to make an honest living. Well, OK, it's not very honest, but we don't hurt anyone. Well, no one who doesn't deserve it . . ."

Gwen reached over and awkwardly gave her a hug.

They watched the screens as Sheehan tiptoed down the stone stairs.

"Look at him. He's like a slug. I'm surprised he doesn't leave a trail of poisonous slime. And the way he just forced that poor security guard up to the tower room and whacked him over the head. There was no need for that. I'm sure he killed him."

Gwen patted her on the shoulder.

"I just hope Letty and Katrina can bring him round. Oh, Gwen, I've never seen Letty look so worried. What are we going to do? I wish Sheehan was dead."

Gwen looked at Dora, switched off the security cameras, disabled the alarm system and stood up.

"Wait there, Dora. Just wait there."

SHEEHAN CAREFULLY REMOVED the final bolt, pulled on the pair of latex gloves and looked at the dogs in their glass case. Feck but they were ugly little feckers. His hands shook a little as he reached out to lift off the glass cover. If that Gwen one hadn't done her job properly, all hell could break loose any time now. But no, the glass came away from the plinth easily. No lights, no lasers, no alarms. As he lifted it off he heard a quiet voice behind him.

"Who are you and what are you doing with my father's dogs?"

Sheehan turned, the glass lid in his hand, and his last sight for some time was a young guy wearing jeans that were far too big for him, one hand holding up his jeans, the other carrying a crowbar which he was wielding like a ninja sword and which was coming towards Sheehan's head at high speed.

KYLE DROPPED THE crowbar, feeling sick. He'd blindsided the grumpy-looking man. He'd just acted on impulse. This was really really not good. Kyle was striving to be a representative of peace, calm and tranquillity and he'd just bopped some man upside the head with a crowbar. Kyle panicked, scooped up the dogs and ran as fast as an armful of heavy metal would allow him.

SHEEHAN GROANED AND tried to open his eyes. His head was thumping and he reached a tentative hand to touch the left side of his head where the little bald guy had hit him. An egg-shaped lump, and the sticky feel of blood. Sheehan's eyes fluttered open. Seven dancing Gwens swayed in front of him in their seven purple velvet outfits.

"Thank feck. Help me up will you?" Sheehan reached out a hand, but the seven dancing Gwens just stared at him blankly. Then Sheehan noticed that the seven dancing Gwens were holding seven colossal crowbars. Sheehan's last sight for some time was the seven crowbars coming towards his head at high speed.

GWEN DIDN'T WANT to go back to jail, she was getting used to life on the outside again. But Dora and Letty were safe again, and that was really all that mattered. She dropped the crowbar by the prone body of Sheehan. Time to go and tell her friends that everything was all right with the world.

SHEEHAN GROANED AND tried to open his eyes. His head felt as though it had been trampled by a herd of wildebeest. He felt his head with his hand. He now had a matching egg-shaped lump on the right side and he could feel the blood trickling down his face. Maybe he would just lie here for a little while. Go back to sleep. It was better when he was asleep. Yep, that's what he would do.

It was the sound of someone clearing his throat that made him open his eyes. Gradually. Painfully. A well-dressed man. Tanned. Posh shoes. Carrying a fecking crowbar. Where were people getting all these crowbars from? Did the museum have a supply of antique crowbars? As the crowbar came towards his head at high speed, Sheehan thought, "Not a-fecking-gain."

STANISLAV HAD NO idea who had hit the old women's chauffeur over the head with a crowbar and left him unconscious. If he had remained unconscious Stanislav might even have left him alive. Although possibly not—he'd never know now, would he? Stanislav also had no idea who'd made off with the gold dogs, but he sure as hell was going to find out. First though, he needed to hide the body for a while. He didn't want the guards to find the body and raise the alarm. In fact, he was going to have to do something about those guards. Right after he had solved this little problem. Effortlessly, still carrying the crowbar, he picked the body up and slung it over his shoulder. Where would be a good place to hide a dead body in a museum? The signpost above his head pointed in different directions—The Impressionists. World War I. Scottish Flora and Fauna. Ancient Egypt. Yes, of course. Stanislav headed towards Ancient Egypt.

KYLE VOMITED INTO the sink in the toilets for a third time. "Oh, Father. What have I done? I've killed a man. How can I make this better? Who's going to look after gran when I go to jail?" He sobbed and looked at his pale and tearful face in the mirror. "Were these dogs worth a man's life?" He heard Quang Tu's reassuring voice in his head. *Are you sure he's dead my son?* No. Kyle rubbed the back of his hand under his nose. He sniffed. Of course. Maybe the man who was trying to steal the dogs wasn't dead. He would go and see. But first he needed to hide the dogs somewhere so that he didn't need to worry about them while he was trying to help the dog thief. He opened the door leading out of the toilet and back into the museum. The Egyptian room. He knew the perfect place.

"WHO THE FUCK was that guy, Dunk? And what was he rambling on about?"

"I haven't a scooby. But did you see what he was carrying? They wee dogs. Come on, Raymie. It's time to leave this stinking hell hole and follow that knob. And then we'll get your honking arse to a hospital."

KYLE SLID THE heavy lid off the sarcophagus and carefully placed the dogs inside as soon as the hole was big enough. The inside of that sarcophagus was creepy. He'd read the information earlier and it said that there was a body in there—a mummy, all wrapped in bandages. It was dark inside the sarcophagus and he couldn't see the body in its bandages, but he could feel it as he gently laid the dogs on top of it. Kyle had seen dead bodies before—he had been trapped in the car when his parents were killed, and he'd touched a few dead sheep. But this body was thousands of years old. So how come it was still warm?

MEGAN BLEW AIR out through her teeth and hesitated at the foot of the path leading up to the museum. She felt like just going back home, opening a big bottle of wine and a box of chocolates and watching back to back episodes of Jeremy Kyle on Freeview. But that wasn't going to make the problem go away. The museum would still have two worthless eyesores made of concrete and plaster and painted with gold paint, and she would still have two gold dogs worth millions. Illegally. Immorally. Really bloody stupidly.

What *had* she been thinking? That bastard Campbell Findlay. He had a lot to answer for. No, she had to go through with this. OK, there were glitches in her plan. She still didn't know how she was going to get into the case. Maybe she could just leave the real dogs in the left-luggage storage room. Not exactly the safest of places but, well, it was unlikely that there was going to be anyone wandering around the museum looking for unsecured antiquities at half past ten on a Saturday night was there? Well, apart from her, that is. And she wasn't actually stealing. She dug out the set of keys and put the first of three in the museum door. It turned smoothly. Megan had recommended a revision of the door entry system—she was glad now that it hadn't been done. Key number two. No, she'd already *done* the stealing part, God forgive her. And in the unlikely event that anyone *was* hunting for antiquities then it was unlikely they would look in left luggage. The dogs should be fine until morning, when they would be found and returned to their rightful place. Maybe it wouldn't be as bad as she thought. It would probably cause a bit of confusion for a while. But hopefully there wouldn't be a big to-do about it. Megan had always looked at things optimistically, and she was managing to convince herself that things would work out. Key number three in the lock now. Actually, the museum would probably want to hush the whole thing up, wouldn't they? They wouldn't want it known that somebody had managed to fool experts into thinking that two ugly concrete dogs were the real deal, and that someone had managed to somehow get into the museum—despite the beefed up security systems in place—and leave priceless antiquities in a room full of ancient, unloved umbrellas, glasses cases, coats, and the odd pair of knickers—for some reason, people found it exciting to have sex on a glass case full of beady-eyed stuffed animals. Actually, Megan hadn't had sex for so long that even that seemed appealing. Concentrate woman. Her mind seemed to drift from lucidity to . . . well, to whatever the opposite of lucidity was.

She tapped in the code on the entry keypad. Campbell hadn't let her down. *MrCool* still worked and the huge door opened silently and smoothly on its well oiled hinges. As an afterthought she opened the control panel and changed the password. *CompleteArsehole.* There.

DUNCAN PACED NERVOUSLY in front of the sarcophagus. "Hurry up and open it and get the wee dogs out. I'll keep watch—make sure he doesn't come back."

"Man, this lid is pure dead heavy, Dunk."

"Stop whining and get them out and let's get tae fuck out of this place. It's giving me the boak. We'll take these dogs back to the Crem and then head to the King Billy for a pint. We'll melt them down tomorrow."

He turned round as Raymie squealed like that fat guy in *Deliverance.* "Fuck's sake, Raymie, you tosser—you trying to bring every guard in the place down here? You see the dogs?"

"Aye, but there's a . . . man . . . there's a dead body in here an' all. A pure dead, dead body."

Duncan shook his head. " 'Course there is, ya tube. You never seen that film with that Boris Karling? *Curse of the Mummy* or something. That's what these sarphocaguses are. Stone coffins. That's a ancient king of Egypt in there. Hunnerds of years old he is."

"This one's no' hunnerds of years old, Dunc."

"Aye, he is. It says so here on this wee sign. King Aga-muppet or something."

"You're the fucking muppet. He's no' a ancient Egyptian King. I've seen this guy before. When he was alive."

Jeez, Raymie was as thick as mince. "He's just well preserved. They used to pickle them in alcohol or something before they bandaged them up. Now get the dogs and let's get tae fuck. I fancy getting pickled in alcohol maself. I can still smell the stink of that huge toley you gave birth to back there. You deffo need to get that arse of yours looked at."

As they left the Egyptian Room, Duncan shivered involuntarily. He'd be glad to get out of this place. He was seeing things now. He could have sworn he'd seen someone hiding behind a pillar. Raymie's shite about warm mummies was obviously getting to him.

MEGAN STOOD IN front of the plinth where the concrete dogs had sat. Nothing. No dogs, no glass case, just an empty plinth. Had they been recognised for the fake little monsters they were, despite her skill? Were they put in the safe every night for additional security? This was totally against the museum's security policy. She would report it if she'd been here legally, but she was skating on rather thin ice. A high-pitched whining had started in her head. Oh, well, at least this turn of events made her task easier. She took out the pink rubber gloves from her rucksack and put them on. Then she lifted out the heavy gold dogs and put them on the plinth looking at each other. Well, *that* was easy. Mission accomplished. In a way it was a bit of a let down. The adrenaline was coursing through her body, every hair on her body felt as though it was standing on end, and it seemed to her as though she could conquer the world. It was scary, but a great feeling. Megan thought she was, perhaps, made for a life of crime after all—she hadn't felt so alive in years. All that pent-up energy and all she had to do was unlock the door and walk in. She started to walk away. Wait. She returned to the dogs and rearranged them. Doggy style. Campbell's favourite position.

DUNCAN BREATHED A huge sigh of relief as the doors of the museum closed behind them. He and Raymie were both carrying one of the dogs under their shell suit tops—usually home for smaller items nicked from shops—razor blades, ciggies, bottles of Buckie. They kept to the darkness amongst the trees, and off the paths leading down from the museum back to the road. It would deffo not do to get huckled by the polis right now. Raymie was struggling a few feet behind him.

"What's up with you?"

"I cannae hold the dog and the rest of this stuff."

"Rest of *what* stuff?" Light dawned and Duncan stopped in his tracks. "Tell me you've no gone and nicked the head of that mummy or something?"

"Fuck's sake, Dunk, what do you think I am?" Raymie sounded indignant.

"Sorry, Raymie, pal. I'm just a bit up to high-do. I didn't really think you would nick anything off of that mummy." Silence. "You didn't, did you?"

"Nothing . . . like . . . precious or anything. Nothing that the museum would really want."

Duncan turned and looked at his dimwitted pal. "Oh, jeez-o—what did you nick?"

"Just his mobi and trainers."

"His *what*?"

"His mobile phone and his trainers." Raymie held up his prizes.

"What the . . . Raymie, ya bawbag, since when did a hunnerds-of-year-old Egyptian king have a Nokia and a pair of Nikes?"

"I *telled* you he didn't look that old, Dunc."

"Shit. Tell me you never touched the body, Raymie."

"Well, no . . ."

"Thank fuck. At least your greasy paw prints won't be all over the place."

"I might just have touched his ankles when I was getting his trainers off, mind. They were practically glued to his feet. But nothing else. Oh, apart from his hands." Raymie put the dog under his arm and dropped the trainers on the floor and rummaged in the pockets of his shell suit. "He was wearing this really class Masonic ring, just like ma da had before he had his fingers chopped off by that mad mental bastard in the Bar-L. I thought I'd get it as a wee present for him, since he doesn't have his no more."

"And where the fuck's he gonnae wear it, you eejit. He's no' got any fingers left."

STANISLAV WATCHED AS the two youths slithered off like a pair of poorly co-ordinated lizards, their nasty synthetic clothing rustling as their thighs rubbed together. He wondered idly whether, if they moved fast enough, the cheap material would spark and ignite. However, it didn't appear that moving fast enough would be too much of a problem as their two speeds seemed to be slouch and stop.

He would catch up with those young men in due course. He was certain he had heard enough to be able to work out where he could find them when he wanted to and he knew what they were planning to do with the dogs and when. A crematorium near a pub called the King Billy. He was reluctant to let the youths—and, more importantly, the dogs—out of his sight, but he mustn't forget that his main aim in all this was to serve justice on the old ladies. The appearance of the youths in the museum was an interesting development, albeit a puzzling one, but it was also one which he felt sure he could use to his advantage in relation to the body in the sarcophagus. How the dogs had also ended up in the sarcophagus, Stanislav was currently at a loss to explain. Again, that issue would need to be relegated to the back burner temporarily. In the meantime, he needed to see how his elderly nemeses were reacting to the fact that the dogs had been stolen from underneath their wrinkled noses.

First, however, in light of recent developments, something needed to be done about the guards. He didn't want them raising the alarm while he was still assessing the new information and its possible ramifications. A frisson of excitement passed through him. Stanislav didn't consider himself a violent man—despite his chosen profession—but he was prepared to use violence if it suited the situation. Flexibility in the face of change. He lived by the maxim of the great General George S Patton, that a good plan, violently executed now, was better than a great plan next week. Given a week, Stanislav was certain that he could take all these new developments and blend them into a plan of stunning proportions. However, needs must, and, given the circumstances, violent execution would just have to do, messy as it was.


LETTY OPENED THE door of the security room. Dora was on her own, sitting in front of the rows of now blank screens, painting her nails a colour that proclaimed itself "Passionate Pink." The smell of pear drops filled the small room. "He's sleeping like a baby. I've left young Katrina to make sure he's OK. We've tied him and gagged and blindfolded him. Don't worry Dora, we've made sure he's comfy. He's going to have an enormous headache when he comes to, mind. That bloody Sheehan. Where is the ferret faced little shit anyway?"

"Dead."

Letty and Dora turned to face Gwen, who was now standing in the doorway of the security room, pale-faced.

Letty raised her eyebrows at Dora and then moved towards Gwen. "What you on about, princess? Come and sit down, you're shaking love."

"Sheehan. He's dead."

"How?"

"I hit him. Hard. With a crowbar."

"A crowbar? Where did you get a bleedin' crowbar from, Gwen, girl?"

"Floor. Next to Sheehan. Lying there dead."

Letty looked at Dora who shrugged her shoulders almost imperceptibly. The message was clear, and a possibility they had considered in the planning stages. Dora thought the stress of the job had made Gwen lose it. Letty felt a pang of guilt. They shouldn't have brought Gwen with them. She was too fragile for all this after everything she had been through.

She touched Gwen's arm. "Let's go and see, shall we, love? Maybe you made a mistake, eh? He's supposed to be down there getting the dogs, seeing as he wouldn't let *us* do it."

"Gone."

Letty pushed Gwen gently towards the door and motioned for Dora to follow. "What's gone, love?"

"Dogs."

"The dogs have gone and Sheehan's dead? That can't be right, Gwen, dear." Dora reached up and patted Gwen on her shoulder. "Come on, let's get this sorted out and then we can get you back to the Castle and get you into bed with a nice glass of brandy."

STANISLAV STOOD, UNNOTICED, behind the two security guards

"That goal was definitely offside."

"Och yer arse. The ref's a diddy."

The security guards hunched over the small television screen in the corner of the basement. How two grown men could be so engrossed in a picture two inches square watching twenty-two other grown men running about like sheep, Stanislav had never understood. But it was to his advantage that they were thus engrossed. Opportunities multiply as they are seized. Stanislav prided himself on being as smoke in the wind. As mist on a November day. Subtle and insubstantial. As Sun-Tzu advised, the expert leaves no trace; divinely mysterious, he is inaudible. Thus he is master of his enemy's fate. Quite frankly, though, the two men wouldn't have noticed a crowd of Tasmanian Devils hurtling towards them screaming, so engrossed were they in the football. Victor Stanislav was *not* a happy man. What was the point in taking pride in your skills in the art of being subtle and insubstantial if the enemy were just too obtuse to appreciate said skills?

KYLE PULLED UP short in the doorway of the Treasures room. He didn't know whether to laugh or cry. This whole thing was completely bizarre. On the plus side, the dead man appeared to have got up and walked away which made Kyle feel a whole lot better. His stomach ceased its churning. He hadn't killed him after all. However, on the minus side, the corpse had disappeared with Kyle's crowbar and that had cost him loads of his gran's money. And, on the minus side again, the dogs he had removed about ten minutes ago and hidden in the big coffin in the Egyptian room had mysteriously lifted the lid of the stone coffin, climbed out and walked back on their little golden legs to their display cabinet, climbed up the plinth and were now having rampant animal sex in glorious golden technicolour. And, another plus side, as part of this mysterious process, the dogs had also transformed themselves into the most beautiful things he had ever seen. He could see just why his father and the other monks revered them so.

Kyle was confused. The dogs couldn't have miraculously changed. Somehow—and he wasn't quite sure how—there must be more dogs. It was easier to believe *that* than the alternative. He would collect these new dogs, pick up the ones he had placed in the sarcophagus, and then go back to his hotel to ponder on the magic. Quang Tu would be well pleased. Instead of the two dogs he was expecting Kyle to bring back, he was now going to get four. As Kyle stepped forward to scoop up his lucky windfall he heard the noise of footsteps. He crouched down and scuttled, crab-like, behind a display case holding an enormous Chinese vase. Glasgow was a weird place. The museum was fuller when it was closed than it was during opening hours.

"OVER THERE." GWEN pointed wildly in the general direction of the display cabinet where the dogs had been kept, her eyes now tightly shut.

"Where?"

"Floor."

"By the plinth?"

"Yeah."

"Gwen, love, he's not there. Look. Open your eyes, doll. I promise you, he's not there. You must have been mistaken. No Sheehan, no crowbar."

"Not right. He was here. Dead."

Letty led her over to the display case. "And look. Here are the dogs. Safe and sound."

Dora gasped. "Letty. Look at those dogs. There's something funny going on here. Look at them! They're beautiful. These aren't the dogs that we've seen on our trips to the museum. These are lovely." She peered closely at the statues. "Even if they are . . . doing it . . . doggy style."

Letty picked one of the dogs up and turned it over slowly, her palms luxuriating in its cool heaviness. The gold felt delicious and sensuous and she couldn't resist stroking it. The stones cast a glow that was both warm and icy under the dim light. Shafts of colour from rubies, sapphires, emeralds and diamonds twinkled and danced as she hefted the dog with some difficulty from hand to hand. "You're right Dor'," she said, almost reverentially. "These are lovely little fellas. Nothing like the ones that was in here earlier. What a queer do."

STANISLAV LIKED TO think that his infrequent smile slashed his face like a scimitar. He could feel its unfamiliarity on his face now. The old con artists stood transfixed. They didn't notice the young man crouched ten feet away, holding his breath, eyes shifting from the women to the dog in the big one's hands. And neither the women nor the young man noticed *him*. He, however, took in the whole scene with interest, before drifting away, smoke and mist.

CAMPBELL FINDLAY ROLLED over in bed under the two goosedown duvets and looked at the clock. He couldn't get the journalist out of his head. She was gorgeous. Louise Lane. He would have to ring her paper and see if he could find her. Maybe she would come up and do a special on him and the museum, given the high profile of the Treasures exhibition. It would be good to see her again. Maybe next time he would actually remember the sex. In the meantime, he needed to get some sleep. He had to get to the museum bright and early the next morning. He was showing the Lord High Provost and his good lady wife around, and he had arranged for

Rentokil to come round and fumigate his office before the visit. The smell was getting stronger. As he shivered in his bed, all the windows wide open, he reminded himself to get them to nip round and do his house at the museum's expense too.

LETTY RELAXED INTO the van's springless front seat as Dora put the van into gear and pulled away from the side road leading up to the museum, leaving the headlights off until she turned onto the main road.

Katrina gasped. "Did you feel that, Dora?"

"Feel what, Katrina?

"Dunno—it just felt as though the van . . . I don't know, bumped or something."

"We must have gone over a rut." Letty smiled. "I didn't feel anything but your arse is skinnier than any of ours, so you'd notice."

Katrina shrugged. "No, I think it was before we even set off. I just felt the van rock a bit at the back. Oh, well, it was probably nothing."

Dora slowed down. "Want me to stop? See if it was anything?"

"Nah, it's OK. Let's just get back to the castle and decide what we're going to do with these dogs. And what we're going to do about Sheehan. He's not going to be happy when he turns up and finds out we've left without him."

# Part Three

STANISLAV SAT BY the open window of the living room of his hotel suite. A warm morning breeze brought the sounds from Pitt Street into the room. The irony that his suite overlooked Strathclyde Police Headquarters was not lost on him, and, in his spare moments, he enjoyed watching the comings and goings of Strathclyde's finest. He had parked his hire car within view of the doors of the police station. Glasgow was, apparently, one of the car-stealing capitals of Europe. Normally this wouldn't bother Stanislav. After all, it was only a hire car, and one that he had rented under one of his many assumed identities and paid for in cash. In normal circumstances, a completely expendable commodity. However, these were *not* normal circumstances since this particular car was special. This one had a dead body wrapped in tarpaulin in the boot. After watching the old ladies leave the museum with the dogs, and the strange young man scuttling after them, he had found a tarpaulin in the basement of the museum and removed the body he had placed in the sarcophagus earlier—now, of course, it was minus its footwear—and put it in the boot of the car. Plans change to suit the occasion and his new plan would have the dual advantage of confusing the authorities and disposing of a loose end. In the meantime, he wouldn't have to worry about the car being stolen because it was now safely under the watchful eye of the Strathclyde police.

Today, the building was a hive of activity. Some fancy uniforms had been coming in and out since the early hours, and it looked as though The Press were starting to gather. A slim woman wearing a scarlet suit that seemed rather risqué for a Sunday morning was leaning against a van marked STV, drinking a large cardboard container of coffee. Stanislav shuddered. Coffee should *never* be served in cardboard containers. He lifted his own cup of steaming hot Guatemalan Elephant coffee—strong and black. The concierge was paid handsomely to keep Stanislav in the finest ground coffee that Whittards in Buchanan Street had to offer.

He ticked off the next pub on his list. Who would have thought that there were so many pubs in Glasgow with names referring to William of Orange. In fact, Glasgow appeared to be a city burdened down with public houses. No wonder there were so many drunks on the streets. They were lurching confusedly from one pub to the next, overcome by the plethora of dark and dingy watering holes smelling of stale yeast and hops.

Running a beautifully manicured finger down the *Yellow Pages* that had been in the bureau drawer next to the Gideon bible, he stopped at the next pub that sounded promising and lifted the phone. His call was answered after eight rings. Poor customer service standards always annoyed him.

"Whit?"

"Ah, good morning—is that The Bold King Billy?"

"Aye—whit ya wantin'?" Stanislav was rather taken aback at the abrupt tone of the publican. What happened to the "hail fellow well met" happy Glaswegian chappie with a smile and kind word for everyone one heard about so often? "C'mon, pal—it's the middle of the morning rush here and ah'm running around like a blue-arsed fly. Ah've no got time to chew the fat ye ken."

"Morning rush?" Stanislav looked at his Vacheron Constantin—for this trip, the *Malte Grande Classique*, in understated white gold and with its diamond hour markers—"but it's only half past eight in the morning."

"Aye, pal, as ah said—the morning rush. Noo, whit ya wantin'?"

"Could you tell me if there is a crematorium in the vicinity of your establishment?"

"A crematorium in the whit of my *whit*?"

"Is there a crematorium near your pub?"

"The Crem—aye, pal, it's just across the road, whit aboot it?"

"Nothing. Nothing at all. Thank you."

"Weirdo."

Stanislav quietly replaced the receiver. The lack of good manners in today's society was astounding. He might just have to pay the barkeep a visit while he was out at the Crematorium. Punch some etiquette into him.

THE TV IN the background was showing the Scottish weather report as Megan curled herself up on the sofa in her pink satin pyjamas and fluffy yellow slippers with their Easter chick faces. Despite the casual dress, she was wearing full makeup and she felt a little weird. She really shouldn't have downed quite so much Shiraz last night, but she was so relieved at having accomplished her mission without a hitch, and full of nervous energy and excitement that she had found herself unable to stop after the first bottle. She'd only managed half an hour's sleep and when she'd checked her face in the bathroom mirror she'd been shocked at the dark circles under her eyes, so at 4 a.m. she'd spent half an hour carefully doing her makeup. Hopefully, a bacon roll with brown sauce and some strong tea, and she would be right as rain in a couple of hours. She picked up her mug from the coffee table and took a large gulp of Earl Grey, reaching out for the remote control as the picture on the screen changed to a familiar sight—the West End Museum in its shady, wooded, park setting.

Not so familiar were the police cars, ambulances, crime scene tape and people in white paper suits. The enormous sunbed-tanned talking head on the screen was saying something. Megan turned the sound up ". . . so that's the situation here at the world-renowned West End Museum. For all the latest developments I'll hand you back to Ellen Bysouth outside Strathclyde Police Headquarters. Ellen."

A blonde in a red suit that would have cost Megan a couple of months' of her previous reasonably decent salary simpered towards the camera. "Thank you, Hector. Well, as you can see, here in Pitt Street activity is frenetic." Behind her a constable yawned and scratched his arse. "The Chief Constable is currently liaising with detectives on the case and we've been promised a statement shortly."

"On *what*? A statement on what?" shrieked Megan, knocking over her tea. She'd seen less forensic experts in an episode of *Taggart* than in the quick glimpse on TV outside the museum. Surely they weren't all there because she'd bought the dogs back. "Dogs that no one knew were missing turn up in their rightful place." Hardly earth-shattering news when there were all those politicians fiddling their expenses and having it off with their secretaries to write about. No, there must be something else going on. And hopefully the simpering Ellen would tell her what it was.

". . . and that's all from Strathclyde Police HQ at the moment. Now it's back to the studio where Donald has a story about a pigeon that flew into a satellite dish in Ruchill and knocked out the residents' tellies for over an hour last night during *Britain's Got Talent* . . ."

"Nooooo!" Megan stabbed at the remote to change the channels. Surely the BBC would have something. But no—*Celebrity Sunday Chef* was showing the vacant looking face of one of the ex-members of a boy band—Megan was unsure which one—as he struggled to make a toasted cheese and tomato sandwich in a TV studio equipped with every cooking utensil known to man.

Megan turned the television back to STV.

". . . have to interrupt you there, Donald," a smug faced Ellen was saying, "Chief Constable McEnteggart is just about to give us a statement on events at the West End Museum last night."

The camera switched to a silver haired man who looked like an older version of Richard Gere. No wonder they wheeled him out for Press calls.

"Last night a serious incident took place in the West End Museum." Megan whimpered. They'd found the dogs and were taking it seriously. "Three security guards were hurt—two of them rather seriously—and all three are currently in the Royal Infirmary where they are receiving medical care and around-the-clock protection pending interviews." Phew, nothing to do with her putting the dogs back then. Maybe they'd had a fight or something. Or it was some sort of a bizarre coincidence.

"The attacks appear to have been motivated by robbery." OK, so nothing at *all* to do with the dogs then, since they hadn't been robbed, but replaced. Megan breathed a sigh of relief. "The theft was discovered at seven this morning when the museum's curator, Findlay Campbell, arrived and tried to enter the museum." Megan snickered—Campbell would be *so* annoyed that they had got his name the wrong way round. Serve him right for eschewing his real first name of Norman and going with his middle name. The handsome policeman continued, hardly using his notes at all. "Mr Campbell found himself unable to access the building . . ." Megan grinned, her work again, ". . . and, on walking around to the back, found a rear door open. On entering the building he discovered the captive guards and, on further investigation, that two exceedingly valuable artefacts have been stolen—a pair of gold and jewel encrusted Chinese dogs—Shih Tzus." Megan threw up on the geometric rug she had recently bought from Ikea. "The public are urged to keep their eyes peeled for these priceless items which are being shown on your screen now." As the dogs—Megan's dogs, not the real ones—flashed up on the screen the muffled voice of the Chief Constable could be heard saying, "Are they *really* worth that much? They look like badly made garden ornaments."

The buzzing in Megan's head intensified and the fake dogs on screen swam in front of her eyes.

THE BUZZ OF conversation died down in the Pitt Street Incident Room as Chief Constable McEnteggart entered. He nodded to Chief Inspector Delaney and went to the front of the room where strategically placed white boards contained photos of the missing dogs, the West End Museum, a map of the area and numerous scribbled notes joined up by lines that looked as though a spider on acid had made the world's worst web. Computers beeped and pinged and hummed throughout the room. The Chief Constable preferred the days when policemen weren't influenced by the high tech aspects of TV crime shows and the bureaucratic "throwing the elephant at the flagpole to see if it sticks" attitudes of modern policing. He preferred the slower, gentler times of *Dixon of Dock Green* or *Z-Cars*, when policemen still used notebooks that came with wee pencils. Either that or the random acts of senseless violence that you could get away with in the '70s, when prisoners were so clumsy that ninety percent of them fell down the stairs in the nick.

Delaney nodded at him. McEnteggart also preferred the days when Chief Inspectors weren't women. Mind you, Delaney didn't look much like a woman, what with her short spiky hair and her complete lack of makeup, not to mention the severe cut of the black skirt suit she always wore. The woman just had to be a Presbyterian. He looked down at her stumpy legs in their thick black tights. Despite the 40 deniers, he could still make out the coarse dark hairs. Aye, definitely Wee Free Church. They weren't allowed to shave on Sundays, were they?

Well, better get on with the task in hand. He perched on the edge of a desk and looked around the room. "Any updates? I gave a statement to the Press about an hour ago as you're all no doubt aware," he nodded at the wide screen TV set in the corner, "but there wasn't much to say at this stage."

"We've had a number of calls to the hotline, Guv." A young Sergeant waved a handful of paper. "Usual nutters and conspiracy theorists. Loads of old geezers out walking their dogs in the park. So far, there have been various sightings—nobody that we've got a great description on—three old ladies were spotted walking away from the museum—probably coming back from the bingo on Great Western Road—be good to trace them—couple of people reported seeing them." A few of the policemen in the room sniggered. "Aye, whatever . . . we can rule them out as suspects, right enough, but they might have seen something. They were there around the right time." He shuffled the papers. "Apart from that, the usual neds hanging about, a woman with a rucksack, couple of aliens, a handsome bloke who was dressed like the Milk Tray Man (according to a gay guy hanging around the park lavvies), not to mention Elvis, Lord Lucan and Shergar." He scratched his nose with his pen. "So, as the papers are so fond of saying, we don't have a lot to go on."

McEnteggart stood and brushed some invisible lint from his trousers. "Yes, well, please make sure that you let me know of any new developments. We need to make sure we're on the ball." He loved these high-profile cases. The rest of the time he sat in his nice tidy office shuffling bits of paper about. At this stage in his career all he had to look forward to were his stints on TV. He would need to put some more gel on his hair for his next TV appearance. "Carry on, Delaney."

THE MAN FACING Nora Delaney across the desk was looking decidedly sick. He kept putting his head in his hands and moaning.

"Is there *anything* you can think of, Mr Findlay?"

He lifted his head off the desk and shook it, as though it was painful to do so.

"Nothing. Oh, my God, I don't believe this. Linklater is going to freak out."

"The owner of the dogs?"

"Yes. Maybe I can just not tell him? Maybe they'll turn up?" Campbell Findlay looked at Chief Inspector Delaney in desperation.

She gazed back at him intently. This guy was a wanker of the first order. "I very much doubt that you'll be able to keep this quiet. The Press are all over it already. There are several reporters and TV crews outside."

"TV crews?" Findlay suddenly seemed to perk up. He adjusted his tie, smoothed his hair and started to get up from the desk. "Maybe I'd better—"

Delaney held up her hand "Not quite yet, Mr Findlay, if you don't mind. I have a few more questions for you. We don't know how the thieves managed to circumvent the security system. You said it's only recently been upgraded?"

"Yes, we beefed it up for the exhibition. It was stipulated by the insurers. These are the most valuable artefacts we've ever had. Oh, dear God, this is a nightmare."

"Is there anyone who may have a grudge against you, or against the museum itself?"

"Against *me*?" Findlay bristled like a priggish hedgehog. "I will have you know that I am universally liked and respected."

Delaney doubted that either was the case. Certainly, in the short time *she* had had the misfortune to make his acquaintance, she had absolutely no respect for the pretentious shit, and she wouldn't piss on him if he was on fire. Some people no doubt thought he was charming, but he didn't fool *her*. "And you can't think of anyone you've had a disagreement with in the last few months? No disgruntled ex-employees? Unhappy ex-girlfriends?" Probably *all* his ex-girlfriends would be happy to be ex.

"Oh, well, possibly, now you come to mention it . . . but nothing of my doing."

"Which? The ex-employee or the girlfriend?"

"Well, both, actually. I had a brief . . . romantic interlude . . . with one of my colleagues." Romantic interlude? Was this guy for real? "She was the Chief Curator before I got promoted into the position due to my superior expertise." Findlay's chest puffed out like a self-satisfied pigeon. "For some reason she felt that I had usurped her position and stolen her ideas. But all the good ones were mine. I was so obviously the man for the job. After I got wind of my promotion I dumped her. She was rather a timid mouse of a woman though. I'm sure she wouldn't have had the wherewithal for anything like this."

Egocentric bastard. Delaney noted down the details Findlay gave her, feeling sorry for the young woman, Megan Priestly. They would need to get around to interviewing her at some point. Delaney turned to a new line of questioning.

"I understand from one of my officers that you had problems with your password when you came in this morning. And has anyone been asking questions about it? Anyone suspicious been seen around the museum? Any unexplained or out of the ordinary occurrences? Any keys or passes gone missing? Any alarms been set off apparently accidentally?"

"No, nothing. I told you. I . . ." Campbell's face suddenly paled.

"What is it?"

"Nothing. It's nothing, I'm sure."

"Mr Findlay? If you can think of anything, no matter how small it seems, you have to tell me. It might be important."

A rosy tinge spread from Campbell's neck up over his face.

"I . . . well . . . I had a . . . well . . . shall we say a . . . tryst . . . with a young lady, Chief Inspector. She . . . asked me some questions about the security systems and around that time that I also lost my keycard. It doesn't have any distinguishing marks on it. I just thought I'd dropped it at home or in the car, so I didn't report it."

Total wanker. Tryst indeed. "Would you like to tell me about this young lady, Mr Findlay?"

"She was a reporter. Absolutely gorgeous. Slim. Lips like Angelina Jolie. Legs up to her armpits . . . oh, you mean . . ."

"Yes." Delaney's tone was dry. It was a good job she herself wasn't some dollybird or Findlay wouldn't be able to concentrate. "What was she asking you? And if you managed to catch her name that would be helpful."

"Louise Lane."

The young police sergeant Delaney had brought with her to sit in on the interview sniggered. She raised her eyebrows at him in a *"some people are too stupid to live"* fashion and ran a hand through her short grey hair in frustration. "Louise Lane?"

"Yes. She worked for the *Independent*, I think it was."

"Don't you think that sounds a little like Lois Lane?" Findlay looked confused. "Tell me, Mr Findlay. Do you ever go to the cinema? Watch DVDs? Read comics?" She wanted to add *"Get your head out of your arse?"* but managed to restrain herself.

Findlay looked puzzled. "Well, I sometimes get to see the odd French film at the GFT. I'm quite partial to a Truffaut from time to time. But really, Chief Inspector, is my taste in films quite relevant just now? Don't you think you should be concentrating on catching these thieves? Besides, to be honest, you're not really my type . . ."

"*Mister* Findlay." Delaney drew the name out as if it was an obscenity. "I'm *not* asking you out on a date." The words "last man on earth" and "no sodding way" sprang to mind. "I'm just wondering how a man of your apparent intelligence wasn't suspicious about this manna from heaven in the form of a beautiful woman. Now, I'd like all the details if you don't mind. If you can, please stick to those little factoids which are relevant. I'm not remotely interested in your shagging techniques unless they have a bearing on the theft."

"FUCK'S SAKE, DUNK, man, it's pure dead creepy in here."

Duncan shrugged, as though being inside the crematorium was an everyday occurrence. In actual fact, he'd sneaked in on a couple of occasions to watch as a body was cremated, and every time he was in here he felt just as nervous as Raymie.

"But where's the bodies, man?" Raymie sounded disappointed. The room was pristine, all white tiles and shiny stainless steel. Only two empty coffins stacked against the wall gave any hint as to what the room was used for.

"What? Did you think we'd be up to our oxters in blood and guts? Have you not seen enough dead bodies to last you long enough? You crapped yerself yesterday wi' just the one, ya arse wipe, and that was hunnerds of years old. They only have a body in here if they're going to be burnin' it."

"Man, it's boufin' in here. What's that stink?"

"Disinfectant. You never smelled it before, you clatty bastit?"

"Shut it, ya hawfwit. Where we going to melt the wee dugs then?"

Duncan pointed over at the furnaces. "I'll switch the oven on so it can be warming up."

"Good idea, big man. Shall I nip over the road and get us a couple of steak pies from Greggs? I'm hank marvin. Could eat a scabby-headed we'an. We could stick it in the oven and heat it up."

Jeez-o, Raymie was a right windae licker. "You put a Greggs steak pie in there and it will be a wee pile of ash in seconds, ya diddy. You can't burn a body at Gas Mark 5 you know. It's like . . . a thousand degrees in they ovens. The guys that work in here all the time told me that the bodies they burn in there just . . . vaporize."

Raymie's eyes shone. "You're kidding me, Duncan, man—really? Just like in *Dr Who*? Aw, that's the berry's man. I'd love to get a swatch at that. Shame we've no' got a body." He hefted the heavy bag containing the dogs onto the table in the middle of the room. They both stood looking at the ugly gold dogs, the jewels twinkling like wee sequins under the fluorescent light.

"They're total mingers, aren't they, Dunk? Really ugly wee dogs."

"Aye, Raymie, they are. But you know what else they are?"

"Yup. Hunnerds and hunnerds and hunnerds of cans of Tennents Special Brew and enough blow to keep us totally off our heads forever." Duncan was impressed. Raymie had never before said anything so profound. That was almost poetic. Maybe there was hope for the big fud after all.

"There a lavvy in here, man? I'm dying for a pish. Or shall I just wallop my tadger in the sink? "

Or maybe not. "Right, let's stick the dogs in the oven. I'm not sure how long they'll take to melt, but we can watch them through the glass door. We'll pick out the stones, and take the stones and the gold to the pawn. It'll be a skoosh." Duncan opened the oven door and slid the heavy dogs into the furnace. He shut the door and pressed the buttons on the panel at the front.

"You sure this is going to work, Dunk?"

"Aye, Raymie." Duncan had no idea why they were both whispering, but it seemed fitting. "I checked it out. The oven's maximum heat is 1150 centipedes. Gold melts at 1063." If they'd had useful stuff like that in Chemistry Standard Grade, he might have done a lot better at school than he had. "I found it on Wikipedia."

As the oven heated up the stones started to slide off the dogs and drops of gold pooled on the base of the oven. "Oh, man," whispered Raymie. "We're going to be so fuckin' rich."

"Let's nip across to the cargo shop and get a bottle of Buckie and a bag of crisps. Then we can come back and sit and watch the wee dogs cook."

"Aye, man. But no Buckie. We're going to be millionaires. We're not going to be drinking Buckfast anymore. It's El Dorado all the way, Dunk."

\* \* \*

KYLE LAY PANTING in the ditch. That clinging-under-the-van scene was not as easy as it looked in the films. He had come out of the museum to see the ladies with the dogs getting into a van. Acting on instinct he had scrambled underneath the van as it started up, and swung his arms and legs around the greasy and oily underside of the van as it started to pull away. Indiana Jones in *Raiders of the Lost Ark* and that actor in *The Terminator* made it look so easy as they hung on for dear life to the underside of a moving vehicle. They came out without a scratch. Kyle was not only scratched, but bruised, burned, scared, and his head was aching where his brains had been rattled around. Maybe it was the wrong sort of van.

He'd begun to wonder whether he was going to fall off the van at high speed as his arms and legs became more and more tired, but had managed to cling on until the van slowed, turning up a gravel road and reducing in speed until he thought it was safe enough to let go.

He'd rolled out from under the van as it came to a halt and he continued rolling into the ditch at the side of the road. His arms were aching, his muscles throbbing. To add insult to injury the ditch was wet, smelly, dirty, and something was slithering up the leg of his jeans. No, Indy never had troubles like that. Maybe Kyle should get a whip. Right now though he just wanted to go home to Creagsaigh and his gran. But he couldn't go home without the dogs. And the dogs were just now being carried into a big castle by the four women from the museum.

"WHAT THE FUCK'S that, man?"

"Raymie, I have no fucking idea." Duncan turned the oven off. Through the glass door of the furnace the dogs, which should by now have been a big puddle of gold and jewels, still stood there. Only now they were grey clumps of what looked like stone—some of which had broken off to reveal a shapeless lump of still-hard metal that definitely wasn't gold.

Duncan and Raymie waited in silence for the oven to cool down and the door to open. They swigged out of the bottle of El Dorado they'd scraped up enough coppers for, and shared a jay. Finally, the door opened and Duncan reached inside and put out a tentative hand to touch one of the dogs. "It's concrete, man. Boiling hot bastarding concrete."

THE COMFORTABLE PARLOUR at Cardieu Castle was a haze of smoke and tequila fumes. "Where the hell's Sheehan?" Letty was worried. It had been ages since they had seen the ferret-faced blackmailing little shit, "If he's got himself arrested we're in trouble. He'll blab to save his own skin. We'll need to find somewhere to hide the dogs—if he *does* come back then we won't have them here for him to take. If he doesn't come back . . ." Letty shrugged, ". . . well, he's either been nicked in which case the cops might be paying us a visit, or he's . . ." she looked at Gwen sitting silently rocking in the corner, as far away from the cigarette smoke as she could get, humming T-Rex's "Ride a White Swan," and lowered her voice ". . . dead."

"Last time I saw him was when he got us to wait in the room with the security guard." Katrina looked over at Gwen and lowered her voice. "Is she all right? Do you think there's anything in her story about killing Sheehan?"

"No, love." Letty took a long drag on the Superking. Nicotine. She needed a really strong smoke. "Gwen's . . . fragile. She's a bit . . ." she tapped her head.

"You know, Letty, I think you're wrong. I think Gwen's a lot stronger than you and Dora give her credit for."

"Look, love, we'll tell you about it some time, but take it from me, Gwen never killed Sheehan. She's . . . I dunno . . . hallucinating or something with the stress of it all."

"Then where is he? Why would he just vanish without the dogs? Without screwing you and Dora out of a small fortune?"

Letty sighed. "Ain't got a bloody clue, doll. But we need to give the dogs a new home for a while." She patted one of the gold dogs, which currently sat one on each end of a small Regency chiffonier. "They're too big to hide safely anywhere in the house. Besides, the only drawers that lock are in here and we know Sheehan's been at these. The cellar locks but Butler's always down there, so it's not ideal. We need somewhere where the staff aren't likely to go. Any ideas?"

Katrina chewed her lower lip. "What about the boathouse?"

"We have a boathouse?"

"It's really quiet, tucked away through the trees, and it doesn't seem as though anyone ever goes there."

Before Letty could answer, Dora came rushing into the upstairs parlour, her face half cleaned of makeup, her eyes looking like a panda that had been watching a sad film. "Turn the telly on! Turn the bloody telly on!"

Katrina jumped over to the set in the corner of the room.

"STV—it's the news."

The four women crowded round the TV. A policeman was giving a Press conference about the theft of the dogs.

"We've seen this already, Dora—it's just a replay of the report they showed earlier. There's nothing new. What's up? Is there news of Sheehan?"

"Look!" Dora's hand was shaking as she pointed at the screen. "I never spotted him before but look—standing in the crowd on the left-hand side. In the long coat. Next to the woman with the stripey top. Can you see him?"

Letty pushed her glasses up her nose and peered at the screen. "Oh, my God, Dor'. It's him . . . it's Victor Stanislav."

"SO WHAT WE gonna do, Dunk?"

Duncan took a long draw on the rollie, his eyes watering as the bitter smoke drifted into his nasal passages. "Well, at least we've still got the jewels. Must be hunnerds of thousands of quids worth here." He patted the zipped pocket of his shell suit top. They had disposed of the remains of the dogs in the bin.

"Man, I can't *believe* those wee dogs were fake. An' after we'd gone to all that trouble to steal them," Raymie said.

"Well, no good hangin' round here feeling sorry for ourselves. Let's get down to the pawn. See what we can get for these." As Duncan pushed open the pneumatic door at the back of the crematorium he turned to Raymie. "Let's face it, wee man. This day can't get any worse at least."

But Raymie was standing stock still—a look of horror on his greasy face. "Oh, aye, it fucking can so."

Duncan spun round and almost tripped over the body that was propped up against the wall. A body whose big toe on the left foot was jauntily poking out of a Rangers FC sock that could do with darning.

"Fuck's sake, Dunk," whispered Raymie. "Do you think he's come back for his trainers?"

STANISLAV WATCHED FROM behind the wall as the two youths stood over the body.

The two nylon-clad reprobates were looking decidedly glum for people who were sitting on a small fortune in gold and jewels—even *before* they had seen the body he had left for them. And they didn't appear to have the gold with them. He had been hoping to do a little swap—the body for the gold which they had so handily offered to melt down for him . . . without knowing it, of course.

It looked as though they were arguing. The tall skinny one who appeared to be in charge was pointing at the corpse's feet. The stocky one with the unibrow looked gormless, which seemed to be a permanent expression. Stanislav eased himself closer—it would be nice to hear what they were saying.

". . . put the trainers back."

"What for? He's not going to need them anymore, is he?"

"You've seen *CSI*, Raymie, you bawbag. They can find wee bits of tracy evidence or something."

"Well, I'll put the trainers back, but I'm keeping the mobile phone. It's a stoater. I've been hanging around the O2 shop for weeks trying to nick one of those. Security is major in they phone shops though. Bastards."

Really, the morals of today's youth—Stanislav shook his head. That was the problem with today's society—it was all easy come, easy go—handouts from the State, no sense of responsibility, lousy work ethic—they simply expected everything to be handed to them on a plate.

"What we going to do with the body, Dunk?"

"You're no' real, you tosser. What do you *think* we're going to do with it? Bury it in the flower beds? The ovens are nicely warmed, we'll burn it of course. Now, come on, you get his feet and we'll stuff him in the fire."

Stanislav smiled to himself. Perfect. He just wondered how long it would be before they asked themselves the obvious question. He watched them as they struggled to pick up the chauffeur's body. Suddenly the tall one let go of the top half of the dead man and the head hit the tarmac with an almighty thunk. Stanislav gritted his teeth. Ouch. That would have hurt like the devil if the man hadn't already been dead.

"Raymie?"

"Aye?"

"How did this guy get here?"

"Well, he never walked did he, ya dobber? Even if he'd had his trainers he still wouldn't be able to. Fuck's sake, Dunk, you call me as thick as shite, but what a stupid thing to say. Someone must have brought him here in a car. Jeez-o, man, this is Glasgow not the set of *Shaun of the Dead*."

"I know he didn't walk. You're no' quite getting the point, Raymie. See that car you so cleverly said he was brought in?"

"Aye?"

"Well, who fucking drove it?"

CHIEF INSPECTOR DELANEY made no attempt to hide her yawn. She had been sitting next to Campbell Findlay as they went through hour after endless hour of video footage from the night of the theft. The thieves had shut down the cameras during the raid, but there was still the footage from earlier on the day of the robbery and for the previous week.

"I recognise that young lad." Campbell Findlay pointed at the screen. Slightly grainy images from the CCTV footage from the cameras in the park around the museum were playing on the screen.

Delaney jumped up and stopped the tape. "You do? From where?"

"He came to see me in the museum. Came with a letter from some monastery in China or something. He wanted us to just give the dogs back to the monastery—just like that—no compensation or anything—apparently they have some religious significance. Ridiculous—who cares about religious significance when they're worth millions of pounds?"

Delaney was finding Findlay's overbearing and obnoxious attitude rather hard to take. As the interview had progressed, the curator had gone from being worried about the consequences to him of the dogs going missing, to talking about the potential for media opportunities, to the possibility of he, Findlay, performing some sort of heroic feat to get the dogs back which would earn him an audience with the Queen, an OBE, a huge reward, his own TV chat show and the undying admiration of a bevy of nubile nymphettes.

"Can you remember his name? Where he is staying? Anything about him?"

Findlay shook his head. "Not really—to be honest I wasn't that interested. His name was . . . Karl? Kevin? Whatever it was it was probably an alias. Oh, my God, I was probably *this* close to getting myself shot by some dangerous Yakuza gangster . . . I'm sure the Press would want to hear about that." He raised a hand to smooth his hair—presumably in anticipation of being interviewed as a heroic figure who had single-handedly managed to defeat a gang of hardened criminals.

"I wouldn't worry, Mr Findlay. I doubt very much he's a gangster, unless it's gangsta rap, looking at those jeans, but we need to track him down. I'll just go and speak to my colleagues about tracing him. If you could just watch the rest of this video and see if there's anyone else you recognise, or anything else that comes to mind. I'll be back soon." Delaney stopped in the doorway. "Have you had any phone calls, by the way?"

"From the Press?"

My God, this man was obsessed. "No, Mr Findlay—from anyone saying they have information about the dogs, or even claiming they *have* the dogs."

"Oh—no. Do you think I will?"

"It's very possible. We've given out a hotline number but people could well contact you directly as you're a public figure." Findlay stuck out his chest and preened like a peacock. Or more like just a *cock*, Delaney thought. She continued. "We'll be monitoring your office number from tomorrow, just in case. But if anyone contacts you in the meantime please let us know immediately." Findlay nodded, as though he was thinking the implications of this through. "No heroics, Mr Findlay. If you *do* get a call, let us know straight away. Is that clear?"

"Of course." Findlay peered closely at the screen. Delaney looked to see what had caught his attention. It was the three bingo-going grannies, closely followed by an attractive young girl with a bob.

"Have you seen them before?"

"I . . . errrr . . . I thought I had but no, I don't believe so."

"OK, I'll leave you to it for a few minutes."

"Right . . . right . . . whatever." As Delaney closed the door, Campbell Findlay drew his chair up closer to the screen and pointed the remote at it.

"SO WE GOING to turn the oven on then, Dunk? Can we stay and watch him vaporise?" Raymie and Duncan stood, their noses glued to the oven door, having manhandled the mysterious body into the oven.

Duncan shook his head. Raymie just didn't seem to get the seriousness of the situation. They could get rid of the body no problem, but that didn't answer the main question. How had the body got there in the first place? Maybe it was the young guy who had come in when they were hiding in the cludgie. He was the one who had put the dogs in the sarcophagus after all. But he looked too slim to have taken the body out of its heavy stone resting place, transferred it to a car and brought it over to the Crem. And if it *was* him, how had he known where to go?

Right now, though, job one was to dispose of this guy. Duncan stood with his hand on the buttons. "Chuck the trainers and the mobi in the oven, Raymie."

"Aw, Dunc, man—"

"I said get the fucking trainers and phone in there *now*, ya knobdobber."

"Can't I just keep the mobile at least?"

Duncan wrenched the phone and shoes out of Raymie's hand, and opened the oven door. But as he was about to throw the ill-gotten gains into the oven, they heard the distinctive sound of the Crem door clanging open.

"What the—"

"Quick, Raymie, get the body out of the oven. We've got to get out of here."

"Where we going to go?"

Duncan looked round, pulling the body out of the oven as he did so. "Cleaning cupboard. Now, come on man, help me with him. He's a fucking dead weight."

"That's cos he is, Dunk."

"Fuck's sake, Raymie, this is no time to get all philosophical on me. Get his fucking feet and help me."

"That toe coming out of his socks looks scary, man—all blue and swollen and that."

"Aye, well, if you hadn't nicked his trainers he wouldn't have cold feet, would he? Now, let's shift, you tosser. And move your arse before whoever's out there comes in and finds us trying to burn a body which doesn't have an appointment."

KYLE CLIMBED PAINFULLY out of the ditch. Somehow he'd managed to fall asleep. It was now daylight, the sun was high in the sky and every part of his body ached. The blood from the cuts he'd sustained during his Indiana Jones-style ride underneath the van had dried onto his clothes and every step pulled the material away from his skin, causing the blood to start flowing again.

His bottom lip trembled. He was cold, wet, sore, scared and he didn't have a clue where he was. The dogs were now hidden somewhere in this castle and he had no idea how he was going to find them. He wanted to go home, back to where he felt at peace, back amongst his friends and everyone who loved him. He hated this city and everything about it. If only he could go back to the island, he would never again long for anything other than his quiet rustic life.

Kyle dropped down onto the verge at the side of the gravel road under a weeping willow tree and felt the tears start running down his cheeks, in tune with the tree. As he sank further into misery, he heard quick, light steps on the gravel drive around the side of the castle. Lying low in the long grass, Kyle peered through the branches of the weeping willow. He slapped a hand in front of his mouth to stop himself crying out with a mixture of joy and shock. Rounding the corner of the castle was a young girl dressed in black jeans, heavy black boots and a tight white T-shirt with writing on the front that said *The Raveonettes.* Kyle had a fleeting moment of wonder about what a raveonette was but his attention was caught by the heavy load the girl was carrying. Tucked under each arm was a small golden dog. All Kyle's aches and pains dissipated and his heart filled with a joyful feeling. The Goddess Nur-Lhamo was smiling on him. This *was* his destiny after all. He felt terrible for doubting what he had been sent here to do. His natural optimism returning, Kyle looked from the dogs to the face of the girl as she hesitated just ten feet in front of his hiding place and glanced around. He'd only seen her from the back before. The sun caught the gold in her hair and danced its beams around her head. The exertion of carrying the dogs had given her cheeks a rosy glow.

Kyle's mouth opened and his eyes felt as though they were about to pop out of his head. Despite the un-godesslike clothing and the heavy boots, Kyle recognised the Goddess Nur-Lhamo when he saw her.

THE CLEANING CUPBOARD was dark, smelled of ammonia, disinfectant and something that reminded Dunk of Raymie's shite, only nastier. The cupboard was far too small for three people—especially when one of them was dead. Duncan and Raymie sat one on each side of their silent companion, holding him steady as they listened to what was going on outside the door. Duncan had been slightly surprised when he had heard the voices of the boss man, Armitage, who had been joined by his second-in-command, Big Shuggie, but very relieved that it wasn't anyone else. The conversation, however, was a bit of an eye-opener.

"What's up anyway, boss?" Big Shuggie had rumbled, his voice sounding as though he was chewing a mouthful of gravel. "Why did you want me this aft'?"

"Those lazy wee shites are onto us," Armitage had said. "They started quizzing me about gold teeth and melting stuff down in the ovens."

"You think they've seen us removing the jewellery and the gold fillings?"

"So it would appear, Shug. We need to clean out the stuff this afternoon, get rid of this last lot, and then I'm going to sack the wee bastards."

Duncan looked at Raymie. Fuck's sake, it looked as though they had stumbled on something without realising it. Raymie looked back at him blankly. The whole conversation had gone over his head. A hamster could run around in Raymie's brain without hitting any obstacles.

"Right, Shug, out to the van and let's get the bags in. I tell you, that pair have really pissed me off. I'm going to give their probation officer a bad report on them. That'll serve . . ." his voice trailed off and the door of the Crem clanged.

Raymie waved a hand in front of his face. "Thank fuck they've gone. You talk about *my* arse being rotten. Yours is minging."

It dawned on Duncan what he was getting at. "Fuck's sake, man—it's no' me. It's him." He pointed at the dead body.

Raymie looked confused. "He's *dead*, ya dobber. He's way past farting, let alone having a shite."

He really was thick as mince. Duncan shook his head. "Right Raymie, let's get tae fuck."

"How? There's only one door?"

"We'll have to climb out the window."

Raymie gestured towards the corpse. "What about him?"

Duncan stuck his hand down into his trackie bottoms and scratched his scrotum thoughtfully. Raymie was an almost totally useless bawbag but his convictions had mostly been for twoccing. A good general made use of his army's strengths. Next to the Crem was Aldo's Van and Plant Hire. Duncan came to a decision. "I have no fucking idea how this body got here, but we're going to take it back and put it where we found it."

Raymie belched. "You mad mental bastard. How we going to get back in that place carrying a dead body and stick it back in that big coffin?"

Duncan had to concede that Raymie had a point. "We'll dump it in the bushes outside the museum. That'll be close enough. Go to Aldo's and nick us something unobtrusive that we can easily transport a body in."


DELANEY STUDIED THE young woman in front of her. Megan Priestly was biting the nails of her left hand, and her hand shook as she picked up the plastic coffee cup. "So you haven't been near the museum or seen Campbell Findlay since you split up?"

"No. Never. Nowhere near. Did he say that I had?" The woman was definitely nervous. A little coffee spilled from the cup and Megan wiped it hurriedly with the sleeve of her flowing multi-coloured top. Megan Priestly was probably an attractive woman, striking eyes, nicely rounded figure and with a slightly bohemian dress sense. But right now, she looked haunted and fraught. Her eyes were sunken and red-rimmed, with dark shadows under the make-up, her skin looked tired and dehydrated. When they had gone to pick her up for the interview she had been up to her armpits in clay and Delaney noticed that she still had some clay on her right cheekbone.

"I understand from Mr Findlay that your split was not exactly amicable and that you were pretty upset?"

Megan's eyes narrowed. Interesting. Her previously placid face suddenly showed a glimpse of passion and fire. "Did he tell you that?"

Delaney shrugged. "I think it was more that I read it between the lines. He's not exactly someone who's particularly sensitive to the feelings of others, is he?"

"You can say that again. Egocentric bastard."

Delaney bit back a smile. "Quite, Ms Priestly." Megan Priestly appeared to have relaxed slightly. "He seemed to suggest that you were the only person who was likely to have a grudge against him?"

"Did he? Did he *really*?"

Delaney tried to read the multitude of expressions that seemed to cross the other woman's expressive face.

"Actually, in a lot of ways he did me a favour. I'm so much happier without him. Besides, he's trampled on so many people to get where he is that I'm sure I wouldn't be the only one with a grudge. He's just too thick-skinned to notice that he's seen as a figure of derision and a pompous git."

"But you must miss the job though?"

"The job, oh, yes. It was much more than that, it was my life." A tear rolled down Megan's face. "That probably sounds a bit melodramatic to you, Inspector Delaney, but that job really was special to me."

"So, would you, or indeed *did* you, do anything to get it back?"

Megan Priestly turned the plastic coffee cup slowly with one hand. She appeared to be giving this question serious consideration. Finally she looked up and stared straight into Delaney's eyes and said, "No, Inspector Delaney. I certainly did not."

"WHAT THE *FUCK* is *that*, Raymie, ya tosspot?"

Raymie beamed and patted his new toy. "It's a belter, isn't it, Dunk?"

"A belter? You glaikit bastard. It's a snowplough. A big, huge bright yellow, eff-off snowplough."

Raymie's grin grew wider. "Aye, it's the bollocks, man."

"*You're* the fuckin' bollix, man. How did you no' get summat . . . I dunno . . . a little less yellow, a little less huge, a little less '*Oh, look, it's a fuckin' snowplough.*' They've got all sorts in that hire place. Vans, forklifts, trailers. Man, they've even got a Mitsubishi Evo. And you nick the bastard snowplough?"

"But, Dunk, man, this is the JCB 3CX. It's pure quality, man. Has all these attachments—buckets, blades, stuff that digs stuff out an' that. Plenty of room for the body in the back and we can even dig a wee hole to put him in, if we use one of the other attachments. I've always wanted to drive one. Besides, it was the only one that had the key in."

"What happened to unobtrusive?"

"They didnae fuckin' *have* an Unobtrusive, man. Nor the Mitsubishi. I looked."

Duncan slapped himself on the forehead several times. It was either that or wanner Raymie right in the coupon. "I *mean* you were supposed to nick something no one would notice. So we could just drive up to the museum, people would think we were workies, and we could dump the body behind a bush."

"Aye. That's what I got. Nobody notices a snowplough. It's like a council lorry or a cleansing lorry. They just do the business and move on."

"Naw, Raymie. It's no' *anything* like a council lorry, ya dobber. Just picture the news tonight. 'Police are wanting to interview anyone who's seen anything suspicious . . . like a big yellow snowplough in mid-fucking-June.' "

CAMPBELL FINDLAY PARKED his red Porsche 928 in its usual quiet spot behind the museum, next to some bushes that led down to the river. There were no other cars around which was unusual for this time on a Sunday, just a noisy yellow JCB of some description pulling into the car park. The museum would generally be a hive of activity right now—the workmen must be taking advantage of the occasion to get some work done. The police had told him he could go back into his office, although the museum would not be opening to the public for a week or so. The small white burger van that was usually doing a roaring trade with the cheapskates who wouldn't pay the museum's prices for superior refreshments was shuttered and secured.

Campbell walked around to the boot of the car, opened it and took out a cardboard box. The box was full of staff files and information the police had wanted to see. He might as well return it to his office while he was at the museum. Normally, he would not be so conscientious, and he would relish the idea of a few days away from work, but there was something in his office that he needed.

One of the security guards was standing outside the back door, smoking a cigarette. He hurriedly ground the cigarette out under the heel of his shiny boot as Campbell approached. Campbell made a note to have one of the supervisors admonish the man for his unscheduled break. He handed the cardboard box to the guard with a clipped "My office," and continued into the quiet, cool depths of the museum.

Campbell took the spiral staircase up to his office two at a time. His goal—the piece of paper on which he had written Louise Lane's contact details—the newspaper she worked for, her phone number— although he was slightly worried that the information might be fake, along with the name she had given him.

RAYMIE WAS BUSY reversing and doing spins in the almost empty car park. Duncan had already tried to get his attention twice. He punched Raymie in the shoulder, almost causing him to swerve into a bed of rosebushes.

"Turn it off."

"What?"

"Turn it off."

"I cannae hear you, Dunk."

"Turn the fucking yellow beast off."

"Hang on, I'll just switch off . . . there, now, what were you saying?"

Duncan bit back a hundred responses. "You see that, Raymie?"

"What?"

"That posh guy from the museum that gave us the evil eye when we were there has left his boot unlatched, see?"

"Oh, aye. We going to see if there's anything worth nicking inside? It's nice and quiet."

"No. We're no' going to take anything out, Raymie. Start the snowplough and pull up behind the car. We're going to leave the twat a wee present."

* * *

DAMN IT TO hell. Campbell Findlay had phoned the number Louise Lane had left. It wasn't *The Independent* as Miss Lane had said. It wasn't *any* newspaper in fact. It was Scotland Yard police headquarters. The little bitch. He knew she'd had something to do with the theft of the dogs. *And* she'd stung him for the hotel room. The hotel room! The hotel would have a record of the name the room had been booked under.

Campbell opened one of the neat and tidy drawers of his desk and pulled out the *Yellow Pages*. Running a podgy finger down the page marked "hotels" he found the number he wanted and dialled it.

"Hilton Hotel? I'd like to enquire about a past guest . . . No, I appreciate you can't give information out but . . . this is . . . Inspector Delaney of Strathclyde Police. This is a murder enquiry, you know, so you'd better spill the beans, young man." Campbell was rather enjoying this. He felt like Dixon of Dock Green.

Ten minutes later, he had cajoled, threatened and bullied all the information he needed out of the young man on the reception desk of the Hilton. In accordance with hotel policy, the room had been reserved by credit card in the name of a Countess Letitzia di Ponzo, along with the room next door—a fact which Campbell found very interesting. And the helpful receptionist had been so excited to have royalty staying in the hotel, that he recalled having taken a call from the Countess' butler the next morning, ringing from Cardieu Castle out by Loch Lomond.

Quite frankly, Campbell wondered how the police had such a poor crime-solving rate. Finding out information was easy. You just had to go about it in the right way. He just wished it was as simple to get rid of the smell of fish. His office really honked.

IF MEGAN HAD been angry before, right now she was thoroughly pissed off. It didn't make it any easier that it was that time of the month and she had a sneaking suspicion she would be slightly more rational if it hadn't been. But right at this precise moment her only goal was to make Campbell Findlay pay. Thanks to him, she'd lost her job, and what she had thought of as the love of her life but now realised was A Very Lucky Escape. She had also been forced to cross the line, steal two precious artefacts, break into a museum and lie to the police. Her mother would be horrified if she knew. Especially about the lying part.

She pulled around the back of the museum in her friend's rusty Volvo, giving way to allow a big yellow tractor thing to pass her as it exited the car park. From her vantage point shaded by the stone fountain, she could see Campbell's Porsche outside the back door.

As she waited outside the museum, hunkered down in the borrowed car, she could feel her heart beating hard and her breathing quickening. She reached down into the messy passenger foot-well and found a brown paper bag which she breathed into to stop her hyperventilating. She really needed something to calm her down. She felt as though she would never, ever sleep again. CDs were strewn on the passenger seat. She picked up Runrig's *Everything You See* and slid it into the CD player and fast forwarded to the last track—"In Scandinavia." Perfect. As the haunting melancholy kicked in, Megan could feel herself calming down and she put the paper bag aside and relaxed into the seat. She had gone to Campbell's house to give him a mouthful but when she had seen that his car wasn't there, she had decided to try him at the museum. On the way, a plan had formed in her head. Talking to him would do absolutely no good at all. No, she needed to do something *far* more drastic that would teach him a lesson. With that in mind she had stopped off at a toy shop and made a purchase. It had been a struggle to find what she wanted—apparently, toy shops were very PC and careful about what they sold these days.

She watched the back door of the museum swinging open and Campbell Findlay strutted out like a fat peacock in his favourite turquoise jacket—a relic from the '80s. Behind him, the security guard holding the door open for the great man raised his middle finger in salute before going back inside and shutting the door. As the drums kicked in on "In Scandinavia" and Bruce Guthro's clear and stirring voice reached a crescendo, Megan felt the adrenaline surge through her body. She turned the volume up on the CD player and now embraced and enjoyed the way her heart was beating three times faster than it should be.

\* \* \*

GWEN OPENED HER well-worn copy of *Anne of Green Gables* and turned to one of her favourite parts, where Anne arrives in Avonlea all excited to be there, not yet realising that Matthew and Marilla want a boy, rather than a girl. But the words swam in front of her eyes and she read and re-read the same sentence over and over. She was worried about Dora. Very worried. The very name of Victor Stanislav seemed to make her shake and turn pale whenever she heard it. And she was smoking far more than was good for her. Drinking too, Gwen thought.

Letty had told Gwen not to fret about it, when she had raised it after Dora had left the room, but Gwen couldn't *stop* fretting about it. Letty and Dora seemed to think that she needed protecting. She knew that she came across as a little odd but she also knew she was stronger than the others thought. And she knew that she needed to prepare for the appearance of Victor Stanislav, as Dora, at least, expected it imminently. It was Gwen's role to protect Dora, it always had been. She'd done it before and had gone to jail for it. But she wouldn't be afraid to do it again.

THE THING ABOUT a Volvo was that, no matter how old it was, it could be relied upon to keep up with a Porsche, especially when the Volvo was driven by a woman on a mission. Megan felt as though the last thirty-seven years of her life had been lived in limbo for this moment. She felt empowered, alive and exhilarated. Her previous Bridget Jones existence had gone—to be replaced by *Indiana* Jones. She had even been shopping for a suitable outfit. Originally, her shopping trip had been to try and take away the distress of the police interview, but as her anger had grown, she had felt a Lara Croft vibe coming over her. She would not usually have chosen the tight cerise jeans and close-fitting pale pink top with no sleeves but today . . . well . . . today she wasn't worried about her bingo-wings. The only item which had been a little difficult to find in mid-June was a balaclava, but she had eventually picked one up in the camping store on Buchanan Street. It was tucked into her pocket, ready to be slipped on when the time was right. Sadly, she hadn't been able to buy a pink one, but she had accessorized in black and was wearing a pair of black and pink Rocket Dogs so the black balaclava would have to do.

As she followed Campbell's Porsche out of Glasgow and along the A82 towards Dumbarton with the rolling hills on the right-hand side, Megan felt a growing sense of invincibility. Her eyes fixed on Campbell's Porsche, two cars ahead, she speeded up. *Come on, punk, make my day.* Who did she think she was? Dirty Harry? Nah, Dirty Harriet more like.

BACK IN HIS hotel room, Victor Stanislav studied the map of Scotland he had bought. He could drive to Cardieu Castle the way he had gone before—along the A82 and up the left side of Loch Lomond through Luss and Aldochlay, but he didn't want to get there too early. He looked at his watch. No, it wouldn't do to get there before dark. He wanted that element of surprise, catch them in their beds.

He would turn onto the A811 at Alexandria, drive through Drymen and come up the other side of Loch Lomond, through Balmaha and possibly stop for dinner in Rowardennan before continuing up to the top of the loch and finally coming back down the other side. A long drive, but a pleasant one. Besides, since he wasn't planning on an extended stay in Scotland after his work was done, he may as well make the most of the opportunity for a little sightseeing.

He looked at his Vacheron Constantin. Just time for half-an-hour's power nap.

CAMPBELL FINDLAY TURNED off the GPS as the voice was in the middle of telling him that he had arrived at his destination. He was at the bottom of a drive on a quiet road. Trees lined both sides of the road and the sun dappled the tarmac through the leaves. The gravel drive to the right bent in a dogleg about twenty feet up and the foliage was so thick that he couldn't see how far up the building was. The Porsche idled throatily as Campbell debated whether to leave the car where it was, or drive up. He looked down at his Kenneth Coles. Definitely drive up. It wouldn't take him long. He would confront Miss Louise Lane or whatever her name was, demand the dogs back, and then drive back to Glasgow.

He turned into the driveway, narrowly avoiding being hit by a cruddy old Volvo that came up behind him. The only question in his mind was whether, after he had rescued the dogs, he would contact the media or the police first. He slowed as he took the bends of the drive, and, glancing in his rear view mirror, he saw the Volvo close on his tail, driven . . . oh, dear God . . . by a huge man wearing a balaclava.

Campbell took his hands off the steering wheel in horror at the same time as he stamped down on the accelerator in a bid to escape. As a result, the car shot off the narrow gravel drive and into the ditch and Campbell's head hit the steering wheel. He must have blacked out temporarily and when he came round he lifted his head off the steering column and groaned. His nose felt as though someone had it in a vice and was twisting hard.

He gingerly raised his hand to his face. His nose seemed to be about four times bigger than normal and his hand came away covered in blood. It would definitely have to be the police first; he couldn't have the BBC taking his photo like this. Feeling woozy, he lay his head back down again. Someone was whimpering and after a few seconds he realised it was him. Then he heard another sound.

"Out."

Campbell raised his head, but kept his eyes shut. "Wha . . . ?" The giant in the balaclava had his head through the broken window of the Porsche.

"Out of the car. Now." The man's accent was American and high-pitched.

"But I . . . help me . . ."

The balaclava stepped back. "Out."

Campbell struggled with the door, eventually getting it open and pushing it against the grass and reeds in the ditch in which the car had ended nose down. He scrambled out of the car and sat, panting, on the bank. Finally, he looked up and squinted against the sun and the pain in his nose. The balaclava-clad head was now surrounded by a halo of sunlight, as though it was the patron saint of terrorists. He? Make that a she. Below the black balaclava was a distinctly rotund body clad in pink, the chubby arms looked huge from Campbell's perspective as he stood below them. They were held out towards him shakily holding onto something. Campbell blinked to clear the blood which had dripped onto his eyelashes from his forehead. Yes. He was looking down the barrel of a huge pink gun.

"I know what you're thinking. 'Did she fire six shots or only five?' Well, to tell you the truth, in all this excitement I kind of lost track myself. But being as this is a .44 Magnum, the most powerful handgun in the world, and would blow your head clean off, you've got to ask yourself one question: 'Do I feel lucky?' Well, do ya, punk?"

He had to be hallucinating. There was something about that voice that he recognised, but he certainly didn't know any terrorists with bad dress sense and flabby arms. "Who . . ." he swallowed, "Who . . . are you?"

"Just think of me as your worst nightmare. Pistol-Packing Barbie, maybe. Now, stand up."

The pink gun waved him towards the gravel road. "Listen, lady, I don't know what your problem is but you'd better let me go. If you let me go now I promise I won't tell anyone about this. I'll say I just drove off the road and—"

"We're not just gonna let you walk out of here."

Campbell feverishly cast around him. *'We'*? Oh, dear God, were there more menopausal, balaclava-clad terrorists out here? He was beginning to regret his bravery in coming out here to confront Louise Lane. "We? Who's we?"

The gun was shoved in his face. "Smith and Wesson . . . and me."

"Look, I'm not rich or anything . . . I don't live in this castle, you know. If you're looking to turn the place over you're—"

"Get in the car."

"In the car? But you just told me to get *out* of the car."

"Not that one, dickhead. The other one—the Volvo. And make it snappy, *Mr Findlay*."

Oh, my God, this wasn't some random carjacking—this mad woman was after *him*. He fell on his knees on the gravel and clasped the woman by the thighs. "Please don't kill me. I'll give you whatever you want. Take the Porsche . . . take anything you want. But please. I'm too young to die. I—"

"Oh, stop being a big baby and get in the car. You're drooling all over my new clothes."

KYLE HAD A dilemma. Mr Findlay from the museum was being kidnapped by a scary pink woman. From Kyle's vantage point in the ditch, the whole kidnapping scene was totally bizarre. On the one hand, Kyle wasn't keen on Mr Findlay because he had refused to give Kyle the temple dogs back. On the other hand, Kyle knew where the temple dogs were and was extremely happy that they weren't with Mr Findlay. He grinned happily. The dogs were safe and Kyle felt it only right to try and save Mr Findlay from the scary pink woman. Quang Tu had always told him to do good wherever he could and to refrain from doing harm where good was not an option. Karma—cause and effect—Quang Tu had drummed it into him in every letter he had sent. But . . . well, again, on the one hand Kyle wanted to stay with the goddess, to bask in her beauty, to worship at her boot-clad feet. On the other, what would happen if the scary pink woman came back when Kyle wasn't around to protect the goddess? Kyle shuddered.

And, truth be told, Kyle quite fancied himself as a hero. He could be just like Simon Templar—smooth and debonair and loved by all the ladies. And Kyle wanted some of that. So, on the one hand, there was the idea of being heroic. On the other . . . well, he was like, a peace-loving Buddhist.

Kyle sighed. Weighing up the pros and cons was hard. And he now had more hands to consider than the Hindu Goddess Kali.

Life was so much easier back with his gran. He needed to make a decision quickly. Mr Findlay was being bundled into the back of a big old car—silver-and-rust-coloured—by the scary pink woman. Mr Findlay was begging and crying and the scary woman was saying "Fuck with me, buddy, I'll kick your ass so hard you'll have to unbutton your collar to shit." Kyle was rather shocked at the language used by women in Glasgow. Of course, he had no other women wearing balaclavas and carrying pink guns to compare this one to, but surely it couldn't be normal?

Kyle made a decision and, as the woman manhandled Mr Findlay into the back seat of the car and tied his feet and arms with some rope, Kyle crawled painfully on his hands and knees over the gravel to the back of the car. He reached up a hand and released the boot catch, raised the boot lid just enough to accommodate his slight frame and clambered carefully inside. He pulled the lid down and lay in the dark, one finger hooked around the lid to keep it down, but at the same time stop it from shutting completely. It was dark, smelly, cramped and unpleasant, but Kyle was most certainly not going to do the whole riding under the car thing again. No, compared to that, this was luxury. Kyle closed his eyes. Having spent the night in the ditch, this was actually pretty comfortable.

* * *

"YES, BUTLER?" LETTY held the Regal King Size behind her back as she peered out of the narrow crack she had allowed the drawing room door to open to. The atmosphere inside was heavy with a mixture of worry and cigarette smoke, and she would rather the staff didn't get a whiff of either. "You know better than to disturb the Signora and I and our guests when we are relaxing in the boudoir. I hope you have good reason for this interruption?"

Butler—Letty could never recall his name, much to Dora's disapproval—bobbed his head deferentially. "Terribly sorry, madam, but I thought you would wish to know. There is a Porsche in the driveway."

Behind Letty, Dora let out a gasp. Letty felt her heart flutter. Despite her reassurances to the others she, too, was worried about Stanislav. "Who is it?"

"Nobody, madam. The car is empty and it looks as though it has been driven into the ditch at the side of the driveway. Would you like me to ask Paul to remove it?"

"Paul? Paul? Ah, yes, Gardener. Yes, please, Butler . . . no, wait. We will go down and investigate before we decide." Never one to look a gift horse in the mouth, Letty liked to take advantage of every opportunity that came her way. A Porsche was rather more of a penis extension than she really wanted, but, still . . . "Come, ladies," she said imperiously for Butler's benefit. She pinched her lit cigarette out with her left hand—ignoring the brief burning pain, pushed Butler gently out of the way with the forefinger of her right hand and led Dora, Gwen and Katrina out of the room and down the sweeping oak staircase like a chintz-covered duck marshalling its wayward ducklings.

"WHERE ARE YOU taking me?" Campbell's voice was muffled. It was no wonder, since his head was stuffed into the brown paper bag Megan had used to stop her hyperventilation earlier, his hands were tied behind his back, and his head was wedged into the space between the back and front seats of the Volvo.

"You talkin' to me?" Megan was running out of Clint Eastwood quotes and had now turned to Robert De Niro for inspiration. "You talkin' to *me*?"

There was a sigh from the brown paper bag.

In actual fact, Megan thought it was an eminently sensible question, and one which she had been pondering for the last ten minutes since she had bundled Campbell into the car. She realised that, in the heat of the moment, the gun and balaclava buying, and her reinvention as Dirty Harriet, she hadn't really thought the whole kidnapping scenario all the way through. Where *was* she taking him? She had automatically pointed the car back in the direction of Glasgow but she had nowhere to go. She couldn't take him home or to her studio. At some point she would need to take the bag off his head and he would recognise both of those locations.

"Please let me go . . . I just want to go hoooooooooooooooooome."

Dear God, he sounded pathetic. However, his whine gave her an idea. With one hand on the wheel, and keeping both her eyes on the road, after all, it would never do to get arrested for reckless driving at this particular point in time, Megan reached out a hand and groped for her handbag. Tipping the contents onto the passenger seat she heard the clink of keys. She cast a quick glance to the side. Yes, there were Campbell's house keys. Hopefully, with all the excitement, he wouldn't yet have changed his locks.

DUNCAN SIGHED HEAVILY as Raymie took yet another bottle of Buckie out of the blue and white striped carrier bag at his feet.

"It's all that museum wank's fault." Raymie idly twisted the metal top from the bottle of Buckfast. The summer rain pinged and bounced on the top of the bus shelter. It was raining quite hard but Duncan and Raymie were the only people actually inside the bus shelter. Both had their feet up on the metal bench and were smoking. Roll-up stubs littered the ground, attesting to the amount of time they had spent in there, drinking Buckfast—well, in Duncan's case, *pretending* to drink Buckfast—puffing away, and idling away the time. Anyone actually waiting for the bus preferred to wait outside—choosing to get wet rather than share the bus shelter with the smoke, alcohol fumes, bad language and occasional insults that wafted their way.

"What is?"

Raymie screwed up his eyes and took a final long draw of the thin rollie he was smoking, coughed, and hawked half his lungs out on the path. "Us losing our cushy number at the Crem *and* our benefits. Now we've got no money. An' if I have to go back to the Bar-L my ma will go fucking mental."

Duncan was still confused. "How was it that museum yoke's fault? Talking of your ma—she got any grub in?"

Raymie hauled himself off the bench and stuck the bottle of Buckie in the pocket of his shell suit top. "Aye, man, and she's at work an' all. C'mon." They started to walk, hands in pockets, to Raymie's mum's flat across the road. As Raymie opened the scratched and battered door of the flat, he continued his moan. "If that tosser hadn't organised that exhibition shite, we wouldn't have got the idea to nick they wee dogs, we wouldn't have tried to melt them down, and Armitage wouldn't have caught us, sacked us, and turned us in to that probation tart."

They slouched into the living room, Raymie booted the Staffordshire bull terrier off the leather sofa and turned the wide screen TV on, flicking through the channels until he found a re-run of *Jeremy Kyle*—"I think your brother's the father of my child—DNA Results." "Aye, it's all his fault, man."

It was a convoluted logic, and Raymie was a total bampot sometimes . . . well . . . most of the time, but Duncan had to admit it made sense. If they hadn't decided to go after the dogs they would still have had their easy community service job at the Crem. "Aye, Raymie, and if he'd been more careful about the crap he was showing off, they dogs would have been real gold and jewels and we would have been fucking minted."

This was a particularly sore point. After dumping the body in the boot of the museum guy's car and returning the bastarding snowplough they had remembered the jewels and headed off to their friendly neighbourhood fence, a local pawnshop owner who gave them a bung for anything they nicked from time to time, no questions asked. So they had taken them down to Stinking Ronnie's, a huge, sweating, greasy-haired creep with a face like a blind cobbler's thumb. The fat turd had taken one glance at the stones and started a weird wheezing laugh, his several chins wobbling. He rocked himself back in his chair, his food-stained T-shirt stretching over his belly. Duncan could see the crispy yellow sweat stains under his arms and had nearly boaked.

When the wheezing stopped Ronnie had finally managed to speak to them. His voice was surprisingly high and thin for such a big man. "Where did youse pair of numpties get these?" Duncan and Raymie had looked at each other and then back at Stinking Ronnie for clarification. Ronnie put one of the emeralds on the floor and maneuvered his chair leg over the sparkling gem. Raymie had jumped up "Haw, ya bawbag . . . what the—" Too late, Ronnie had ground his bulk down on the stone using the chair leg. The stone had fractured and cracked and ground into hundreds of tiny pieces.

Ronnie had started his wheezing laugh again. "Glass, ya pair of fannies. Now, get tae fuck out of here, ya haufwits." His laugh had followed them out of the shop. Duncan had wanted to give the arse piece a good gubbing. And now, here they were, as Raymie had summarised—no money, no community service, and probably headed back the the Bar-L as soon as the probation officer found out they'd been given the heave-ho. Duncan sighed and lit up. Raymie turned the TV up as a local news report showed a photograph of the guy whose car they had put the dead body in before cutting back to a live feed of the museum, a blonde bird standing outside holding a microphone.

". . . of the West End Museum has been reported as missing by his secretary who tried to get in touch with him on an urgent matter and was unable to contact him. Strathclyde Police have released a statement saying that they feel the disappearance of Mr Findlay is not un-connected with the disappearance of a valuable exhibit over the weekend." Raymie and Duncan looked at each other and grinned. "Ports and airports have been put on alert in case Mr Findlay tries to escape with the stolen items. We have Chief Constable McEnteggart here. Chief Constable, would you like to comment on latest developments?"

A silver-haired man came into view "Well, Miss Bysouth, as I am sure you reported, my earlier statement indicates that we are looking for both Mr Findlay and the dogs and we will not rest until both are found."

"And are you sure Mr Findlay has the dogs?"

"At this particular time I couldn't possibly comment."

"Has Mr Findlay's home been searched?" The museum was replaced by a shot of Findlay's house, panning out from the front door to a street sign saying Hyndland Road.

"We have been to Mr Findlay's home and ascertained that there is nothing fishy there," McEnteggart hesitated. "Apart from a strange smell of fish."

"Is there a possibility that Mr Findlay has been kidnapped?"

"We have not ruled out *any* possibilities and are pursuing all lines of enquiry."

"Do you think there will be a ransom demand for Mr Findlay's return?"

"As I've said Miss Bysouth, we are pursuing all lines of enquiry and haven't ruled anything out at this stage."

"Do you think that if he *has* been kidnapped that the kidnapper also has the dogs?"

"That's all I have to say right now, Miss Bysouth. As soon as we have any further news we will hold a further Press conference."

The blonde looked miffed. "Thank you, Chief Superintendant. Back to the studio."

"Well, there's a fucking belter of an idea, Dunk."

"What?" Duncan leaned down and picked up the can of Special Brew Raymie had got for him earlier from his ma's supply in the fridge and tipped half of it surreptitiously into Raymie's wee brother's potty which was next to the sofa. Being a non-drinker was sometimes a right pain in the arse. He'd tried, but just didn't like the taste.

"Well, we know that *no-one* has the dogs, 'cos we had 'em and we are the only people who know they're fake. So we kidnap that dick, hold him for ransom, and get a big wad of cash for him."

Raymie contemplated the suggestion. "Only one thing wrong Raymie, mate. He's already missing."

LETTY RAN HER hand over the shiny paintwork of the Porsche.

"Who would leave a car stuck in the middle of a ditch?"

"Dunno, Katrina, love."

"Maybe whoever owns it has gone off to get some help."

"Why didn't they come up to the house first?"

Dora peered in through the broken driver's side window. "Good point, Katrina. And the keys are still in it." She pulled them out and waggled them at the other three. She held the keyring out. "Whoever the car belongs to is 'Hot Stuff' apparently."

Letty snorted. "Thought so. This car belongs to some fat bald guy having a mid-life crisis. Chuck the keys over, Dor'. Let's have a look in the boot."

Dora threw the keys in a ladylike underarm throw which Letty caught with one hand. She turned the keys in the lock, but it was open already. She unlatched the boot and the four women moved in to peer inside.

"Oh, holy shit."

Letty raised an eyebrow at an atypically foul mouthed Dora. "Yep. Holy shit indeed. And holey socks too. I recognise those." She reached in and pulled the tarpaulin away from the face of the neatly wrapped body inside.

"I told you I killed him." A single tear ran down Gwen's left cheek. She looked at Letty. "They're going to take me back inside, Letty."

Dora moved over and reached up to give her a hug. "No, they bloody aren't, Gwen. Are they, Letty? We're going to sort this out, aren't we?"

"You take Gwen inside, Dor'. Call all the staff into the kitchen on some pretext and then give us a buzz on the mobile. Me and Katrina will sort this out, yeah?" Letty motioned to Katrina to help her lift the body out of the boot. "When you've rung, we'll carry him round the other side of the house down to the boat, take him out and throw him in the Loch Lomond. Shame it's not Loch Ness—he would make a nice snack for the monster. Come on, Katrina, doll. Help me get him out and we'll put him in the weeds under that tree for now. We can get some rope from the garage to tie him down so he don't float back up."

Dora nodded and started to lead Gwen off. "Oh! Letty, what if this is Stanislav's car? Do you think he's watching us from somewhere?" She scuttled over to the car, leaned in and opened the glove compartment. Taking out the car's owner's manual she read the name. "Campbell Findlay."

Katrina gasped. "Christ. Now we've got *two* of them after us. No way we can just wait here and let them come for us. What are we going to do?"

Letty, who prided herself on being able to think on her feet, smiled with more confidence than she felt. "I've got a plan. Unfortunately, it *does* involve waiting here for Stan. But don't worry. We ain't going to be sitting ducks."

MEGAN HAD DRIVEN twice around the block. There were no police cars anywhere around, no suspicious cars parked in the vicinity containing two burly blokes drinking coffee, no mysterious white vans with aerials on top. Megan was glad she lived on a diet of cop shows and action films. Campbell's house had that unmistakeable air of emptiness about it. She was probably being over-cautious anyway—it was unlikely anyone would have missed him yet.

With a last glance around for police activity, Megan turned the Volvo into the narrow lane behind Campbell's house. She pulled in just past his back gate.

"Up."

"Where . . . where are we? What are you going to—"

"Up" Megan lifted Campbell by his shirt collar, his weaselly words becoming a strangled gurgle. She was enjoying this. This must be what people meant when they talked about taking back your life. "And keep quiet. Nobody can hear you except me, and, if I do hear so much as one whining peep out of you, you'll get this." She pressed the toy gun into his fleshy stomach and pulled him out of the car, shut and locked the doors and opened Campbell's back gate.

The paper bag was sucked in and out as Campbell breathed heavily. "Who are you? And what do you want with me?"

"Me? Oh, I'm no one. Just a fly in the ointment. A monkey in the wrench. A pain in the ass. But right now . . . I'm your worst nightmare. Now, walk." Megan took Campbell roughly by the arm and shoved him in front of her.

He stumbled up the path to the back door, whimpering and whining. My God, how could she ever have found this snivelling little shit attractive? This was really therapeutic. Megan put her hand in front of his chest to stop him, slid his key into the back door and turned it. She stepped inside the kitchen ahead of Campbell and stopped in the doorway to listen. The fridge buzzed quietly and a clock ticked on the kitchen wall, but otherwise there was nothing but the silence of an empty house. She hooked a hand around Campbell's arm to bring him in, and led him down the hallway, their footsteps sounding loud and harsh on the hardwood floor.

As they moved further into the house Megan's nose started to detect the unmistakeable smell of dead fish and she grinned to herself. She unlatched a door under the staircase up to the first floor and led Campbell inside and carefully down a set of dark, narrow stairs. She recalled the basement from the time Campbell had once sent her down for something. It was a place that he chose not to go, due to his claustrophobia. It would be perfect.

"Oh, my God—it's cold here. Have you bought me to some chamber of torture to kill me?" Campbell's voice was falsetto with panic. She led him over to an old kitchen table that was the only piece of furniture in the room.

"Strip."

"What?"

"Strip. Take your clothes off. Divest yourself of your outerwear. Put yourself in a state of dishabille."

"You're going to rape me, aren't you? That's what all this is about. You're going to keep me here and use me as a sex toy?" Campbell sounded hugely relieved.

"Campbell Findlay, if a woman were to ever love you as much as you love yourself, it would be the greatest romance in history. Now, take your clothes off and get that unappealing pale, flabby, hairy arse up on the table."

"How am I going to undress when my hands are tied up. Besides, how do you know my arse is hairy?"

Whoops. She needed to be more careful. She had disguised her voice up until now, putting on a fake American accent. Megan had no idea where she was going with this whole kidnapping lark, but she knew that she wasn't really going to do anything awful to Campbell. So she definitely didn't want him to recognise her. She pulled the balaclava out of her pocket and pulled it on and then undid the ropes binding Campbell's arms behind his back. "There. Now get undressed and lie on the table. Everything off."

Campbell peeled off his clothes, coyly turning away as he took off his red silk boxer shorts—his trademark, Megan remembered. He put his hands on the paper bag over his head. "Do I take this off?"

"Nope." Megan poked him in the side with the toy gun and his flesh jerked away. "Just get on the table."

Campbell scrambled up. "Ouch."

"What?"

"I think I've got a splinter."

"Good."

"You're a bit of a bitch, aren't you?"

"You better believe it, baby."

"Why are you doing this?"

Megan tied the ropes around Campbell's body, tying him to the table. "Because I can."

"Is it money? Is that it? You want money? I'm a powerful man. How much ransom have you asked for?"

"Twenty-five."

"Thousand? Is that *all*?"

Megan wound the rope tightly around, back and forth, holding Campbell tight on the table. "Pence. And they refused to pay up." She leaned forward and gave the rope a final tug. "There. Piggy's all tied up nice and tight." She took the red silk boxer shorts, lifted the bottom of the brown paper bag, and stuffed them into Campbell's mouth.

Campbell started to thrash and try to speak through the boxers. Maybe he was finally getting some backbone. She took the gag out of his mouth. "Make it good."

"You'll regret this, you know. Have you any idea who I am?"

"Yep. A total and complete arsehole." Megan stuffed the boxers back in his mouth, turned away, and walked back up the cellar steps.

KYLE WAS DESPERATE to stretch his legs. The car had stopped some time ago and, from what he could hear, the woman with the gun appeared to have led Mr Findlay off somewhere. He was doing a lot of whining. Kyle had wanted to poke his head out of the boot and tell him to pipe down. But he had kept his cool and stayed curled up.

After a few minutes he had inched the boot lid up and started to ease his aching body out, only to hear people stopping by the car.

"I think this is it, Raymie. It's what they said on the telly anyway."

Kyle eased the boot lid back down very slowly, his finger hooked underneath again.

"Aye, four houses in from the main road. This'll be it. Looks well smart, man. Bet there's loads of good gear inside there."

"Fuck's sake, Raymie, we're not here to nick the guy's stuff. That's, like, penny-ante stuff. We're here for the big score."

"Aye, man, but no reason we shouldn't make the most of it while we're in there."

Kyle realised that he would have to stay where he was for a little while longer. He folded his legs back into their previous position as quietly as he could, wincing at the jolts of pain the movement sent through him.

"What are we waiting for, Dunk? Let's just go in."

"Best not open the gate just like that, there might be someone there. Here, give me a leg up and I'll look over the wall."

"How come?"

"What?"

"How come I get to be the one doing the lifting?"

"Fuck's sake, Raymie, sometimes I think you're just no' right in the head. You're a fat bastard."

"Bit personal, Dunk. And you're a skinny wee wank, but I wouldn't dream of saying that and hurting your feelings."

"No, you tosspot. You're about twice the weight of me. Now, put your hands out and give me a lift up."

For a couple of minutes Kyle could hear nothing but grunts.

"Jeez-o, Dunk. That's my bawsack you just crushed. Watch where you're treading, you dobber . . . what can you see?"

"Nothing. The door's shut and there's nobody in any of the windows."

"Do you think it's safe to go in?"

"Looks as though it might be. Lower me . . . wait, there's someone opening the—"

Kyle heard scrambling and cursing, followed by a heavy thunk on the boot lid. He only just managed to move his finger out of the way in time.

"What the fuck did you let go of me for?"

"You said let you down."

"Aye, 'let me down,' not bastarding drop me. Now leg it. There's some bird on her way out of the back door. We'll come back in a bit."

Footsteps slapped on the tarmac as they ran off. Now Kyle had his opportunity. He pushed against the lid of the boot. No movement. The body falling on the lid had locked him in.

The next moment, the driver's door slammed, and the car set off.

VICTOR SLANISLAV TOUCHED the corner of the napkin to his mouth. What could be more pleasant than fish caught freshly that day, in the loch just outside the restaurant he was sitting in, and cooked to perfection by a chef who obviously knew his trade?

He checked his watch. He still had plenty of time. He would have some cranachan and a small glass of Glayva with his coffee and be on his way.

MEGAN PARKED THE Volvo close to the kerb, got out of the car and ran up the steps to her flat. She couldn't cope with Campbell's whining anymore, so she had put the gag back in his mouth, ensuring that he could breathe, and had left him tied to the table. She would go back and rescue him in the morning. By then he might be suitably humble. She had absolutely no intention of causing him any physical harm, she just wanted to scare him a little. OK, a lot.

She would go back tomorrow and untie his arms, leaving him to untie his own legs. By the time he'd done that, crawled up the stairs and discovered he was in his own basement, she would be well away.

As Megan entered her flat she looked at the clock in the hallway and yawned. God, she was tired. Fresh air, a nice drive out into the country, and a spot of kidnapping were obviously more strenuous than they seemed. She made her way to the bedroom, peeling off the pink outfit as she went. Maybe, just maybe, she would get a good night's sleep. Or just *any* sleep.

She crawled into bed. So tired, but sleep still wouldn't come. So many questions. Had Campbell recognised her? Would he be OK down there overnight? Had she locked the back door before she left? Megan started to cry. She'd just thought of another question: would she ever sleep again?

CAMPBELL FINDLAY STRAINED against the ropes tying him to the table. He let out a muffled sob. There was no give at all. The mad bitch who had kidnapped him had told him she was in the Girl Guides and had earned her knot-tying badge. She had turned the light off when she left. He had managed to get his head free of the paper bag, but it was so dark that he still couldn't see anything. It was dark, cold, claustrophobic, and he was going to choke to death on his own boxer shorts. He tugged at the ropes again. It was useless. All it did was cause his body to burn in all the places the ropes chafed. Campbell turned his head to one side, trying to spit out the boxer shorts. As they had become soaked with his saliva, they seemed to have become more compact. If he could empty his mouth he could call for help. Or consider it, at least. His captor had told him that no-one would hear him if he made a noise, but he had to try. She was going to kill him anyway, he knew it. Either that or subject him to humiliating sex acts twenty-four hours a day.

Campbell stopped his ineffectual movements. Voices. More than one. He lifted his head as far as he could and strained to hear.

". . . nice pad, man . . ."

Campbell sobbed with relief, redoubled his efforts, and was rewarded by the soggy boxer shorts popping out of his mouth and hitting the table with a squelch.

"Down here . . ." his voice was rough and dry, and came out as no more than a whisper. Campbell cleared his throat. "Hey, down here!"

Silence. Then the door at the top of the stairs opened, letting in a shaft of light which silhouetted two figures in the doorway—a gorilla and a beanpole.

Campbell could have cried with happiness. "Help me. Untie me." He was going to be saved. He would be free. And the first call he would make would be to BBC Scotland. They would surely want to interview him.

"Fuck's sake, Raymie, somebody's left the museum tosser all tied up and ready for us."

LETTY BREATHED IN deeply, plucking up the courage to admit to something she had been keeping to herself since shortly after they had seen Stanislav on television. Katrina's shoulder was covered in Dora's foundation as she hugged the crying woman. She looked at Letty with a worried look on her face, and patted Dora's knee, as if she wasn't quite used to being a source of comfort. Gwen hovered over them both, gnawing at her fingernails.

Dora raised her tear streaked face to Letty. Her waterproof mascara obviously wasn't. Letty thought Dora looked like an aging panda that had gone mad in the dressing up box. Dora's lip trembled. "He's going to kill us all, I know he is." Gwen moved forward, as if to say something and Letty put out a jewel covered hand to stop her.

"He's not, Dor'."

"Of course he is, Letty. He's a trained killer. We're just . . . old ladies." Letty felt as though her heart would shatter. Dora had never admitted such a thing before. Dora reached out a shaking, liver-spotted hand, looking at that moment every day of her seventy-five years. "We should leave while we still have the chance, Letty. I'm glad you told the staff to go—at least we don't have to worry about *them* when Stanislav arrives." She squeezed Katrina's arm. "I just wish you and Gwen would leave, love. Stan's got no beef with you. It's . . . it's me and Letty he wants."

Letty picked up an Edinburgh Crystal tumbler filled to the brim with tequila and downed it in one swallow. "Look, as far as Stan's concerned, we don't even know he's after us. He'll be thinking he's got the element of surprise. When, in fact, it's us with the upper hand."

"How do you work that out?" Katrina took a break from comforting Dora to light a cigarette.

"Well . . ." Letty hesitated. Dora was going to sodding kill her. "I bought us a little something when I went into Glasgow." She pulled out a ladylike sub-machine gun. "This is a MAC-10, commonly known as a Big Mac. But so much tastier."

CAMPBELL HAD FINALLY come to the conclusion that this pair of Neanderthals had not come to rescue him. Instead, it would appear that they, too, had come to kidnap him. However, unlike the mad pink American bitch in the balaclava they weren't going to subject him to hours and hours of humiliating and depraved sexual acts. At least, he hoped they weren't.

"What do you want with me?"

The tall, weedy one surveyed him thoughtfully. "You heard of the duck that laid the golden eggs?"

"Goose. It was a goose."

Weedy's eyes narrowed. "Alright, smart arse. The duck that laid the golden goose." Campbell opened his mouth to speak but thought better of it. "Well, you're our duck. And you're going to lay us some golden dogs."

Campbell closed his eyes. He was going to wake up from this bizarre dream at some point. "But . . . I don't *have* the dogs. They were stolen from the museum—didn't you hear?"

"Aye, by us . . . but they were fakes."

"What?" Campbell almost strangled himself trying to lift his head up.

"Like you didn't fucking know that already, you tosser. So we're going to hold you, and they wee dogs, for ransom."

The one advantage Campbell felt he had over his captors was that the intelligence levels of this pair seemed to be subnormal. Surely a man of his intellect—even under the rather trying circumstances of being naked and tied to a table—could find a way to escape from these Neanderthals.

"What are you going to do if that woman with the gun comes back?" From the looks on their faces they obviously hadn't considered that possibility. The blubbery one paled under the spots and pimples that covered his face.

"He's right, Dunk."

"Fuck's sake, Raym . . . I mean, Ronnie . . . I told you not to use our real names. "

"I forgot. Who are we again?"

Weedy sighed and explained patiently. "We're Ronnie and Reggie, after the Kray twins. Them big London gangsters, man. I'm Reggie, you're Ronnie."

Campbell couldn't help blurting out, "They got caught." Two pairs of vacant-looking eyes were turned his way.

"What?" Weedy broke the silence.

"They got caught." Campbell turned his head to look at Blubbery. "And you might like to know that your friend gave you the name of the mad, gay one. I wouldn't be very happy about that if I were you."

"Is that fucking right?" Blubbery moved towards Weedy who backed off, holding his hand in front of him. "I'm not a fucking arse bandit. We'll need to swap names."

Weedy took a swig out of a can of Special Brew. "Oh, for fuck's sake, Raym . . . Reggie . . . Ronnie. Right, you come up with some good aliases then, you dobber."

Blubbery screwed up his face as though he was struggling to pass a kidney stone. "OK, Dunk. I'm Clyde. You're Bonnie."

"SO, WE ALL clear then?" Letty looked around at her team one by one. Three serious faces looked back at her. "Katrina, you and Gwen head off and get some kip and Dora and I will take first shift. Any sign of Stan and we'll come and get you,"

"But why *don't* we just leave, Letty?" Katrina rubbed the back of her neck.

"Katrina, doll, Dora and I are staying put. You and Gwen are free to go . . . and I wish you would." Katrina and Gwen both shook their heads. Dora's eyes filled with tears and she leaned over and kissed both women in turn.

"The dogs are safe in the boathouse, yeah?" Letty looked at Katrina for confirmation.

"Yep. I hid them in an old fishing net under a tarpaulin. They'll do there until we can get them away somewhere else. That boathouse isn't obvious."

"And you put the Porsche in the old garage at the back of the garden?"

"Yep."

"Good. If Findlay doesn't turn up to pick it up we'll drive it back into Glasgow and leave it near the museum . . . God knows what happened to him."

"And what about . . ." Dora rubbed her temple, "after . . . ?"

Letty slapped her on the back. "After we see Stan off, we'll dump him in the loch to keep Sheehan company and then sit tight on the dogs for a while until things cool down."

THE THICK ONE had gone out to get cigarettes, leaving the really, really thick one to guard him. Campbell was fuming. He had discovered that he was being held captive in his own basement. How on earth had that bitch got hold of his keys?

To add insult to injury, the two criminals had raided his drinks cabinet and were now working his way through his wine collection.

Even worse, Blubbery had made the comment "This is shite. Have you not got any Thunderbird, ya dobber?"

As well as going for cigarettes—taking the money from Campbell's wallet to do so—Weedy was also going to get some bread to make some sandwiches from the "meat paste" he had found in the fridge. It had taken Campbell a minute or so to register that the meat paste was actually the *pâté de foie gras* he had spent a mint on at Peckhams a couple of days before. He had no doubt that Weedy would be coming back with a processed sliced white loaf.

Blubbery was swigging out of a bottle of particularly fine Cabernet Sauvignon Shiraz. A selection of goodies from the kitchen was spread out in front of him on the top of an old heater. He put a black olive in his mouth and promptly spat it out. "Aw, fuck's sake, man, that grape's minging."

"I need the bathroom." Campbell wanted to get out of the basement.

"What, bawbag?"

"I need the bathroom."

"You think I'm gonnae wash your hairy arse for you while you have a bath?"

"No, I need to use the toilet."

"Why didn't you say that? Here," Blubbery put a wine bottle into Campbell's hand. "See if you can aim into that."

"It wouldn't do any good. I don't need to urinate, I need to . . . defecate."

"Eh?" Blubbery moved closer, a look of intense puzzlement on his face.

"I need to move my bowels."

"You need a shite. Jeez-o, man you talk a lot of pish. You'll have to hold it in—I can't let you go to the lavvy until Dun . . . Bonnie comes back."

"I'm desperate. You have to let me go."

"Tortoise's head out?" Blubbery moved away, making a disgusted face. "Aw, man, you can't shite there, it will be honking. Put us right off our paste sarnies so it will."

"Then just untie me and let me go to the toilet."

"I cannae, man."

"Oh, dear, I think with all this stress I've got diahorrea." Blubbery looked blankly at him. "Diahorrea. The runs . . . I could shit through the eye of a needle."

KYLE WAS DREAMING of a huge pizza being fed to him piece by piece by the Goddess. Not the one back in the statue on his chest of drawers, but the one he had seen at the big house. The pizza was covered in ham and chicken and pineapple and pepperoni and ground beef and peppers and mushrooms. And tons and tons of cheese. And so was the Goddess. She was dripping with gooey cheese. Mmmmmm. Kyle woke up, his mouth watering, his stomach grumbling and his muscles protesting at the cramped conditions in the car boot.

He willed himself to go back to sleep again. He wanted the dream to continue. Perhaps he would eat the cheese off the Goddess. He drifted back off into unconsciousness, a happy smile on his face. This time, he was being eaten by an enormous pizza that covered the floor like a huge carpet. It folded him into its warm and cosy wetness and he had to eat his way out. It was brill.

He woke up again, and realised he was so very very hungry that he was almost tempted to eat the damp blue carpet that lined the boot. Everything ached. He was cold and uncomfortable. And a really loud couple appeared to be having sex on the car. Strange grunting and groaning noises and the rhythmic slapping of flesh were accompanied by the bouncing up and down of the car and the "bang, bang, bang" of the boot lid. Kyle felt seasick. He put his hands over his ears and thought of something more pleasant. The first thing he was going to do when he got out of here was have a pizza. And then he was going to go back to the castle and speak to the Goddess.

"I WISH YOU'D get to bed, Gwen. It's been a tough old day and we need you and Katrina fresh for the next shift.

Gwen shook her head. "I wouldn't be able to. I'd rather be in here with you and Dora."

Letty looked over at Dora who was sitting hunched up gazing into the empty fireplace, looking just like the old woman she really was. Letty sighed heavily and lit yet another cigarette from the one she was already smoking. She absently took a long drag and blew out the smoke in a thin stream. Gwen coughed and waved a hand.

"I'm sorry, doll. I'll put it out. I've been smoking far too much this evening—it's nerves."

"Don't do that." Gwen heaved herself up out of the armchair. I can't settle anyway. I'm going to go out for a walk by the loch, get some fresh air. It'll do me good—clear my brain and my lungs." She nodded meaningfully at the still figure of Dora. "Look after her, won't you?"

"I'll go and make us all a cup of coffee."

"Put some brandy in it. I won't be long."

"WHAT DO YOU mean, 'he's fucked off'?"

Raymie looked sheepish. "He escaped."

"He *escaped?* What, like Harry fucking Houdini? Just got out of the ropes all on his own? Raymie, you fud, you untied him, didn't you?"

"Well, aye. But he was going to shite all over. You know that gives me the boak. I've got a weak stomach."

"It's not the only thing that's weak, you halfwit. And why are you just sitting here drinking? Do you think he's just going to come back?"

"He might."

"Fuck's sake, Raymie. He'll be halfway to the polis by now. Let's get tae fuck out of here."

"Can I grab his telly on the way out?"

"WELL, WELL, LADIES. How *lovely* to see you again at last." Victor Stanislav had seen the fake Contessa silhouetted in a third floor window as he crept, on panther paws, up the gravel driveway, making not a sound—a skill of which he was extremely proud. He had circled the castle, surveyed the lie of the land and then simply walked into the castle through the open door. They were obviously very trusting out here in the country. He had silently entered all the rooms, like drifting smoke. There was no-one anywhere apart from the young girl. How thoughtful of the old crows to make things easy for him by getting rid of their staff. Other than the girl, the only sign of life he had seen outside the room in which he knew his quarry were was an unmade bed.

He had placed a hand over the girl's mouth as she slept and led her to the room were the old women were. His hand still over the girl's mouth, he had pushed her ahead of him into the room, letting the hags see the gun pressed into the girl's back.

The Signora dropped the delicate china cup she was holding and it smashed into smithereens on the hearth of the handsome fireplace she was leaning against. She stood completely still, her hand held out as if the cup was in it.

Stanislav bowed. "Whoops. I do hope that wasn't part of a set?"

The Signora looked as he remembered her—slim, neat, and with a fashion sense belying her advancing years. Her face, however, was a mess—streaked with make-up, her lipstick smudged. The Contessa, on the other hand, was a totally different kettle of fish. She was almost unrecognisable as the tweed and silk clad battleaxe of a woman he had known in Australia. She wasn't wearing a stroke of make-up, her grey hair was piled in a rough knot on top of her head, and she was dressed in combat trousers and black T-shirt covered in skulls—she looked remarkably like a tent he had slept in once in Angola. She had paused in the act of lacing a pair of enormous boots.

"Victor." Her voice was low and emotionless. He was disappointed. He would have preferred a reaction more like her sister's.

"Yes indeed, dear lady. It is I. In the flesh."

"How did you—"

"Get in? The front door was wide open. Very hospitable of you, if a tad over-trusting. I understand that Scotland has high crime levels. You never know who might walk in uninvited."

Theodora whimpered like a beaten cur. Victor focussed his attention on Letitzia. She was the one who would be the most trouble. He watched her face as it ran through a gamut of emotions— puzzlement, fear, anger, worry . . . finally all transitory changes were replaced by a look Victor recognised very well—a look he had seen on his own face in the mirror on many occasions— a look of sheer animal cunning. Ah, she was, indeed, a worthy foe. It made Victor feel much better to know that he had been outsmarted by such a worthy opponent. But only once. This time he would not be bested.

The young girl struggled in his grip and he tightened his hold. The little bitch was trying to bite him.

Theodora suddenly put a hand to her mouth and gasped. "Where's—"

"Dora!" Letitzia smartly snapped out a warning that shut her much more placid sister up immediately.

Victor smiled. He knew the reason for both the half-finished question, and the warning. And he also knew the reason for the look of relief and complacency that he had seen on Letitzia's face.

"You might want to look out of that window." He gestured with his eyes to one of the curtained windows on the far wall. "Slowly, if you please, and keep your hands visible at all times."

Letitzia backed over to the window, watching him all the time, and stopping to place a large but reassuring hand on her sister's shoulder as she passed her.

She lifted the red velvet drape and looked outside. Victor was rewarded by the sagging of her shoulders, and her crumpled face as she turned briefly to look at Dora. She suddenly looked as though she had aged ten years.

"Yes—your strange friend. She's fine . . . for now. I only gave her a light tap on the head. But it *does* mean that she won't be the cavalry you expected her to be."

DELANEY HAD DECIDED that she hated this case.

"I *really* don't know how many times I have to tell you this, Chief Inspector. The *first* time I was kidnapped was by a sex-crazed Amazonian woman carrying a gun."

"I thought you said she was American?"

"She *was*. I mean Amazonian in the sense of huge, threatening and scary."

"And this was just outside Glasgow, correct?"

Something flickered across Findlay's face. He was definitely keeping something from them here. "Yes, I'd gone for a drive and stopped at the side of the road to stretch my legs and they jumped me." Had he been going dogging, perhaps? Was that the reticence Delaney sensed in him? "Oh, my God, my *car*." Campbell's lip trembled. It was the first sign of real emotion she had seen in him the whole time.

"Don't worry, Mr Findlay, I am sure we'll find it. Now, are you sure this woman had a real gun? Her outfit sounds a bit . . . Are you sure it wasn't just hen-night hi-jinks?"

The white paper suit rustled as Findlay heaved a huge sigh, sucking every bit of oxygen from the small interview room. "Look, Chief Inspector, she said she would kill me if I didn't tell her where the dogs were . . . I still can't believe you thought *I* had taken them and run off to Brazil or somewhere like some common Ronnie Biggs character by the way." He sounded more offended that he was being likened to Ronnie Biggs, rather than accused of stealing the precious artefacts.

"We were just pursuing our enquiries, sir. Now, please tell us again how you bravely escaped from this crazed lunatic." The sergeant sniggered, covering it with a cough and then a sip from his mug of steaming tea, to disguise the smile.

The sarcasm which Delaney believed had dripped from her voice like arsenic-laced honey passed Findlay by. "I keep *telling* you. The second lot of kidnappers rescued me from the first one . . . in my own house, the very cheek of it . . . can you believe it?"

"And this Amazonian woman just disappeared never to be seen again?"

"Yes."

"Are you sure someone hadn't fed you some drugs? Some peyote from South America for instance?" the sergeant sniggered again.

"As I've already said, Chief Inspector, when I say Amazonian woman, I don't mean that she literally came from the Amazon. I just mean that she was large and fearsome."

"And sex-starved."

"Yes, sergeant. And sex-starved."

"Sounds like my ma's friends after an Ann Summers party and a couple of bottles of Bacardi Breezer."

Delaney turned to her colleague. "Thank you, sergeant, for that titillating insight into your family life. Carry on, Mr Findlay, please tell us about the second gang."

"Oh, my goodness. Well, these were serious Glasgow gangsters. They were going to hold me to ransom and they thought I had the dogs. Just like you, Chief Inspector. Oh, my God, don't tell me it's been on the news that you thought *I* had the dogs?" Findlay's face paled to match the paper outfit. "My reputation will be in shreds."

"Did the woman also tell you she was going to hold you for ransom?"

"No . . . no, she never actually said what she wanted . . . it was more like it was a . . . I don't know, a sport." So he did notice things after all. "How many were in this second gang?"

"I saw two, there may have been more. Large. Muscular, glowering men with facial scars. It was a testament to my savoir faire and guile that I managed to escape their violent clutches. Have you been round to my house?"

"Yes, there was nobody there." Something had definitely happened in the house. Forensics were currently going over the basement where Findlay had been kept. "The back door was open. They probably legged it pretty smartish after you escaped."

"Did they take anything?"

"The telly's gone and the fridge door was open." Delaney shrugged. "That looks to be about it until you can confirm otherwise for us. Did they have guns too?"

"Probably. Guns, knives, baseball bats, machetes, samurai swords. I tell you Chief Inspector, they were violent and dangerous criminals. I narrowly escaped with my life after outwitting them and fighting them off."

It had to be done. "OK, Mr Findlay, please tell us again this tale of derring-do of how you outsmarted your captors and how we found you wandering the leafy streets of Hyndland at two o'clock in the morning, naked and hysterical."

"I only became hysterical *after* your men manhandled me into the back of a police car." This stung. Oh, it definitely stung. "I can't *believe* they arrested me for indecent exposure."

As Campbell Findlay launched into his *Boy's Own* tale of capture and escape at the hands of a murderous Glaswegian triad, Delaney leaned back in her chair and let the soothing hiss of the interview tape wash over her as she shut out Findlay's pompous drone.

"SO, LADIES, I think what we will do now is have a little chat about these dogs. And then we'll see what we're going to do with you." Victor had led the three women at gunpoint to the dining room where he had tied them up with workmanlike efficiency with some strong nylon rope he had brought especially for the purpose, and then gone outside and fetched Gwen who was still sleeping. They were all now lined up in front of him, securely tied into a set of Hepplewhite shield-back, mahogany dining chairs, upholstered in sea-green velvet. Victor had felt a pang of dismay at having to tie the rope so tightly around such a fine example of Georgian furniture, and then to secure the chairs to the heavy original radiators that lined the room, but it had to be done. "Where are the dogs?"

"And if we don't tell you?" The Contessa . . . Letty Huggins, as he now understood she was called, glared at him with disdain. He would knock that out of her. He moved swiftly over to her and hit her on the side of the head with the gun—hard enough to draw blood, not hard enough to stun.

"Letty! Oh, my God, Letty." Dora Huggins sobbed. "Please, Victor, don't hurt her."

"It's OK, Dor'." Letty looked up at him, still defiant. "I'm OK, love. You can fuck off, Stan—we're not telling you where the dogs are."

"Really? We will see about that." Victor prided himself on his intuitive reading of human nature, helped along by a degree in psychology from Heidelberg University. For some reason, the old bags were very protective over the woman they called Gwen. Still asleep, her head was resting on her chest, her mouth slightly open and an unsightly thread of drool darkening the purple velvet of her shapeless top. Victor placed the barrel of his gun to the top of her head.

"If you don't tell me, I will splatter this woman's brains all over the carpet. And I really don't want to do that." He looked at the deep pile of the carpet under his feet—pinks, beiges, cream and delicate blues. "It's a Savonnerie, if I am not much mistaken. Neoclassic . . . Empire style. Not as fine as the Louis XVI or Louis XIV but still a fine piece nonetheless. It would be nigh on impossible to get blood out of it."

"Letty, we have to tell him. After what he just did to you, he won't hesitate to kill Gwen." It was the first time the young girl had spoken. She was a bit of an enigma, very calm, taking everything in, throwing concerned glances at Dora from time to time.

Letty nodded. "I know, love, tell him where you hid them. Then he can be on his way, can't you, Stan?" Despite her position, Letty's voice held a flinty note.

Victor was impressed once again. She was, most definitely a worthy opponent. He would enjoy a little game of cat-and-mouse with her. He bowed, deeply. "Of course, your ladyship."

Katrina looked straight at him, her eyes like flints. "They're in the boathouse."

"Exactly?"

"Underneath a tarpaulin right at the back, wrapped in some old fishing nets."

Victor nodded. "Casual, but good." He looked at Katrina thoughtfully. "I think I will take you with me. If you're lying to me I can then squeeze the truth out of you . . . and then continue squeezing."

Katrina gasped. "I'm not lying. That's where they are. I put them there earlier."

Victor untied her with one hand, professionally and skilfully. As if he had done it before. Which, of course he had, on many occasions.

DELANEY RUBBED HER eyes. They felt gritty and were stinging from lack of sleep and cigarette smoke. She had to leave the interview room every half an hour or so for a cigarette and some fresh strong coffee. She glanced at her watch—5 a.m.—she had been up for forty-eight hours straight. "Right, Mr Findlay, you can go. As I've said, one of the policemen at the house will be staying there with you."

"Do you think either of the gangs will come back?"

Delaney shrugged. "Hard to say. Amazonian women are so unpredictable." She raised her eyebrows at the sergeant. It was increasingly hard to remain polite. This turd was probably the most annoying person she had ever met. She wondered whether anyone would actually *pay* a ransom to have him returned. She made a note to investigate all his family and friends. Maybe one of them had taken advantage of the situation with the missing dogs to have him offed. Quite frankly, she wouldn't blame them. They'd probably get away with manslaughter on the grounds that being in his company would be enough to drive even the sanest of people up the wall.

"Well, I hope I am going to have police protection around the clock."

Delaney idly wondered which of her subordinates had pissed her off so much recently that she would subject them to Findlay. "Of course, Mr Findlay. We are taking this very seriously." As Findlay stood up she added. "Oh, and the Press are outside. Someone saw your early morning streak down Hyndland Road and called the *Daily Record*. I would caution you against speaking to them."

"Oh, my God—and look at the way I'm dressed." Findlay gestured to the white paper suit, which, Delaney was pleased to see, had a big rip, right up the arse. "I can't meet my public like this. You must have something else I can wear to go home in."

Delaney sighed. This tosser was not going to heed her request that he not talk to the Press. No, if she knew him, his first move would be to run into their welcoming arms and tell them about the hordes of marauding Vikings and Huns he had battled single-handed. "I'm sure the sergeant can find you something suitable from lost property."

As she left the room for her sixteenth cigarette of what had been a very long night, Findlay's annoying voice followed her up the echoing corridor. "I can't wear nylon, it chafes my skin. Make sure the sergeant knows I can't wear nylon."


"I HAVE NO idea where they are! That's where I hid them, I swear." Victor was surprised to find that he believed her. She had looked as shocked as he had when they had entered the boathouse to find the tarpaulin and fishing nets tucked into a dark corner, but no dogs. He had dragged her back to the dining room and tied her up again. Letty and Dora had obviously been stunned by the revelation too.

"That only leaves her." Victor gestured to Gwen, who was now showing signs of waking up.

"No way. There's absolutely no way Gwen would take them. She's devoted to Dora and me."

"Perhaps she simply moved them."

"Why would she do that? No. She's not touched them, Stan."

"What about the staff?"

Letty considered the possibility before shaking her head. "Nah. None of them had any reason to suspect there was something up. I'm not sure most of them even know there *is* a boathouse."

"Has anyone else been here?"

"Nope. We're . . . oh, shit."

"What?"

"The Porsche, the bloody Porsche. The museum curator's Porsche, but he wasn't in it. It was in the driveway. With the body of our chauffeur in the boot."

Victor tried to assimilate this confusion of information. He had left the chauffeur's dead body at the crematorium. By what means had it found its way back to the castle?

MEGAN DISSOLVED A headache powder in a glass of milk. She had a pounding headache and, of course, hadn't slept a wink. She put her thumbs into her eye-sockets and pressed hard, trying to push away the pain. It wasn't working and she felt sick. She downed the milk and headache powder mixture, feeling her face screwing up at the taste. She pushed the plunger on the cafetiere and poured coffee into a mug—strong, black, bitter—just what she needed this morning. Blowing on the coffee she took it into the lounge and switched on the TV.

Why the hell had she kidnapped Campbell? It had all seemed appropriate yesterday and, actually, quite good fun. But, in the cold light of day, with the onset of a migraine, she was regretting what she had done. She groaned and sank down on the sofa, pulling her towelling robe around her more tightly and resting her head on the big fluffy cushion.

She pointed the remote at the TV and muted the annoying advert that had a woman talking to a finance company on the phone, asking for a ridiculously large loan. A thought struck her—a thought which made her really happy. Instead of going back to Campbell's and facing both him and the mess she had made, she could just ring the police. Just phone and let them know that there was a man tied to a table in his own basement who needed rescuing. That way she wouldn't have to see the slimy toad again. What was the name of the policeman in charge, the good looking one on the telly? As Megan looked up the telephone number of Strathclyde Police Headquarters she racked her brains for the name. Mc-Something. Mackenzie? No. McEnteggart, that was it. She dialled the number, dialling 141 first to disguise her number.

"I'd like to speak to Chief Constable McEnteggart, please . . . no, I'd rather not give my name . . . I'd really like to speak to him, it's about the theft of the dogs at the museum. Well, strictly speaking it's about the kidnapping of the curator of the museum . . . what do you mean, 'again'? . . . Yes, I'll hold." Megan took a gulp of her coffee as the woman who had interviewed her earlier came on the line. She asked Megan her name in a rather husky, tired voice.

Megan reverted to the American accent she had used when she kidnapped Campbell. "No, I've already said I'd rather not give my name. Just think of me as someone who fights for truth and justice and the American way . . . no, sorry, I'm not American, it's a quote from *Superman*. Anyway, I'd like to report a kidnapping . . . no, not me . . . Campbell Findlay, the curator of the museum those gold dogs were stolen from . . . I don't understand what you mean by 'again?' . . . No, you'll find him tied to a table in his basement . . . What? . . . He *did?* . . . But I . . ." Megan quietly put the phone down. How on *earth* had Campbell escaped?

THERE WAS A television set in every room of this castle. Normally, this would have offended Victor's sensibilities. However, on this occasion it was actually useful. He had eventually gagged his captives so that he could think about his next move and once he had meditated and allowed his brain to work through the problem he had subsequently turned on the television to see if there was any news. On the hour, he was rewarded by a news report from the steps of a house. The number on the door read 53, and the apparent owner of the door was standing outside it. Victor had recognised the man as the museum's curator and possible possessor of the dogs, since by all accounts he had been the only person in the vicinity of the castle other than its residents. From the strangled noises behind at least two of the gags, it would appear that his captives also recognised the man. All five of them were now watching the screen with rapt attention. Victor thoughtfully turned up the sound.

A blonde reporter in a green suit held out a microphone. Her job was made easier by the volubility of her subject.

"I was kidnapped first by a drug-addled female, high on amphetamines and carrying an automatic weapon. She told me that if I so much as sniffed she was going to kill me. Dangerous, violent women like her cannot be allowed to walk the streets. I, myself, on my own, managed to bravely overcome her and she fled from my home."

The interviewer managed to squeeze out a question.

"Why do you think she kidnapped you?"

Campbell Findlay looked straight into the camera. "I think she wanted to use me for her own warped sexual practices. It happens to virile, handsome men in positions of power."

A POOL OF coffee spread around Megan's feet, gradually creeping out over the wooden floor and oozing in between her naked toes. She was utterly gobsmacked. Drug-addled? Violent? She should have stuck the gun up his bum, then he would have seen who was violent. Given him an enema with the pink Barbie water-pistol.

And to think that he had convinced himself that she had kidnapped him for sex? She had never even *mentioned* sex. And she could have done. Oh, yes. She could easily have said he was the most useless, limp-dicked lover she'd ever had in her whole life and that his willy was the size and consistency of a Milky Way. Only not as tasty. And it didn't stay anywhere near as hard either. And she would have had every right to say that—the man was totally useless in bed—he was always in it for his own gratification. But did she say anything of the sort? Did she torment him when he was tied to the table? No, she bloody didn't. And to think that she had even phoned the police because she had felt bad about leaving him tied up there.

If it wasn't for the fact that it would get her arrested she would go down to the police station and turn herself in. She would ask the police if she was violent and drug-addled and sex-crazed. And show him up for the lying little toe-rag he really was.

This was bloody war. She couldn't go round his house—she had spotted a couple of policemen lurking in the background on screen. But she knew where his car was, and if she knew that slimy little rat Campbell she knew he would head for his pride and joy. And she would be there waiting for him. Without even bothering to go and get dressed, Megan zipped up her pink towelling dressing gown covered in gambolling lambs, stuck her coffee soaked feet into her fluffy yellow chicken slippers, and picked up the keys to the Volvo.

RAYMIE'S MUM SLAMMED down a plate of jam sandwiches in front of them. Duncan had been starvin' marvin only the minute before but now he and Raymie sat glued to the TV screen, the sandwiches forgotten on the cracked plate.

Some snooty bird was asking Findlay. "And the second kidnapping?"

"Ah, well, a vicious gang of thugs burst into my home and held me at knifepoint. Disgusting, mouth-breathing yobbos who couldn't string two words together. They beat me, pulled guns on me and threatened to kill me."

"What does mouth-breathing mean, Dunk?" asked Raymie, breathing through his mouth.

"Shhhhhhhh."

"How did you get away?"

"Well, they thought they were tough but I was tougher. When it came down to it they were cowards of the first order. I am twice the man that they were. A whole team of so-called hard men and I still managed to fight them off. Hard? I showed them who's hard."

"Fuck's sake, Dunk, the fucking fud's a fucking pie. He never fought me. He just ran off when he went for a pish."

Duncan snorted. "He couldn't look hard even if he'd taken Viagra eyedrops. He's about as hard as my first shite."

They looked back to the screen. The blonde piece was nodding. "And did the gang tell you what they wanted?"

"They were going to hold me to ransom. And they wanted the missing dogs. That's the problem with the youth of today. They have it too easy—they don't want to work and make their way up like the rest of us do, they just want everything handed to them on a plate. Things have gone to the dogs in this country since the Labour government came to power. I think it's time to bring back National Service. And hanging. It's a dis—"

"Mr Findlay, do you have any idea who any of these kidnappers were?"

"I was able to give the police two of the kidnappers' names. I managed to extract this information from them using guile and cunning."

"And can you tell us what those names were?"

"Duncan and Raymond. They were the two most vicious, most stupid, and most reprehensible members of the gang. And I've told the police that I believe they have the dogs. It's certainly not *me*."

"Oh, you pair of useless gobshites." Duncan and Raymond turned to see Raymie's ma in the doorway, a cigarette in one hand and a strawberry jam-covered knife in the other. As she bent down to wipe up a big blob of jam from the faded carpet a thick streak of dark brown and grey showed at the parting of her bleached-blonde hair. She straightened up and stuck the jammy finger in her mouth with a slurp. "What the fuck have you shitey wee arseholes done *now*?"

"WELL, WELL, WELL." Stanislav leaned back in the wingback chair, crossed his legs carefully, and flicked a speck off dust off his charcoal grey Ted Baker trousers. "I think we have found our dog-napper." He laughed at his own joke. The four women, however, did not look in the slightest bit amused. He considered the situation. He couldn't take them all with him while he went to liberate the dogs—that would be too much to cope with. He also couldn't leave them all tied up—there was no guarantee that some of the staff wouldn't come back. He would need to do something about that.

No, he needed to do something which would guarantee their compliance but which would leave him free to do what he had to do. He looked at each of them in turn. Letty—big and brash—she looked relaxed despite the dried blood crusting in the deep wrinkles on her cheeks. Dora—strain showing in her face, and the veneer of respectability finally washed away along with her thick foundation. Katrina—the girl had been staring at him constantly while the TV report had been on. He had felt her eyes boring into his head. And then there was Gwen—the big, shapeless woman in purple had been sinking in and out of consciousness—he must have hit her harder than he had thought. Yes, Gwen, that was it.

"What we're going to do, dear ladies, is that I am now going to untie you." Letty's eyes flickered. "I think I can rely on your co-operation, can I not?" It was a threat, rather than a question. "Then I am going to drive back into Glasgow and get the dogs from that pretentious nonentity of a museum curator." The look of animal cunning was back on Letty's face. Victor smiled to himself. "And you, dear ladies, will wait nice and quietly here for me to come back." Katrina and Letty looked at each other. Victor moved closer to Letty, hitched up the knees of his trousers so as not to spoil the sharp crease, crouched down in front of the chair she was sitting in, put a hand on each padded arm of her chair and said quietly. "I know you aren't going to call the police because of your involvement in all this, but hear this . . . if you leave, I will find you. I will hunt you down to all four corners of the earth. And I will make you watch as I rip your friends apart limb from limb." Yes, it was melodramatic. Yes, it was below him. But it needed to be said.

Letty still looked contemptuously at him, holding his gaze with cold, defiant blue eyes. "And, just to make sure of your willing compliance," Victor raised his voice so that they could all hear him clearly, "I am taking your friend Gwen with me as security for your good behaviour. But don't fret—she'll be very comfortable in the boot of the car."

FOR THE LAST three hours Kyle had been working at a piece of carpet in the boot of the Volvo using a rusty old nail he had found. Sweat pouring down his face, stinging his eyes, he had wriggled and jabbed the nail into the edge of the carpet, slowly but surely weakening the material and exposing a panel behind the back seat of the car. Using his fingers he had unscrewed the screws holding the panel in place. It had taken ages to get even a small bit of movement. His nails were torn and the ends of his fingers were blistered and bleeding but the panel was now starting to move, he could feel it give as he turned the third screw. He would be out in a matter of minutes. He was sure that when the panel was off he would be able to squeeze into the back seat of the car and then let himself out. A quick trip back to his hotel for a shower, change of clothes, ring his gran so she wouldn't worry about him, and one of the hotel's magic breakfasts and he would be raring to go. He could then try and find his way back to the big house and the Goddess and the dogs.

He wiped the sweat away and renewed his efforts on the screw. But the noise of a key in the car door halted him mid-twist. He heard a sobbing voice from the front of the car. It was muffled by the panel and the back seat, and the sudden and ferocious revving of the engine, but he was sure the voice said "I would *never* use my bare breasts as weapons."

CAMPBELL STEPPED OUT of the shower and wrapped himself in one of his luxurious fluffy towels. As he towelled himself dry, he looked at himself in the full-length mirror, sucking in his stomach and turning sideways. He would need to wear his control underwear before his next TV slot. His interview with the icy blonde from STV had gone well, he thought. He felt he had come across as brave but self-effacing, a pillar of the community and a local hero. That the blonde had turned down his offer of dinner had been a minor disappointment. There would be plenty more totty where she came from.

The phone had been ringing off the hook since he had made his live TV appearance. The police were going to put some sort of monitor on his phone just in case any of the kidnappers, or the person who had the dogs, called him, but they hadn't done that yet. In the meantime, newspapers, radio, TV—they all wanted to interview him. Nothing national yet though, just the locals. His mind flicked back to Louise Lane. He would be more careful when it came to the national press—no-one would pull the wool over his eyes on that score again.

The phone rang and Campbell bounded down the stairs, knocking aside the police sergeant that had been tasked with guarding him as the policeman reached out to pick up the phone.

He panted into the phone, slightly out of breath from running down the stairs, hitching the towel up around his hips. "Campbell Findlay—museum curator and local hero. How may I help you?"

"Ah, Mr Findlay, good day to you. My name is Victor Smith, and I'm calling from *The Times*." The voice was cultured and polite.

"*The Times*?" Campbell's heart started to thud. You mean the London *Times*, as opposed to the *Glasgow Evening Times*?"

"The very same, although I am in Glasgow at the moment, covering the story of the heist at the museum. I was wondering if you would consent to giving us an interview? Tell us about your horrific ordeal?"

Yes, I'd *love* to be interviewed by you . . . I'm free now, can you come round now? Will there be photographers?"

"Would it be possible for you to come to us, Mr Findlay? We are on a bit of a deadline and I'm expecting my photographer back at any moment."

Campbell looked round. The policeman was hovering in the doorway, biting his thumbnail and looking distinctly bored. Campbell turned away and lowered his voice. "No, there's a policeman here . . . They won't let me out of the house on my own, I have to have a round-the-clock bodyguard."

"That would be a shame. I am *sure* you could use the guile and cunning you have so ably demonstrated to lose your police nanny."

Campbell listened to the well-spoken voice and preened. "Yes . . . I'm not really sure I should, though. I've been kidnapped twice, and by some *very* violent people you know. Maybe it would be better if you came round . . ."

"Oh, dear, that is a pity. We were looking to do a three-page spread on the exciting events. And possibly a front-page photograph. Ah, well, never mind . . ."

"A *three*-page spread you say? With a photograph on the front page? Yes, of course I'll come. Where do you want me to meet you?" Campbell was already scrambling through the *Yellow Pages* looking for taxi numbers.

"Do you know Clydebank shopping centre? The car park at the other side of the pedestrian tunnel that leads to Asda?"

Campbell stopped mid-search. "Isn't that a bit of a strange place for an interview? . . . Maybe you *should* come here."

"I do believe we may also be looking at the possibility of a book deal, Mr Findlay."

"Really? I'll be there in half an hour."


DUNCAN HAD BITTEN his nails down to the quick. If Raymie didn't stop pacing he was going to go mental.

"What the fuck are we gonnae do, Dunk?" Raymie peered out of a crack in the nicotine-stained curtains. "The polis are gonnae check they computers and find us."

"Look, man, they only know our first names. How's that going to lead them to us?" Despite his outward bravado Duncan, too, was worried. The cops had their first names, and that big shitebag of a museum tosser had told the cops that *they* had the dogs. Where did the fat fuck get off doing that?

He joined Raymie at the window. The dirty net curtains gave the bright summer day outside a brownish haze. Duncan looked out into Islay Street from Raymie's maw's ground floor flat. The long grass tickled the bottom of the window sill of the flat and the broken windows of the wheel-less car on blocks in the small front garden. Across the way Raymie's twelve-year-old brother hung round with a gang of his mates in the doorway of the ugly grey concrete high flats, smoking and chatting to several of the neighbourhood girls, whose braying laughs echoed up the deserted street. They all posed and preened like nylon-clad pigeons, their skip caps pecking as they went through their rituals. Duncan was beginning to see these people he had lived amongst all his life in a new light. One which made him dissatisfied with his lot.

It was the sort of place where nobody had even seen a game of baseball but everyone had a bat, and even the dogs moved in teams. The graffiti on the doors and walls and over the metal shutters on some of the empty flats exhorted the residents to "fuck the polis" or give them the big news that "macca takes it up the bahookie."

Duncan sighed. He needed to get out of this shite hole. He was sick of all this crap. He wanted something bigger, better, brighter. He and Raymie had been so close to getting their dream of a wee pub in the Drum or Milton. If those dogs hadn't been fake they would have had it. And if that tosser hadn't escaped they would have had a big wad of cash. They needed a big score. And that big fandan of a museum curator was still their best chance of getting it.

He punched Raymie in the arm. "C'mon, Raymie, let's get out of here. Tell yer maw to make us a piece on egg and we'll head off."

"Where we going, wee man?"

"Back to the scene of the crime, Raymie."

"Oh, aye, right." Raymie paused in the process of pulling his stained white Reebok shell suit top on over his Rangers T-shirt. "Which crime?"


LETTY SHIVERED. GIVE Stanislav his due, he *had* let them loose from the chairs. However, after forcing Letty and Dora to phone all the staff to tell them not to come in for a few days, they were now locked in the cavernous wine cellar with a pile of sandwiches and over six hundred bottles of dusty old wine. No tequila, but Letty was making the best of a bad situation. She had so far tried, and rejected, six bottles of white and three bottles of red.

She was now sniffing the cork of a dusty bottle of red from 1946. Letty had picked it because it was the year when, at sixteen, she had been forced, pregnant and desperate, into an unhappy marriage with a family friend, a man much older than she was, just to keep the good name of the family. It was all pointless, since she had ended up losing the baby after her loving husband had punched her in the stomach one too many times. She had run away from him a year later and taken to the streets. Letty wiped the bottle neck before taking a swig of the dark and fruity wine. It tasted of sweet plums and cherries. Dora had joined her shortly after, escaping from the unhappy family home.

They had been happy in the brothel. Life was different then, in the fifties and the swinging sixties. Much freer, easier, and a lot more fun. Even the gangsters had been good for a laugh—until you had crossed them. Letty and Dora had tried to keep it fun when they had taken over the running of the brothel in the late 'sixties, and they had done so for a good decade. The protection money to the cops and the gangsters had been a small price to pay, the punters had been manageable, and there hadn't been the drug problems.

And then . . . things had changed. And for her and Dora things had changed forever when Dora . . . Letty looked over at her sister. She was slumped in a corner, her usual vitality had left her. Letty knew she was worried about Gwen, and she felt she was to blame for what had happened to her—both now and thirty years ago—but she seemed to have lost every spark of . . . well, anything that made her Dora. Katrina was fussing around her and trying to get her to eat something but the most Dora had taken since they had been locked down here was a glass of water.

Letty took a large gulp out of the wine bottle and lit a cigarette with her Zippo. "Come on, love, you've got to pull yourself together. This isn't helping Gwen any. We've got to think of something for when Stan comes back. He might have taken that smashing gun I bought but this place is full of stuff we can use. After everything that's happened, we're not going to just lie down and accept whatever he has in store for us. There must be some way of getting out of this cellar. Shouldn't castles have secret passages?"

THE TAXI DROPPED Campbell off outside Matalan in Clydebank. Campell looked around. He had sneaked out of the back door of the house, having told the policeman he thought he had heard a noise upstairs. The taxi met him, as arranged, two streets away. Campbell was almost certain he hadn't been followed. He felt a mixture of excitement at having escaped his police bodyguard and fear at the telling off he would get from the prickly Delaney when he went home.

She was a bit of a hard-nosed bitch, and, besides, Campbell wasn't used to dealing with women who were immune to his charms. Although he was sure that if he *had* tried his charms on her she would have melted. He just didn't fancy her, that was all.

The journalist had told him he would be driving a red Audi A4 Avant, and that he would be parked close to the tunnel at the far end of the car park. And there was the car, parked right at the back, tucked out of the way. Leaning nonchalantly against the car was a tall, tanned man smoking a cigar. Campbell had the impression that he had seen the man before. Perhaps he was also a TV journalist, as well as a newspaper one. He was certainly handsome enough. His casual clothes looked smarter on him that many people looked in business suits. He was wearing a pair of well-cut grey slacks and a baby-blue sweater that looked like cashmere or mohair. Campbell's fingers itched to stroke it. It was a warm day but the man looked as cool as a cucumber.

The man held out his hand. "Mr Findlay? Please, do get in. I thought I might take you to lunch—a little ride out into the country."

Campbell looked at his watch. He would be missed by now, the police would be looking for him, and he was beginning to feel a little nervous about his unannounced departure. He was about to tell the journalist that he didn't have time when the man spoke again.

"Cameron House Hotel, OK? I thought we might have lunch by the loch. I've told the photographer to meet us there."

"Perfect," said Campbell, easing himself through the passenger door which was politely being held open for him. He had his mobile on him—he would call Delaney and let her know where he was—after it was too late for her to protest, of course. He surveyed the handsome profile of the journalist. Depending on how well they hit it off and how amenable the chap was, he might ask him to drive the few extra miles up to Cardieu Castle so that he could pick up his Porsche.

"So, tell me more about this publishing deal, Mr . . . ? I'm sorry, I forgot your name, Mr . . . ?"

The journalist turned and smiled at him, his perfect white teeth sparkling like a toothpaste advert. He said in an accent Campbell couldn't decide was Australian or Eastern European, "Please just call me Victor, Campbell."

\*       \*       \*

"YOU SEE WHO that is, Raymie?"

"Who is it?"

"That posh twat who was at the museum. Findlay's getting into his car. We need to follow him."

"Fuck's sake, Dunk. My maw's man's gonnae kill me as it is. I'm not supposed to be driving his motor."

"Raymie, you bawbag, you're not supposed to be driving at *all*."

"Aye, but if I get nicked by the polis I'm only going to get community service and another twelve-month ban to add to the two I've already got. If Mental Malky catches me he's going to rip my bollocks off and feed them to his pitbulls."

"How much have you had to drink today, Raymie?"

"No' enough, man, no' enough."

Duncan was slightly fearful of being in the car with Raymie driving, but he was intrigued by developments. They had spotted Campbell Findlay legging it down the lane behind his house, puffing and panting like a water buffalo with a rocket up its arse. They had followed behind him and watched him jump into a waiting taxi a couple of streets away. They had then followed him here, despite Raymie's shite driving. Cheeky bastard wouldn't let Dunk take the wheel. Duncan didn't like being behind the wheel of a car anymore, after he'd killed that couple but rather that than put up with Raymie's shite driving.

"Got to be something to do with they wee dogs, Dunk. An' that lying toerag said he never knew anything about them . . . an' he told the polis and everyone it was us."

Raymie sounded positively offended. Duncan didn't like to remind him that, technically, they *had* stolen the dogs. He didn't think Raymie would be able to wrap his brain around that philosophical debate—especially not when he was driving. The big fandan had trouble telling his left from his right.

They followed the Audi as it pulled smoothly out of the car park, Raymie's ma's boyfriend's clapped out old Sierra belching smoke. Its holey exhaust pipe gave a hiccupping growl as Raymie revved the engine like a boy racer.

"Calm down, ya dobber. They'll think they're being followed by a Boeing 747 if you keep making that racket." The Audi turned right at the bottom of Kilbowie Road, onto Dumbarton Road.

"Hang a couple of car lengths back, Raymie, like they do in the films." This was pure mental. Duncan's heart was beating like a drum. He felt as though he was in an episode of *The Bill.*

"What are we gonnae do now there's two of them, Dunk?"

Duncan snorted. "What . . . some posh twat and that museum dick? Nae problem, Raymie, mate, it'll be a fucking skoosh."

DORA HAD FINALLY fallen into a fitful sleep and Katrina and Letty were sharing a sandwich and a bottle of wine.

"Better not have too much more of this, doll." Letty's stubby fingernail tapped the side of the bottle. "We need to keep a clear head for when Stan comes back."

"What do you think he's going to do to us, Letty?" Katrina sounded worried, and much less confident than she had done before. She'd put a brave face on when Stan was there.

"I dunno, love, I really don't know. He's a vicious bastard though. Dora's right to be afraid of him." Letty didn't want to sugarcoat things. It was best that the girl knew what they could be facing.

"Do you think Gwen's all right?"

Letty sighed. "I hope so, doll."

They sat in silence for a couple of minutes.

"What is it with Gwen, Letty? Why is she the way she is, and why are she and Dora so . . . I don't know . . . protective of each other?"

Letty reached over and tucked a wayward strand of air behind Katrina's ear, letting her hand linger on the girl's slightly feverish cheek. "Well, you know Gwen was in jail, right?"

"Yeah, I gathered as much, although none of you ever talk much about it, especially in front of Gwen."

"Well, it was on account of Dora that Gwen got herself banged up. She always looked up to Dor' when we were managing the girls. Gwen was a brass, too, you know. A real quiet girl, plump and healthy and hearty and unrefined, where Dora was always delicate looking and fragile." Letty smiled over in Dora's direction. "Tough as old boots she was though, our Dora. Much tougher and harder than me back in the day. She ruled the roost with a fist of iron in a velvet glove. If she had a go at you it felt more like she was stroking you. The girls loved her, but none of them would ever dare cross her. And they had too much respect to, anyway." Letty gazed off into the distance, memories flooding back.

"Anyway, there used to be this punter back in the 1970s. He was in his late thirties. Bit mental. Derek Abrahams his name was." Letty couldn't stop an involuntary shudder. "He had a thing for Dora, even though she were a good bit older than him. He used to come round once a month or so for a good time and always used to ask for Dora."

"I thought you and Dora gave that side of things up in the late 'sixties, and concentrated on the management end."

"We did, love." Letty grinned. "But Dora always loved a bit of the old slap and tickle, and this Abrahams bloke was hung like a donkey." The grin faded. "He was always a bit edgy, though, liked to play a bit rough, you know? That was another reason Dor' always obliged. She didn't like him putting his big mitts on the girls. A few times when Dora wasn't around, he had to settle for one of the other girls. Always led to a black eye, or some cuts and bruises. Once he broke a girl's arm." She paused and took a large swig of wine.

"He never ever laid so much as a pinky finger on Dora, though. Well, it was shortly after the arm-breaking incident that Dora told him he wasn't welcome anymore. Unfortunately, she did it when she was alone with him. Thought she could handle, him, see? Since he was never rough with her. Well, she was wrong—the guy went apeshit. Put his hands around her throat and near enough squeezed the life out of her."

Katrina raised her hands to her own throat with a gasp. "Yep. We thought she was a goner. And if it hadn't been for Gwen, she would have been. Gwen was finishing up with a punter next door when she heard the commotion—Abrahams shouting, Dora screaming before he got her by the throat, furniture crashing. So Gwen steamed in, all guns blazing. Naked as a newborn baby, she was. She found Abrahams with his big hands circling Dora's throat, and Dora's face turning blue. So she grabbed the first thing that came to hand—a big marble ashtray— and belted him over the head with it. And she didn't stop until his head was all caved in like a squashed watermelon."

"Oh, God, Letty, that's horrible! Poor Dora. And poor Gwen."

"Yeah." Letty blinked away the tears that swam before her eyes. "I'll never forget it. It was a bloody nightmare. Literally. He was dead, of course, and for days we didn't know if Dora was going to pull through. She was dead for a while, the docs said. Starved of oxygen from being strangled. But the tough old bird made it."

"But how come Gwen went to jail for so long? Surely it was justifiable in the circumstances?"

Letty rubbed her forehead and snorted. "Yeah, well, you would think so wouldn't you? But one thing I never mentioned was that Abrahams was a cop. A crooked bastard if ever there was one. He was one of those on the take—and not just from us. He was making a mint from Soho, so he was. But the boys in blue rallied round and protected their own. Who's going to believe the word of a couple of brasses when the whole of Scotland Yard is doing a whitewash job, and making that bastard out to be some sort of saint?"

"That's sick."

"Yeah, ain't it just? So, Gwen got put away for a good long stretch. Me and Dora got out of the game. It just wasn't the same by then anyway. Drugs, gangs not from our manor, girls being forced on the game, the Eastern Europeans just starting to take over. Things had changed. And Dor' . . . well, she was always a bit delicate after that, you know? She's a game old bird, though. Still tough in a lot of ways, and she never lost her warped sense of humour. But I know for a fact she still has nightmares."

"That's all that cheese I eat, Letty, love." Letty and Katrina turned to where Dora was now sitting up, a wan smile on her face. Her bottom lip trembled slightly. "Now, will you pair of miserable-looking tarts cheer yourselves up, for pete's sake." She stood up gingerly and walked over to the wall of wine bottles. "Now, if I remember rightly it's nine across and six down . . . or is it . . . six across and nine down?"

"Dor', this is no bloody time to start doing crossword puzzles." Letty was worried. Had this all pushed Dora over the edge?

"Not a crossword puzzle, Letty, dear. Just where Mr Dixon keeps the spare key to the wine cellar. Now, help me look. We need to be ready for when Stan comes back so that we can kick his Armani-clad arse into next Tuesday."

\*　\*　\*

MEGAN WHISTLED THE theme tune from *The Good, the Bad and the Ugly* for the twenty-third time. For some reason she just couldn't seem to get it out of her head. She was a little worried about the state of her mind. First of all she had stolen priceless treasures from the museum she loved so much, then she had kidnapped her former boyfriend and curator of said museum. OK, so he was an arsehole, but really, she was better than that, she should be able to rise above it.

And now, well, the red mist had descended again and she was on her way to . . . do *what* exactly? At the very least sabotage his car. At the very worst . . . who knew? Maybe she was ill. Perhaps she needed a patch of some sort, or a pill. Maybe this was the early onset of some hormonal breakdown. Oh, God, she was too young for the menopause, wasn't she? Did this mean she was going to start growing a moustache and shrivelling up into a dry, sexless harridan?

No. All this was Campbell Findlay's fault. He had stolen her job, passed off her ideas as his own, and cast her aside like a pair of old slippers.

He deserved everything that was coming to him.


CAMPBELL COULD FEEL the tears soaking into his shirt. This was just not fair. The man who had passed himself off as a journalist had turned out to be a kidnapper. Campbell was not sure if he was allied to either of the two previous gangs, but he, Campbell, must be the unluckiest person in the world if he wasn't. There was something about this Victor person that sent a shiver down Campbell's spine. He was definitely far scarier than the two earlier kidnapping teams.

When the banging had started in the boot, Victor had pulled the car into the side of the quiet road that wound beside the loch, swiftly but calmly tied Campbell to the passenger seat and got out of the car, presumably around to the boot. What was this man—a serial kidnapper?

Campbell had managed to extract a hand from the ropes binding him and was now desperately trying to reach into his pocket. He could just feel the smooth back of his mobile, but his fingers were slick with sweat and he couldn't get a purchase. He sobbed in frustration and made a desperate lunge, the ropes on his arms burning as they bit into him.

His hand closed around the cool plastic and he pulled it out, clumsily stabbing Inspector Delaney's number into the keypad. The phone was answered after two rings. Campbell twisted around in his seat at the sound of further thumping sounds from the back of the car, but he could not see Victor. He crouched down in the seat and put his mouth as close as he could to the phone.

"Inspector?" It was half whisper, half sob.

"Who's this?"

"Campbell Findlay."

"Speak up, man, I can't hear you. If this is some heavy breathing pervert, you've picked the wrong woman to mess with."

"No! It's me. Campbell Findlay." Campbell raised his voice slightly.

"Oh, *is* it indeed, Mr Findlay. And would you like to explain why, exactly, you found it necessary to—"

"Never mind that right now, Inspector. I've been kidnapped."

Delaney sighed. Campbell could almost feel the frosty breeze on his cheek. "Yes, we are all aware of that, Mr Findlay. You've been kidnapped. Twice. Once by a bevy of Amazonian beauties . . . blah blah blah—"

"No. I've been kidnapped *again*, Inspector."

Silence on the other end of the phone. Then, "Look, Mr Findlay. I don't know what sort of Walter Mitty-type fantasy you've got going on here, but I seriously suggest that you get your arse down here ASAP before I put a warrant out for your arrest."

Campbell's half-formed response was cut off as the phone was gently but firmly removed from his greasy fingers. A well-manicured thumb jabbed the "end call" button.

"Tut, tut, Campbell—that wasn't very clever now, was it?"

THE CAR DRIVEN by the intermittently sobbing and hiccoughing woman bumped and rolled and clanked, causing Kyle to hit his head on the lid of the boot. It finally stopped with a judder. Kyle heard the door open and shut quietly. He pulled aside the panel he had unscrewed and clambered over the back of the seat into the car. He was so relieved to be breathing fresh air, and to be able to stretch his legs at last. He lay panting for a second, letting his legs get used to the freedom. A painful pins and needles sensation ran through them.

Lifting his head until he could just see out of the window he registered his surroundings. His eyes were drawn to the only movement in the vicinity. Kyle squeezed his eyes shut, shook his head and wondered if he was hallucinating after his enforced captivity in the dark boot of the car. A woman in a long pink robe covered in little furry, happy-faced sheep was creeping away from the car. She was carrying a gun that matched her outfit. Worse still, on her feet were two dead chickens—bright yellow, combs flapping over her toes, beaks pecking the ground as she walked. Trippy.

Kyle watched the woman as she moved slowly—hiding behind a tree and then scuttling out, crouched down, tripping over the yellow chickens until she reached another tree. Somehow Kyle doubted that the trees were good hiding places in the circumstances—a pink that bright would be hard to disguise in a whole forest, let alone the thin trunks of her hiding places.

She had driven the car into some high grass, well away from anything resembling a road. Kyle lifted his head further. He grinned happily and blessed his good fortune. The Goddess must have been smiling down on him—it was totally karmic. He could see the big house in the distance—the Goddess in her human form, and the dogs, were both here waiting for him. He was nearing the end of his quest, he could feel it.

MEGAN SAT ON the floor behind the Porsche. She was slightly puzzled as to how it had come to be hidden in this tumbledown garage, tucked away at the back of the property, but here it was, and at some point soon that weasel Campbell would be coming looking for it, and she, Dirty Harriet, would be waiting for him. She blew down the barrel of the pink plastic Barbie gun. Come on, punk, make my day. This time Campbell would know who she was—she wanted him to know who it was bringing him to his knees until he begged and pleaded for her forgiveness.

And then she knew exactly what she was going to do—the idea had come to her as she had driven the Volvo into its hiding place and had opened the glove compartment in the car and seen the pad of lilac writing paper and the pen she kept there. It had suddenly struck her. She was going to force Campbell to write a letter—just a short one as he would need to copy it out several times. It would be a letter of resignation, explaining that he was a thief, a fraud, and a useless waste of space. It would explain how he had achieved his position at the museum by seducing the poor, innocent incumbent (that would be *her*, of course), stealing all her good ideas and passing them off as his own, and how he was ill-suited to be a curator—being a slimy tosser of the first order, a pompous shithead, and a back-stabbing bastard who wouldn't know his Ming Dynasty from his Tang Dynasty if it jumped up and bit him on the bum. OK, so she might have to rethink the wording slightly, but the general gist was there. She would get him to write copies not only for Glasgow City Council, but also for the *Glasgow Herald*, the *Evening Times*, Radio Clyde, STV and the curators of the Kelvingrove Museum and Art Gallery and the Burrell Collection. That way it would definitely get to *everyone*.

Now she just needed to sit back and wait. He would soon turn up for his car. She could feel the stress beginning to lift. She felt calmer than she had done for a long time.

VICTOR PRIDED HIMSELF on his calmness in the face of all eventualities, learned during his time in China where he had studied the art of Tai Chi at the feet of one of the masters. He could generally meditate his way past any stress. But Campbell Findlay's whining was seriously getting on his tits. He turned the radio on, to try and drown out the incessant drone of the pretentious curator. It was a news report on Radio Clyde: ". . . are still searching for the curator of the West End Museum, Campbell Findlay . . ."

"There, I *told* you the police would be searching for me. I'm an important man, you know."

". . . believe that Findlay has absconded with the missing treasures and may, by now, be abroad . . ."

"No! Oh, my God! Turn round and take me back *now*. My reputation is in *shreds*."

Victor sighed and turned off the radio. "Mr Findlay, if you don't shut your annoying mouth right now, your reputation won't be the only thing that is in shreds."

LETTY WAS ORGANISING her troops. Katrina had been sent out to the boathouse to pick up ropes and the fishing net, Dora to Sheehan's bedroom to pick up some of his socks and to the snooker room for some snooker balls, and Letty was now standing in the castle's Great Hall. She looked at her watch. They needed to be back in the cellar in fifteen minutes. It would not do for them to be found wandering around when Stanislav came back, particularly as they did not know what he would have done with Gwen. They had the spare key to the wine cellar and therefore the upper hand was with them.

Letty looked wistfully at the claymores criss-crossed on the walls of the Great Hall. No, there was no way she could shove a couple of those down her knickers, no matter how big her knickers were. They would have to make do with more modest weapons. It was a shame Stan had taken her lovely new gun. However, she'd found a couple of sharp knives in the kitchen—to be used judiciously in view of Stanislav's superior strength and obvious masculine advantage, but they might come in useful for cutting through ropes if he tied them up—and they would have Dora's homemade coshes. She just hoped that they would get a chance to use them.

Katrina burst in, panting. "Here's the ropes and net. What do you want me to do now?"

Dora manouvered the stepladder she was holding over into position under the chandelier and handed Katrina a screwdriver. "Now, listen carefully . . ."

"FUCK ME, DUNK. Is this where the queen lives?" Raymie and Duncan had pulled the rusty Sierra in to the side of the road when the Audi turned off up the gravel driveway and had followed on foot, scuttling from tree to tree. Duncan had made them both slap mud on their faces so that they would be camouflaged, although he wasn't sure that it worked particularly well—thinking about it as he looked at Raymie, their faces blended in nicely with the scenery, but his navy Kappa shell suit, and Raymie's white one, not to mention Raymie's Burbery skip cap, sort of stood out like a sore thumb. Oh, well, they couldn't be expected to be prepared for all eventualities.

They clambered their way down into the ditch, ignoring the oozing mud beneath their trainers, and worked their way along the ditch, closer to the huge fuck-off castle. As they watched, crouched down in the mud and grass, the Audi pulled to a stop in front of the castle, kicking up a storm of gravel, it had barely stopped before the well-dressed shite was getting out of the car and waving a huge gun at his passenger.

"Oh, fuck, Dunk, that knob's got a gun." Sometimes Raymie stated the fuckin' obvious.

The guy from the museum got out of the passenger seat "There's no need to talk to me like that—" His voice trailed off as the smart guy said something to him. Duncan couldn't quite catch what it was, but the museum guy turned white. The bloke with the gun went to the back of the Audi and opened the boot. He lifted out a big purple roll of carpet . . . no, wait . . . it was a sleeping woman, all the while keeping the gun trained on the museum fud. He threw the woman seemingly effortlessly over his shoulder and motioned the man at gunpoint to the front door. They disappeared inside.

"What we gonnae do now, Duncan, man?"

"It's easy, Raymie—we're going in."

"Oh, fuck, I was worried you were gonnae say that, man. Can we no' just go home and forget about all this?"

"What about our dreams, Raymie? The pub? The beer-flavoured ciggies, all the fanny we can pump?"

"Dunk, after seeing that gun, I'm no' sure I'll ever be able to get it up again in my puff, so all the fanny in the world is not going to help."


"LADIES, I'VE BROUGHT you a new plaything." Victor pushed Findlay down the cellar stairs in front of him.

"Plaything? Oh, my God, what *is* this? Some sort of torture chamber? Am I going to be ravaged, used, abused and discarded when I'm spent?"

"Don't flatter yourself." Letty snorted as Katrina muttered under her breath.

Finlay turned in Katrina's direction. "You! Louise Lane. What are *you* doing here?"

"Louise Lane?" Victor laughed a huge belly laugh. This man Findlay was absolutely the most ridiculous man he had ever met.

"Where's Gwen?" Dora had recovered somewhat since he had left them here. There were a few open bottles of wine—maybe they had been on the Dutch courage. He would need to watch them.

"She's perfectly fine. I've left her tied to a chair in your hallway for the time being. Right now, I needed somewhere to bring Mr Findlay so that we could have a little chat about where he has hidden the dogs."

"I've *told* you! I don't know *how* many times I told you on the way here—I don't *have* the dogs. These . . . women . . . have the dogs. Or the Amazonian woman. Or the Glasgow gangsters. But not bloody *me*!" Jesus Christ—did the man just stamp his foot like a little boy? Stanislav closed his eyes and shook his head. "Mr Findlay, I want you to tell me where you hid the dogs or I will have to be slightly less polite and resort to violence." His voice turned icy. "And I don't think you want me to do that, do you?" He looked at Letty, Dora and Katrina in turn. Maybe the women *did* know more about the dogs after all. He would leave them locked up down here to think about that while he had a look around the castle. Just in case.

MEGAN WAS STIFF, bored, pissed off, and she thought she was getting piles from sitting on the cold concrete floor of the old garage. She wished Campbell would hurry up. She was also thirsty and hungry. The only liquid in the place was a couple of gallon cans of petrol, and she had nothing to eat. And she was totally exhausted. Every muscle, bone and nerve ending ached. A dirty old tartan rug, oil stained and torn, lay in the corner. She couldn't stretch out behind the car because Campbell would see her if he came into the garage. However, she *could* spread it out *underneath* the car. That way she would still be hidden and she could wrap herself in the rug and just rest. Close her eyes and relax. Gather up her strength. She felt remarkably calm. As she curled up on the rug all the tension left her body and a warm, relaxed feeling spread up from her toes. She closed her eyes.

LETTY WAITED UNTIL the key had turned in the lock of the cellar door. "Right, let's get to it. We know Gwen's in the hall, so our first priority is to get her safe and out of the way. Next, we'll try and lure Victor into the Great Hall, as agreed. Any questions?"

Dora and Katrina shook their heads. "Excellent, then we'll—"

"Actually, *I* have one." They all turned and looked at Findlay. "What? Am I not allowed to ask a question? I have just as much right. I've been kidnapped not once, not twice, but three times. I've been tied up, stripped naked . . . and not in a good way, drugged . . ." Findlay looked sternly at Katrina who grinned and waved her fingers at him. "So I think I have every—"

"Oh, get on with it, you bloody blowhard. What's the sodding question?" Letty felt she had given him long enough. They had a job to do, after all.

"He's just locked us in, so how are we going to get out of here? He's got a gun, so what the hell do you think we're going to do? And what does he want with me, anyway?"

Letty held up three fingers "One—we have a key. Two—we have a plan. Three—we don't give a shit." She turned to Dora and Katrina. "Now, ladies, let's get out of here."

"What about *me*?"

"What part of 'we don't give a shit' do you not understand?"

"DUNK? WHY'S THAT woman in purple sitting in that chair?"

"How the fuck should I know, Raymie?"

"We goin' in?"

"I guess . . . wait . . . where did those old birds come from?"

"That young one's a tidy bit of stuff."

"Fuck's sake, Raymie—we're not here to ogle the fanny. They've locked that door behind them, look. Let's go and see why. Maybe that's where the dogs are."

As the women disappeared around the foot of the stairs, to the front of the castle where the woman in purple was slumped in a chair, ropes keeping her tied in place, Duncan and Raymie slipped out of their hiding place by the kitchen door and crept to the cellar door where the big key still sat in the keyhole. They unlocked the door and made their way downstairs.

"Oh, thank *God*," said a familiar voice in the darkness. "Have you come to rescue me?"

"OH, BUGGER ME, I forgot to bring the key from the cellar door. Ah well, never mind. At least Findlay can't get out."

"THIS IS A nightmare, an absolute nightmare. Are you here to kidnap me *again*?"

Ignoring Findlay, Duncan and Raymie wandered around the cellar. "Fuck's sake, Dunk," Raymie's voice was positively revererential, "look at all this bevy."

"Naw, Raymie, c'mon. We need to go and see what's happening ya dobber."

As Duncan put his foot on the bottom stair, the ominous sound of a key turning in the lock at the top of the stairs stopped him in his tracks. And Findlay had disappeared.

"Fuck. We're locked in."

"Aw well," Raymie hoisted a couple of dusty bottles of red out of their slots and waved them gleefully. "Least we've got something to do while we wait. 'Mon, Dunk, man. Let's wire in."

LETTY AND KATRINA made their way quietly to the Great Hall. They had left Gwen in the pantry, sleeping off the effects of whatever Stan had done to her, with Dora looking after her. Now they needed to carry out the rest of the plan.

THERE WAS THE Goddess, with one of the elderly ladies. Kyle could feel his heart beating fast in his chest, like a baby bird drumming to get out of his rib cage. It was a feeling that was at once pleasurable and full of pain and Kyle was worried his heart might actually burst. What was this feeling? He scuttled from one window to the next, watching through the window as the women made their way across the black and white tiled floor. The Goddess placed her hand on the old lady's arm and smiled at her. Kyle gasped. As he watched the smile spread across her face it was as though someone had woken the sleeping sun.

VICTOR CROUCHED AT the top of the grand staircase, gun in hand, Letty in his sights. How had the women got out of the cellar? And where were they going? He glided down the stairs, like smoke on water, and peered over the bannister as Letty and Katrina opened the door of the Great Hall and sidled in, shutting the door quietly behind them.

CAMPBELL ROUNDED THE bottom of the staircase and watched as Victor opened the double doors of the room in front of him.

"Well, well, ladies. And aren't *we* the clever ones?" So, the ladies were in the room too? Campbell tiptoed to the door. Victor was standing just inside the large empty room, training his gun on one of the old women and the girl who had pretended to be Louise Lane. Campbell had taken it all for far too long now. There were limits to a man's patience. He had lots to be mad about, but the man Victor was probably the one who had made him maddest. Well, apart from the Amazonian woman but she wasn't here.

He crept up behind Victor. The old lady was focused on Victor, but Campbell saw Katrina's eyes widen and her mouth open as she spotted him over Victor's left shoulder. Campbell put a finger to his lips but it was too late. As Victor turned and trained the gun on him, Campbell dropped instinctively to the ground. He slid along the shiny parquet floor and headbutted Victor in the knees.

The old woman shouted to the girl "The rope! Pull the rope!"

Victor fell with a yelp and the gun swung wildly in his hand. Seconds later, the huge chandelier in the middle of the ceiling came crashing down, crystals smashing around them all like huge hailstones. Campbell's ears rang and a sharp pain went through his right shoulder. He lay on the floor and ran his left hand down his arm. His fingertips came away red and sticky. He'd been shot—oh, my God, he was going to die. He reached out to Letty as his head swam—buzzing and dizzy. "Tell them . . . tell the media I died a hero."

Campbell gazed up, as the elderly woman leaned over him. He could smell the cigarettes on her breath, along with strong red wine fumes. Her face was wavering in and out of focus but he could see the smudged lipstick as it bled into the wrinkles around her mouth. She spoke. The words didn't seem to match the movememnts of her mouth, like a badly dubbed film. "Oh, bear up, you big wuss. It's just a scratch."

THE CRASHING STOPPED and Kyle rubbed the window with his sleeve, clearing a space where his breath had fogged the glass. He had been fixed to the ground and unable to move as the scene unfolded before him. The Goddess was safe. The old lady was safe. The museum curator was safe—clutching his shoulder, but sitting up. Only the body of the smartly dressed man was unmoving under the big glass and metal structure which had fallen from the ceiling as the Goddess had untied a rope attached to one of the curtain hooks on the wall. All Kyle could see were the man's legs. The rest of his body was covered with chain and brass and twinkling shards of glass.

Kyle watched as the other old lady he had seen before came rushing into the room with the woman in purple. The four women gathered around the immobile man on the floor. No-one but Kyle saw the museum curator as he slowly stood up and staggered out of the room like a drunken monk. The curator crossed the hallway and left the castle by the front door.

RAYMIE PAUSED MID-SWIG, and lowered the bottle. "Whathefuckwasthat?"

Duncan had his ear pressed to the door at the top of the cellar stairs. "Shhhhhh. I'm trying to listen. I'm sure I heard a shot."

THE FOUR OF them stood around Stanislav's body.

"Is he dead, Letty?"

"I think so, Dor'."

Katrina reached out a foot and poked the body with her toe. "Are we going to chuck him in the loch, along with Sheehan, like we said?"

"Mmmmmmmmmmm." Letty was unsure. "I don't know, doll, maybe it's not such a good idea—one body in the loch could be accidental. Two looks a bit suspicious if they're found."

"His car." They all turned and looked at Gwen. "His car—the Audi he drove here in. We could put him in it and make it look as though he crashed somewhere."

Letty nodded slowly. "That could work, Gwen, love. That could deffo work. Come on, let's get him into the car. Katrina, you follow us in the Daimler and we'll find a nice quiet spot further up the side of the loch."

THE WOMEN SURVEYED the devastation that was the Great Hall.

"Bugger me, Dor'. How are we going to explain this away to the letting agent? This is going to look *really* suspicious."

Dora was about to answer when they were surprised by a banging and shouting from outside the room. "Fuck's sake—let us out of this cellar, will yous?"

"Letty, I do believe we still have a big wad of fivers in the drawer upstairs, do we not?"

DUNCAN PICKED HIS nose, deep in thought. The old birds had explained it to them several times. Twenty grand in used fivers, which were fucking minging, by the way—really honking of shite—and all they needed to do was admit to a bit of vandalism.

"And now, young man, one of you needs to go and find a quiet spot to hide this in." The old one in charge held out a Sainsburys bag, stuffed full of notes. "Then we'll call the police and say we found you on the premises, drunk, and you'd caused all this damage. I'm sure with the British justice system being as it is, you'll get away with a slapped wrist. *Et voilà*," she shook the bag, "you're twenty grand richer."

Duncan knew there must be a catch. "How do we know you'll give us the money?"

She held the bag out. "We're giving it you now. One of you hide it and we won't know where it is, will we?"

Duncan looked at Raymie, who shrugged. "Sounds good to me. Want me to go and hide it?"

Fuck's sake. Duncan wasn't trusting Raymie with *this* job. He stood up and took the bag. "I'll do it, ya dobber."

CAMPBELL'S HEAD WAS spinning. The blood had stopped flowing from his shoulder but he must have lost a lot. His sleeve was covered in it. Well, not exactly covered, but there was loads of blood on it. A bit, anyway. He didn't like the sight of blood—especially his own. Made him feel faint. He was tired. So tired, as though every ounce of energy had been drained from him. He just needed to find somewhere for a little nap. There, that building in front of him, coming towards him. No, that was wrong. The building wasn't coming towards *him* . . . *he* was going towards the building. Yes, that was it. Campbell pushed open the door of the building. It was stiff, the door dragging on the floor as he pushed.

He stood stock still. Maybe he was hallucinating. He staggered forward a few steps and put his hand on the bonnet. The bonnet of his lovely red Porsche. It was a miracle. He would get in and drive it back home. Give interviews to the media. Tell them what a brave boy he was. A brave boy, just like his mummy had always said. Wait, he was older now, wasn't he? Not a boy anymore? That's right. He was a man. A big, important man who was now a hero. Campbell couldn't quite remember *why* he was a hero, but he knew he was.

A nap. He just needed a little nap. He opened the door of his lovely red Porsche and scrambled in. He pulled the blanket he kept behind the seat over him and lay down. A lovely wee nap in his lovely red Porsche. That's it. Night night. Sleep tight. Bed bugs don't bite.

FUCK'S SAKE, MAN, this spot was the berries. Right out of the way of the castle, tucked in through undergrowth that looked as though no-one ever went there. And it would be dry and the money would keep out of the rain. Perfect, man. Duncan opened the door of the old garage and stepped inside. As his eyes adjusted to the light he saw the Porsche and grinned. Even better. They would come back and get their dosh in a couple of days when they were out on bail and drive home in style. He reached up and tucked the Sainsburys bag behind a rusty old piece of car exhaust on a high shelf. Minted. He carefully closed the door behind him and headed back to the castle.

MEGAN WOKE UP and stretched. Sleep. She'd finally slept. The stone floor wasn't very comfy but it hadn't made any difference. For the first time in ages she felt as though she'd had a deep and restful sleep. She eased herself out from underneath the car and stood up a little bit at a time. Her favourite chicken slippers were dusty and grimy. That bastard Campbell Findlay obviously wasn't coming for his car. She would have to change her plans. She glanced around the old garage and her eyes lit on the cans of petrol. Perfect. She took first one can and then the second, splashing the liquid all over the car and throwing the empty cans into a corner. She stood on tiptoes and grabbed the large household box of matches that was sitting on a high shelf between an old jam jar full of nails, a piece of rusty exhaust, and an old Sainsburys carrier bag. She shook the box. Plenty of matches inside. Megan eased herself out of the door of the garage, took a match out of the box and struck it against the side of the box. She threw the lit match at the car and ran.

A hundred yards or so away she paused and turned towards the garage. Nothing. Maybe it hadn't caught. How disappointing. She took one step back towards the garage, taking another match out of the box.

Woooooooomph. The satisfying yellow and red brightness of flames lit up the small window high in the garage wall and the glass exploded outwards as the fire crackled and boomed. Nice. Time to drive home.

AS THEY WATCHED the police car driving off with Duncan and Raymie in the back seat, and Mr Franklin . . . or was it Mr McIlroy? . . . of Franklin, Franklin, McIlroy and Franklin had departed, sobbing over the state of the parquet floor and the chandelier, the four women stood silently by the oak door of the castle. "Well, I guess that's it, dolls." Letty sighed. "Bit of an eventful few days and bugger all to show for it. Time to move on, no? Somehow I'm thinking that we're going to be *persona non grata* around these parts. We've made a right mess of this place."

"Well, we had fun, didn't we?" Dora had her arm around Gwen and gave her waist a little squeeze. "And we made an absolute killing from the usual scam. So I think we can consider this a successful trip."

Letty was glad to see that both Dora and Gwen seemed to have bounced back. She had been so worried about them earlier.

Katrina sat down on the step and put her feet on one of the pillars. "Make's you wonder though, eh?"

"What's that, doll?"

"What happened to the Campbell Findlay? Last we saw him he was locked in the cellar with those two neds."

"Bugger me, there's something else we're missing."

"What's that, Letty dear?"

"The dogs Dor', the bleedin' dogs."

Dora turned with a scream as a voice from inside the hallway of the castle said, "If the Goddess will permit me . . . ?"

The four women turned to look at the slim bald young man in the doorway. Letty was the first to get her voice back. "Goddess, love? Bleedin' hell, it's a long time since I've been called a goddess."

"Not you." The young man apparently realised that this sounded rude. "Sorry, madam. I mean the Goddess Nur-Lhamo here."

"*Me?*" Katrina sounded gobsmacked.

"Don't knock it doll." Letty gestured at the young man as he prostrated himself on the ground in front of Katrina. "Enjoy it while you can."

The young man lifted his head. "I followed you to the boathouse by the water, Nur-Lhamo, and I watched you as you hid the dogs. And then I . . . moved them." His face fell and his eyes filled with tears. "You can have them. Quang Tu will be *very* disappointed, but *you* are the Goddess."

Letty bent down and took the young man by the hand. "Come on, love. Why don't you get up off the floor and tell us all about it?"

THE PARAMEDIC SLID down the last three feet of the rockface and was propelled by gravity to the resting place of the Audi. The man inside was still. His head was covered in blood and broken glass from the windscreen. It was going to be a tough one trying to get the body up the top of the hill and into the waiting ambulance. At least they wouldn't have to worry about being careful with the bloke. They could maybe strap the body to the stretcher and hoist him up. The paramedic gasped as the fingers on the steering wheel twitched. He put his hands around his mouth to make a megaphone. "He's alive! Damn . . . the guy's *alive!*"

MEGAN RUBBED THE brass of her new office in the basement of the West End Museum. *Megan Priestly—Museum Curator* spelled out in a beautiful cursive script. She gave Campbell Findlay one final thought. She felt a niggling stab of guilt. She'd had no idea he was in the car when she set fire to the garage. She must have been in such a deep sleep that she hadn't heard him get into the car. The police reports had put the death of Campbell Findlay down to suicide while the balance of his mind was disturbed. Despite the guilt, Megan realised she had slept the sleep of the innocent every night since then. Obviously, inadvertently killing someone wasn't that stressful. Megan idly wondered if she should seek help. Perhaps she was turning into a psychopath.

She picked up the phone. Her first job as Curator would be to call Mr Linklater and tell him that the police had given up on finding the dogs. That was only fitting. Where *had* the dogs got to, she wondered.

*　　*　　*

THE FIRST CLASS lounge at Glasgow airport was almost empty. "Are you OK, Kyle? You know which departure gate you need to go to, don't you?"

"Yes, Goddess. And thank you again. My father, Quang Tu, will be so happy to see these. He's coming over to the island to visit next week. He'll take them back with him then." Kyle hoisted his hand luggage with some difficulty.

"Don't thank me, Kyle. Thank Letty and Dora. They're the ones who decided you should have the dogs, to give them back to your Quang Tu." Katrina gave Kyle a hug. "Look after yourself. And remember to phone me to let me know you got home safely."

"I will." Kyle bowed low over Katrina's hand. "Goddess?"

"I wish you wouldn't call me that . . . it's Katrina."

"Goddess Katrina. Are you sure you won't come back with me?"

"I'll come back and visit you very soon, Kyle." Katrina nodded over to where Letty, Dora and Gwen were sitting in their comfortable chairs drinking tequila and watching *Ocean's Eleven* on the big screen. "But me and the ladies are off to Rio for a wee holiday."

Kyle nodded and they hugged silently. Katrina watched him as he shuffled off to catch his flight. She grinned as he hitched his trousers up and made her way over to the three elderly ladies who were engrossed in watching George Clooney scam the Las Vegas casino out of a fortune. She put a hand on her chest—her heart felt as though it was expanding. They'd been so lovely to her, these old tarts. "We've made an absolute mint with the horseracing scam, doll," Letty had said. "And these dogs are a bit hot for us to try and unload. So we were thinking of giving them to your young man to return to the monastery. What do you think?"

"What do I think?" Katrina asked. "I think you're the most wonderful, kind, sweet, lovely women in the world, that's what I think."

Letty had blushed. "Soppy tart."

And Dora patted her knee. "Just think of it as an early wedding present, love. Young Kyle is smitten with you."

It had been Katrina's turn to blush.

She sat down as the closing credits for *Ocean's Eleven* scrolled up the screen. Dora turned to her sister, her eyes sparkling. "Letty, do you know if they have casinos in Rio?"

# Epilogue

QUANG TU HUGGED the young man in front of him. "My son, you are an inspiration. You are welcome to our humble temple at any time. The other monks will be so glad to meet the person who returned our precious dogs to us. We will never be able to thank you enough."

His young protégé beamed. "I'm happy I was able to do it, Father. They belong with you."

Quang Tu patted the case containing the dogs. "They are coming home, my son. After far too long. And it's thanks to you."

"That's OK—I had a great time getting them. It was an adventure. And thank you for the robes."

Quang Tu nodded. He had taken Kyle a set of robes and some Tibetan gifts. "We do not have much, my son, but everything we have is given with love." He looked round as the tannoy blared. "That's my flight being called. I had better go. Bless you my son. Tell your grandmother she should be proud of you."

KYLE WATCHED THE dignified monk make his way slowly to the departure gates. He watched until the slim frame in its saffron robes disappeared from sight and then returned to his gran, waiting anxiously on the concourse at Glasgow airport. "It must have been very strange for such an unworldly man to come over here and experience all this," she said, taking his arm. "It was very thoughtful of you to suggest that we accompanied him back from the island, to make sure he was safe."

Kyle nodded. "I was worried about him, carrying the dogs like that all the way back to Glasgow on his own. I'm sorry to tell you this, Gran, but there are a lot of thieves and bad people about."

IT WAS REALLY bloody cramped in the lavvy cubicle, but Albert Fleck managed to unwind himself from the yellow robes he had been wearing for the last week, his boarding card clamped between his teeth. Thank fuck for that. It was like dressing in bedsheets. He'd almost gone arse over tit several times on this trip. He took a pair of jeans and an AC/DC T-shirt out of his hand luggage and eased himself into them with a sigh of relief. He took his boarding card out of his mouth and wiped off the spittle and then unlocked the clasps of the hard silver case which housed the dogs. It had been a nightmare trying to check in for Birmingham when Kyle had thought he was checking in for Tibet. Albert felt a bit of a twinge in his chest when he thought about Kyle. The lad had been dead nice. But so naïve. Albert almost felt guilty at deceiving him like that. He looked at the dogs, nestled on velvet cushions in their case. Nah. He didn't feel guilty at all and neither would his millionaire Japanese buyer.

# The End

# Acknowledgements

THERE ARE LOTS people I need to say "thank you" to. First of all, to my agent and friend, Allan Guthrie. You're brilliant.

At MaXcrime and John Blake—Maxim Jakubowski, John Wordsworth, Peter Lavery, Rodney Burbeck and John Blake.

At Busted Flush Press—David Thompson.

For eagle eyes, for beautiful cover art, for the people who gave me such wonderful blurbs, for the people wo took the time and trouble to read the manuscript, and for friendship and support—Graeme Andrew, Nicola Barton, Karen Blaney, Paul Brazill, Steve Brewer, Ken Bruen, Donna Buchan, Declan Burke, Bill Crider, Chris Ewan, Christa Faust, Jean G, Kieran Gallagher, Ann Giles, Dorte Jakobsen, McKenna Jordan, Elliott Kastner, Rob Kitchin, Louise McAulay, Russel McLean, Jennifer Muller, Norman Price, Keith Rawson, Kat Richardson, Dan Rouse, Bobbie Rudd, Brad Wyman, Julie Zarate. And to 4MA and Friendfeed Crime and Mystery Fiction Room.

And last but not least, lots of love to Joyce Moore, Patrick Moore, Darren Moore and Ewan McGhee. Thanks for putting up with me, and sorry about all the swearing, Mum.

# About the author

**Donna Moore** is the author of ...*Go to Helena Handbasket*, winner of the 2007 Lefty Award for most humorous crime novel. She has short stories in various anthologies, including *Damn Near Dead* and *A Hell of a Woman* (both Busted Flush Press). Donna runs the blog Big Beat From Badsville (bigbeatfrombadsville.blogspot.com), which focuses on Scottish crime fiction